DUNGEONS _and_ DRAMA

Also by Kristy Boyce

Hot British Boyfriend
Hot Dutch Daydream

DUNGEONS
and DRAMA

Kristy Boyce

DELACORTE PRESS

Text copyright © 2024 by Kristy Boyce
Cover art copyright © 2024 by Liz Parkes

All rights reserved. Published in the United States by Delacorte Press, an imprint of Random House Children's Books, a division of Penguin Random House LLC, New York.

Delacorte Press is a registered trademark and the colophon is a trademark of Penguin Random House LLC.

GetUnderlined.com

Educators and librarians, for a variety of teaching tools, visit us at RHTeachersLibrarians.com

Library of Congress Cataloging-in-Publication Data is available upon request.
ISBN 978-0-593-64701-1 (pbk.) — ISBN 978-0-593-64702-8 (ebook)

The text of this book is set in 11.5-point ITC Galliard.
Interior design by Ken Crossland

Printed in the United States of America
4th Printing
First Edition

MIKE, THIS ONE IS JUST FOR YOU.

Chapter One

O f all the punishments my parents could have chosen, I can't believe they went with this one.

"Riley," Mom says from the driver's seat of our SUV, "I don't want to see you sulking today. You brought this on yourself, and part of the agreement is that you're going to have a good attitude."

I sink farther into my seat, the memory of myself and my best friend, Hoshiko, in these very seats still strong in my mind. Only a few days ago we were blasting the original Broadway cast recording of *Waitress*, laughing and debating whether the actors would come out for autographs after the show. And now . . .

"Are you sure we can't rethink this, Mom?"

"No." She glances at me and back at the road. "I still don't think you're understanding what a dangerous decision you made Friday night. How are your father and I supposed to trust you at home alone after this?"

Okay, it wasn't the *best* decision to take Mom's car without her permission while she was out of town on business. And yes, I drove multiple hours on the highway at night to get to Columbus, with Hoshiko . . . and without a driver's license. But we didn't get pulled over or get in an accident! In fact, you could argue that I should've driven faster because then I would've beaten Mom home and I wouldn't be getting this lecture right now. I don't think I'm going to use that argument on her any time soon, though.

"But working at Dad's *store?*" I whisper.

She presses her lips together like she wants to sympathize but is fighting it. "Your father suggested you spend the afternoons with him since I'm too busy at work to be home after school with you. It's not my fault he's so attached to this store of his."

The tinge of bitterness when she mentions Dad's store only adds to my frustration. Mom has never liked the store. It was one of the main reasons for their divorce, and I've always been firmly on Mom's side about the whole thing. It never even occurred to me that she'd agree to have me work there as a punishment. I really figured Mom would understand about my love for musical theater outweighing my logical decision-making (and state driving laws). Where Sara Bareilles is concerned, there is no line I'm unwilling to cross.

I'm about to argue more when she pulls into the parking lot. We both sit for a second, taking in the store. It's not a particularly pleasant sight, despite the blue skies and sunny September weather. His store is in a run-down shopping plaza in Scottsville, my rural Ohio hometown, which has more than its fair share of run-down plazas. Quite a few of the other storefronts here are empty, though there is a local pizza place next door, and some of the letters have fallen off the signage. It's not inspiring me to be in a better mood.

"Your father's waiting," she says.

I haven't been in this parking lot since we drove by five years ago when Dad first scouted the location and they were still married. A dark, sinking feeling falls over me as my feet hit the concrete.

"Shannon." Dad nods to her as she steps onto the sidewalk.

She nods back, though she keeps more of a distance than is strictly necessary. "Hey, Joel."

They couldn't be more different. Mom is as stylish as ever, with her blond hair pulled back in a low bun, wearing a blouse, wide-legged trousers, and heels that are too high for most people to pull off. Dad, on the other hand, has on ill-fitting jeans and a T-shirt with Deadpool riding a unicorn. I have no idea what brought them together to begin with, but it certainly wasn't a similarity in looks—or interests either.

"And how's my pumpkin?" Dad asks, his big smile reserved for me.

Hesitantly, I walk over and give him a hug. "Hey, Dad."

"Ready for your first day as the newest employee at Sword and Board Games?"

He grins broadly at the idea, as if I'm joining him for summer camp instead of spending the next eight weeks working here as "probation," grounded from extracurriculars and friends. I can only grimace and stare at the cracked concrete sidewalk.

"Sure you're up for this?" Mom asks Dad, and juts her

chin at me like I'm a convicted criminal ready to dig my way out of prison with a rusty spoon.

"I've been trying to get Riley to come here for years. I was hoping it wouldn't take a rap sheet to make it happen, but I'll take what I can get."

I groan. "Okay, for the last time, I didn't *steal* Mom's car! I just . . . borrowed it for one evening. It was more like joy-riding, not grand theft auto or something."

"Are you certain about that?" Dad asks with a raised eye-brow.

I am, actually. Hoshiko Googled it once we were on the highway and headed for the show.

"Well, you won't be doing any joyriding for the next two months, young lady," Mom says with a shake of her head. "Or having much *joy* at all."

"I'm choosing to think of this as a twisted type of bless-ing," Dad says, careful to look at me rather than at Mom. They almost never make eye contact. "I get to spend quality time with my daughter, and you can broaden your interests while you're here."

I sigh and hunch my shoulders. Half of me wants to kneel on this sidewalk next to the discarded napkins and cigarette butts and beg them to rethink this, but I bite my tongue. The other, rational half knows my punishment could've been worse. But the thing is, I don't want to spend more time with Dad, and I don't want to work at his game store. For the past five years I've spent every other weekend at his apartment—watching TV, eating frozen pizza, and barely talking—and that's all the bonding time I'm up for. He made his priori-ties known when he chose this store over Mom and me. He shouldn't be allowed to have his cake and eat it too. But it's clear that the time for debating this is over.

"Well . . ." Mom rocks back on her heels. "Have a good first shift. I'll be back at nine to pick you up."

I wave goodbye and try to keep a neutral expression as I follow Dad to the entrance. In the grand scheme of things, eight weeks is nothing. A blip in time. And luckily, preparations for our high school's annual spring musical won't start until late fall, so—if I'm on my best behavior and win back their trust these next few months—I should be ready to earn my place as the show's student director before Starbucks stops selling PSLs.

"Here we are!" Dad says loudly, making me jump.

I peek over his shoulder. The store is dim and quiet, though it's bigger than I thought it would be. It kind of looks like a hole-in-the-wall from the outside, but the interior is actually spacious . . . or it would be if it wasn't absolutely crammed with stuff. There's a long checkout counter to the left that's up on a platform, maybe so the employees can see the entire floor. The rest of the space is filled with wooden shelving units. They don't look professional, so maybe Dad built them himself. I vaguely recognize some of the games, like Warhammer, from Dad's apartment. There are tons of D&D manuals and figurines, boxes of Pokémon and Magic cards, and displays of brushes and paints in every color for the tabletop game models Dad loves to collect.

I try to conjure a smile on my face, but I'm struggling. For years, Dad's been asking me to come to this store. He's obsessed with gaming. Board games, role-playing games, video games, it doesn't matter. I don't mind a round of Monopoly during the holidays, but that's about as far as my interest goes. Over the years, it's led to lots of frustration and disappointment for both him and me.

Dad walks me through the store, pointing to all the products and telling me a bit about each. I'm dizzy from it. How am I supposed to learn all this stuff? What if someone comes in asking me for a board game? He doesn't exactly sell Candy Land here.

"Hey, Joel? Which of these would you recommend for a twelve-year-old?" calls a skinny man in his late twenties from across the store. "Forbidden Island or Ticket to Ride?" He holds up two board games I've never seen before and gestures for my dad to join him and a middle-aged woman who stands next to him. A little boy, probably no older than five, is with her. The woman looks as bewildered by the shelves as I do.

"Just a sec, Riley," Dad says, and walks over. I shove my hands in my pockets and follow behind. "Well, Forbidden Island is great if you like cooperative play, but if you're looking for something more competitive, I'd recommend the other." The woman nods, but I recognize that expression. It's the same one I make when Dad spouts off facts about 40K armies.

"Um, what do you mean by *cooperative*?" she asks.

Dad and the younger man share the slightest of looks before Dad launches into an explanation. In her concentration, she's let go of her son's hand and he wanders away. I take a few steps in his direction. There's merchandise precariously stacked on the shelves, and a little kid could do a lot of damage very quickly. I'm not interested in reshelving on my first day here.

"Pikachu!" he cries, and grabs a box of cards sitting on the checkout counter.

I step up to him, not sure what I'm supposed to do but knowing that I need to do something. He stares at me. "You're bright."

I look down at myself. Today's OOTD isn't even one of my bolder styles—I was mostly going for comfort after a rough few days. I'm wearing orange jeans with a cobalt-blue ruffled shirt, chunky jewelry, and my favorite purple checkerboard Vans. I know my style isn't like most people's, but I decided long ago that I want to wear clothes others will notice. No black, beige, tan, or navy for me. I don't like blending in.

"Well, thank you." I point at the cards. "Do you play Pokémon?"

"No, but I watch the cartoon."

I smile and nod. I did too when I was younger. You don't grow up as the daughter of a serious gamer without being introduced to a lot of IPs.

"My favorite was always Jigglypuff."

He squints at me. "What's Jigglypuff?"

I feign shock. "Only the cutest Pokémon ever! It's pink and round and loves to sing, but whenever it does, it puts people to sleep. And then it gets grumpy and puffs up its cheeks like this." I puff out my cheeks like I'm a squirrel with too many nuts in my mouth. Then I hit my cheeks with my hands so all the air blows out. I smile to myself, remembering how I would do that with Dad when I was little. Those were better times between us.

The little boy giggles and pulls my attention back. "You're making that up."

I'm really not, but there's no time to argue because he's already wandering off again. I remember a candy bowl I saw behind the counter.

"Do you want a lollipop?"

His eyes shine. "Um, yeah!"

"Excuse me, is it okay if he gets a sucker?" I call to his mom.

She nods thankfully. "That would be great."

I lead him over to the checkout counter to grab the candy bowl but jump when someone else squeezes behind me. It's a white kid from my high school—Nathan Wheeler. He's got on a black T-shirt and jeans, his dark hair is flipping in different directions like he's run his fingers through it too many times, and his wide black glasses are falling down his nose. We've been in school together since junior high, but I barely see him around. I don't think he's involved in much—definitely not in the music or theater programs where I spend all my time.

He quickly grabs a sealed pack of cards from behind the counter and slides them into his back pocket. He nods when he sees I'm staring, then grabs a lollipop from the bowl.

"Root beer's my favorite." Then he takes off toward the back of the store.

I'm dumbfounded. Did he actually come behind the register without asking? And take something? I look at Dad, hoping he saw that, too, but he's still with the customer. I can't believe someone stole from him in my first five minutes of being here.

"Just a second," I say to the boy, and walk toward Dad.

"What about my lollipop?"

"What?" I turn back to the boy, who is pointing at the counter. "Oh, um, sure." I grab the bowl and lower it to him, keeping my eyes on Dad while also making sure Nathan hasn't snuck out of the store yet.

The man with Dad gestures for the woman to follow him to the register, and Dad waves me toward a door at the back of the store. I frown and follow him.

"This is the game room, where we hold events during evenings and weekends and where people can come to play with the products," Dad explains as soon as I'm close enough to hear him. We walk into an open room filled with large tables and chairs. A gigantic dragon head is mounted to the wall. "We have a lot of regulars who use the space." He gestures to two men standing by a table in the back corner.

"You finally got a new girlfriend?" one of them calls, and waves at me. He's got thinning gray hair and an Ohio State sweatshirt on. My eyes fly open in horror at his words.

"Behave yourself, Fred. This is my daughter."

"Nice to see a new face here. I'm used to staring at this old fart all the time," the other man says, and points to his table mate. He's shorter and round with an old Batman shirt on.

Dad chuckles and lowers his voice. "That's Fred and Arthur. They're both retired, so they're here almost every day playing Flames of War."

I shake my head in confusion. I can't keep up with the

names for all the games, particularly when I'm distracted by what happened with Nathan. Should I interrupt Dad now to tell him or wait to find someplace away from customers?

"That's a tabletop game where they reenact war battles," Dad explains, completely oblivious to my uncertainty. He's clearly excited to show off his store after I've avoided it for so long. "Personally, it's not my favorite. I've always liked a little fantasy element in there myself. Anyway, terrain for the tabletop games is in the back, and we have a little vending situation. It's on the honor system." He points to open boxes of chips and candy and a cooler of sodas along the back wall before turning his attention to a group of boys huddled around a table. "Look who's here. Nathan, come over a second."

My eyes widen—I've been too caught up in my thoughts to notice him.

He trots over. "Is everything okay?"

"Better than okay!" Dad exclaims, and claps him on the back like they're old friends. "Riley is joining us at the store." He turns to me. "And I'm sure you already know Nathan from school?"

My mouth opens a bit and I look from Dad to Nathan. Oh no, this just got so much worse. Dad's friendly with this jerky kid who steals from him, and now *I* have to be the one to break the news?

I narrow my eyes at Nathan, who's standing serenely next to Dad like he doesn't have a care in the world. I might not be on the best of terms with Dad, but that doesn't mean I think it's cool to watch other people blatantly take his products and hurt his business.

"Hey, actually, I need to go talk to Curtis about the latest Warhammer shipment," Dad tells us. "Nathan, maybe you can help Riley get settled?"

Dad heads for the front before either of us can respond, looking weirdly pleased with himself, and I put a hand on my hip. "Look," I whisper. "I don't know what's going on with you and my dad, but just give me what you took and maybe I won't tell him what happened."

Nathan blinks slowly behind his glasses, looks back at the table where his friends are ignoring us, and then pats the front pocket of his jeans. "Hmm, I still have this. Will that do?" He holds out his lollipop wrapper to me.

"Very funny. You know I'm talking about those cards from behind the counter."

Now he laughs, and I might have been charmed by the way he throws his head back if it weren't for the fact that the action makes me feel as small as one of the miniature models Fred and Arthur are playing with on the other side of the room.

"Wow," he continues. "Way to jump to absolutely bizarre conclusions without asking a single question. You do realize I work here, right? And that I bought those cards with my own money? Or did you seriously think I stole them in front of you and then *stayed in the store*? What kind of petty thief do you take me for?"

"I . . . well . . ." He's an *employee*? I glance around frantically, desperate for anything to save me from this exchange. "A pretty bad thief, I guess?"

"The worst thief to ever walk this earth."

I gather the fraying threads of my dignity and point at

him. "Now, wait a second, don't turn this around on me. How was I supposed to know what was going on? I didn't see you pulling out any money. I come in and two minutes later you're walking behind the counter and taking something without a word!"

He waves away my argument like there's nothing to be explained. "Joel said you're joining us at the store—please tell me he meant you're visiting for the next five minutes before leaving forever and not, you know, *working* here."

"Say hello to your newest colleague." I grin spitefully and put my hands out to my sides.

"Seriously? But you play, at least, right? Board games, tabletop, cards, something?"

"Nada."

He groans. "Ugh, not one of those. Of course you don't play."

"Excuse me?"

"You can't work at a game store and not play. Or worse, be *disdainful* of games," he replies.

"I'm not disdainful."

But my tone gives me away. It's not about the games themselves. I'm sure this stuff can be fun; otherwise Dad couldn't afford to live on his own, even if it is in a small apartment. But whenever I think of this store, I think of my parents' divorce. I'm sure they must've been happy at some point, but what I remember is Dad getting it into his head that he wanted to start his own store and Mom trying to talk him out of it because of the expense and time commitment. He had a good job in IT before that. But he was so obsessed with the idea that it tore them apart. I always wished that

Dad would just give up the games. How much could they matter? More than Mom? More than me? The answer was pretty clear.

I look up defiantly. "It's not my thing. I guess I didn't inherit the gene."

"Great. Well, I'm absolutely thrilled to work together, then."

He stalks away and I have the urge to bolt out the front door and into oncoming traffic.

Chapter Two

I've never been so happy to be back at school. Mom didn't go so far as to take away my phone, so I spent Sunday night catching Hoshiko up on everything that happened at the store and lamenting that we won't be hanging out at each other's houses until after my probation is done. This stupid punishment makes me extra grateful to be sitting by her side in choir on Monday.

"I'm so sorry, Riley," she says for the hundredth time. "I should have talked you out of driving to the show. Some-how."

I raise an eyebrow and she laughs and plays with the ends of her long fishtail braid. Hoshiko is a master at braiding her long black hair and usually comes to school with a different braid each day. She and I don't exactly have the same style—most days she's in yoga pants and a T-shirt from one of the many dance and theater camps she's attended in past summers—but I like that we each have our own way of expressing our creativity.

She shouldn't blame herself for what happened. We both know I can be impulsive, and nothing and no one was going to talk me out of taking Mom's car when Hoshiko's broke down. We hadn't spent hundreds of dollars and the last two months talking about seeing the touring production of *Waitress* just to let the opportunity slip through our fingers. And honestly, even after getting in trouble with my parents, my grounding, and that horrible interlude with Nathan yesterday, I would do it again in a heartbeat. Nothing compares to getting autographs afterward and having the lead wish me luck with my student directing. It was a dream come true.

"So, just work for two months, huh?" Hoshiko asks with a sigh. "And you're sure you'll be allowed to quit this job by the time the musical gets going?"

"Yes, absolutely. There's no way I'm missing that."

Hoshiko's shoulders relax. "Good. I don't want to do it without you."

It's kind of her to say that, but there's no way I would let her miss the musical no matter what was happening with me. Hoshiko is the most amazing performer. Her parents chose her name because it means *star child* in Japanese, which is perfect for her because she's definitely going to be a star. In fact, if she hadn't been my best friend since fourth grade, I'd probably be ridiculously jealous of her. She's smart and gorgeous, she's an amazing singer, and she's an even better dancer. She takes ballet, jazz, and tap classes every week, and she's even taken classes on Broadway dancing.

"Which musical do you think they'll choose this year?" She nods to the musical posters from previous years that encircle the cream walls of the choir room. They go back for more than fifteen years—long enough that the oldest ones are looking a bit yellow and dated.

"I don't know. It's hard to say without Mrs. Bordenkircher around anymore. But with any luck maybe I'll be able to help with the choosing."

Hoshiko and I have been involved with the high school musical for two years, but our love of theater goes back to when we met at a theater summer camp as nine-year-olds. I was immediately drawn to her joy and the fact that I never had to tone myself down around her. I could be as over-the-top extra as I wanted, and she never got embarrassed or annoyed. In fact, watching her kill every performance while also being the only Japanese American girl in our camp taught me what it meant to be truly confident onstage. Since then, we've never left each other's sides.

Now that I'm a junior, though, my dream is to become student director for our musical. Well, actually my dream is to be a stage director for Tony Award–winning Broadway musicals, but we all have to start somewhere. Unfortunately, the school's longtime choir and musical director retired, so now I have to prove myself all over again to someone new.

I frown and look down at Miss Sahni from my chair on the tiered risers. She's sitting in front of a piano, laughing and chatting with a few of the other students before class starts. She's much more stylish than most of our teachers, and her bright jewelry and red ankle boots speak to my soul. She's very young—just out of college—and I already have a feeling she's going to be super popular. It would probably be a good idea to let her know how enthusiastic I am for this year's production, but we're less than two weeks into the school year and I don't want to overwhelm her.

The other students Miss Sahni was talking to go back to their places on the risers and I stand decisively. "All right, I'm going to say something before we get started."

But before I can take another step, someone's moved in front of me and blocked my way. I recoil when I see who it is. Paul—my ex and the absolute *last* person I want to see.

"Hi, Hoshiko. Riley, how are you?" He asks me the question like I've had a sudden death in the family.

I bristle at his tone. I've managed to mostly avoid him since Disaster Day—my term for the day back in June when Paul broke up with me after he scored the lead role in the community production of *The Music Man* and I didn't get a part. I've been seething ever since, particularly about his patronizing tone when he told me he wouldn't have time for me anymore.

"What do you mean?" I ask.

"I was just wondering how you've been since, you know . . . everything with us this summer. It feels like you've been avoiding me."

Um, *of course* I've been avoiding him. It's just self-preservation to avoid any tool who makes you wipe snot bubbles away while telling you that your talents could be better utilized as part of the stage crew. But also, does he really think that our breakup is equivalent to an actual traumatic event in my life? I have to hold back the impulse to pretend-barf at his feet.

"I'm great." I lift my chin and give a wide smile.

"Yeah?" His eyes fill with rage-inducing pity. "I thought about you over the weekend and hoped you weren't too upset about everything."

I hesitate for a second before I realize what he's likely talking about. *The Music Man* held its last show over the weekend. Yeah, I'm sure he gave me a ton of thought while he was basking in the standing ovations for his lead role and flirting with all the actresses his age.

Hoshiko elbows me. "We had an amazing time on Friday."

I nod. "Yes, incredible. We saw *Waitress* in Columbus. And we got autographs after."

"Whoa, cool. That's a great show—my parents and I saw it in New York when Jessie Mueller was still performing with the original cast. I'm sure the touring cast was good as well, though."

I cut my eyes to Hoshiko—she's trying to control her annoyance, but seriously, what did I ever see in this guy? I don't remember him being like this when we were together. But, let's be real, I know exactly what I saw in him. He's 100 percent swoony lead actor material. He looks like Zac Efron during his old *High School Musical* days, all wavy brown hair and white-toothed smile. And, unfortunately, he's just as talented as Zac too. I can already imagine him taking the theater world by storm as soon as he graduates and moves to New York. The thought makes me tighten my hands into fists.

"Listen . . ." He glances at Hoshiko and steps closer to me as if to edge her out of the conversation. "We're cool, right? We never really got a chance to talk. I hope you aren't still upset about the breakup—it just made sense given how busy I was going to be. With all the rehearsals, I wouldn't have had time to hang out anyway."

"Yep. Not upset in the least. In fact, now I'm super busy myself."

He squints in confusion. "Really? With what?"

"I have a job after school," I blurt out before I can think better of it.

"Where at?"

I silently kick myself. I should've walked away as soon as he came over. I have zero interest in explaining about my new job (or why I had to get it), but I also can't stand letting him think I'm alone and pining over him while he's off living his best life. I take a deep breath and roll my shoulders back.

"Sword and Board Games."

"You're working at your dad's store? But you don't like gaming."

"Sure I do." I take a step away from him. "I have lots of interests I never told you about."

Paul opens his mouth to say something else but is interrupted when Miss Sahni claps her hands twice, calling our choir group together. At that, we start our warm-ups and I'm saved from any more commentary from Paul.

Typically, Miss Sahni uses every available minute of class time for choir practice since we only have an hour together, but today she stops us ten minutes early. She sits down on the piano bench in the front of the room and surveys our group.

"Hey, everyone." She waits a few more seconds until

there's complete silence. "Listen, before we end, I have some news I need to share. As you know, Mrs. Bordenkircher retired as musical director last year, and it seems that the school's faith in our musical program retired with her. From what I've been told, the administration feels that interest in the spring musical is fading. Fewer students are participating, there are fewer community donations, and lower ticket sales." She scans the room, her head tilted and her eyebrows scrunched in sympathy. "Given the lack of interest, they've decided to save funds by cutting the musical from the budget. So, while we'll still have choir, that means the spring musical has been canceled."

There's a simultaneous gasp from the students that could only be pulled off by well-trained singers with strong lungs. Hoshiko's hand grasps mine and squeezes tightly, but I can't pull my eyes from Miss Sahni's face. No spring musical? That's not possible. We've had a musical at the school for almost twenty years now. Even when other high schools started dropping their musicals and extracurriculars, ours stayed strong. They can't just *cut* it out of the blue like this.

"I'm so sorry to have to break this news to you, particularly when we're only a few weeks into the school year. I know this is a huge shock. But money is always tight in the arts, and one thing we can agree on is that the show must go on in one form or another. So we'll show off all your talents at the winter choir recital instead."

As soon as she finishes speaking, the room explodes with noise as everyone turns to each other.

"This is so unfair!" Hoshiko's voice is wobbly and I know she's just as brokenhearted as me. She can be shy and soft-spoken during everyday life—it's only onstage that her real power and confidence come out. I know how important this show is for her.

"We can't let this stand," I say.

She bobs her head miserably. "I know. It's horrible."

I turn to her. "No, I mean it. This can't be the end. There has to be something we can do."

She squints at me. "I wish, but it sounds pretty decided."

"Things are always decided until you find a way around them," I mutter, and stare down at my checkered Vans. Hoshiko was willing to give up on *Waitress*, too, and I found a way to get us to the show. Sure, I'll be paying for that choice for the next eight weeks, but the point is that I *did* something. And I'm going to do something about this too.

"Can you believe this?"

I don't have to look up to know it's Paul again. I bet he's especially happy he got to perform in *The Music Man* this summer now that we've all lost out on our musical. I don't even acknowledge his question.

"I'm going to talk to Miss Sahni," I tell Hoshiko.

"You and the rest of the choir," Paul says, and gestures down at the piano. Sure enough, a lot of students have already surrounded her, and it looks like several are crying. It's understandable, but not the most productive way to use their energy.

"I'm not giving up," I say, still pointedly looking at Hoshiko and not Paul.

Paul steps closer again, like we're a little team. "Listen, if you want my advice, you should bide your time on this. No one's going to be swayed by a bunch of high schoolers whining. But money talks and that's how you sway them."

I purse my lips, frustrated by the fact that Paul is making sense. Complaining to Miss Sahni isn't going to do anything. Looking around the room at the distraught students surrounding me, it's clear there's still plenty of interest in our musical. But Mrs. Bordenkircher hadn't been choosing musicals we were particularly interested in—last year we did *Pirates of Penzance,* which isn't exactly looping on our Broadway musical playlists—and she was a total drill sergeant about rehearsals. Only the most dedicated of us had stayed.

But that could all be changed. If we choose a fun, more modern musical—something that can show off our talents but reuse sets and costumes from past years—I bet we could get a lot more interest. Miss Sahni would be a much more popular teacher to direct it, and I would happily step in as student director to help as well. And a more popular musical would mean more ticket sales. A swell of excitement fills me. This is totally possible, and I'm not giving up hope for it.

"Looks like you're plotting, Riley," Paul says as he studies me. "I want to help, but my community theater director asked me to run acting workshops this fall, so I'm obviously swamped."

Yes, *obviously.* I roll my eyes. Leave it to Paul to douse my excitement with his overflowing ego.

"Luckily I don't need any help." I walk around him, Hoshiko quick at my side, but rather than heading to Miss Sahni, I stride to the other side of the room by the double doors to the hall.

"Sorry, but he's the absolute worst," Hoshiko says.

"Don't apologize to me—it should be the other way around. I can't believe I forced you to hang out with him last spring."

"Well, if it makes you feel any better, he was a lot less jerky when you two were dating."

I snicker. "That makes me feel exceptionally better." I look over my shoulder at Miss Sahni. "So, I have an idea, but I think it might take time to pull together. Should I run it past Miss Sahni anyway?"

"The bell's going to ring any second."

Choir is the last class of the day, and Dad's likely already waiting outside to drive me to the store. Part of my "probation" means no extra time after school and no friends driving me anyplace. And even though I *really* hate to admit it, Paul probably is right. Talking to her when I'm unprepared isn't going to do anything to help the cause. I need details and plans.

Sure enough, the bell rings and makes the decision for me.

"Okay, I'll start pulling together a plan and then I'll talk to her." I grab my book bag and we push out into the hall with the crowd. "But I'm not giving up until you're back on that stage beaming under the lights."

"And you're getting a standing ovation for your brilliant stage direction."

We grin at each other, and visions of next spring fill my mind. One way or another, I'm going to make this happen— for both of us.

Chapter Three

D ad is once again waiting in the parking lot for me the
following afternoon. I duck into his car. "Are you sure I
can't have Hoshiko drop me off one of these days?"

He shakes his head. "No can do. Anyway, I like picking
you up. It makes me think about how I used to drive you to
elementary school. Do you remember how we'd hold hands
and walk into the school together?"

I roll my eyes. "I'm not six anymore, Dad."

"Don't I know it."

If I'm being honest, I do remember that. I have a lot
of happy memories from the Before Days, but they feel so
long ago. They've been pushed back into the recesses of my
mind by the last five years of stilted conversations and sepa-
rate holidays and weekends. If he's unhappy with how things
are between us, he only has himself to blame.

"Riley? Hello?"

"Sorry, I was thinking about . . . my history paper."

"Anything interesting happening at school?"

I grimace, remembering Miss Sahni's announcement from yesterday. I've spent the last day ruminating about it and I haven't gotten control of my emotions yet. Without the musical . . . what is this school year even going to look like? I'm already missing so much at the beginning of the year because I'm stuck at this annoying store, and now the rest has been decimated too. Usually my whole year centers around the musical. Reviewing the roles and prepping for auditions with Hoshiko, anxiously waiting for the cast list to be announced, sourcing costumes, helping with sets, and then rehearsals that fill up my spring in the best way possible. And now? Nothing.

Tears prick at the corners of my eyes, but I stare out the window and clamp my mouth shut. There's no way I'm sharing a word of this with Dad. He might have come to my performances over the years, but he knows nothing about musicals and he's never tried to learn. Conversation topics with him are limited to pizza toppings, passing thoughts about my homework and teachers, and why I'm tired and need time alone. No emotions and discussions about broken dreams, thank you very much.

"It's just school," I say quietly. "There's nothing to say."

Dad scowls. "All right. Well, I was thinking that when the store is quiet, you should study up on our inventory."

And here we are. Back to his favorite topic, as usual.

"You're going to need to know the difference between Settlers of Catan and Carcassonne," he says, and flips on his turn signal.

I raise an eyebrow at him.

"What about Dungeons and Dragons versus Pathfinder?"

"I've heard of Dungeons and Dragons," I say, shrugging.

He snorts. "Well, I'd hope so."

We pull into the parking lot and I follow him inside, but school is still on my mind. If I'm going to be taken seriously, I need a compelling argument. I glare around at the store. I'd have plenty of time to pull together a plan if only I wasn't here every freaking evening. Instead, I have barely any free time between school, homework, and store hours.

Nathan stands to my left, looking at a board game. His dark hair is in desperate need of a cut, and as usual, he's wearing a gamer T-shirt, this time with a video game I don't know. I roll my eyes at his new presence in my life. Why is he at the store when he's not scheduled to work today? And somehow he even beat Dad and me here.

"Hey, Nathan, you got a second?" Dad calls.

Nathan looks up from the game, his eyes flicking to me before focusing on Dad. "Sure. What's up?"

"I know you aren't on the schedule today, but a shipment of new games came early and I'd like to get them out on the floor. Do you mind taking Riley through that process before your game starts? Unless that Algebra Two course is already kicking your butt and you need the time for homework?"

I squint in confusion. Dad knows Nathan's *class* schedule? I'm not even sure he knows my schedule—but then, that would require us having real conversations. I shouldn't be surprised he's closer with Nathan given how much they have in common.

"Yeah, I can do it. No problem," Nathan replies. Maybe

it's my imagination, but he seems annoyed before replacing his scowl with a politely neutral expression.

"Great!" Dad claps him on the back and looks between us. "This is terrific. You two will finally have the chance to get to know each other better."

Lucky me.

We stare stonily at each other, and Dad's voice falters. "Er . . . well, I'll be on the phone with distributors if you need anything."

Dad leaves and we stand for another second in silence. Dread fills me. I was already frustrated, and now I have to work directly with Nathan? Tonight just went from mildly annoying to absolutely miserable.

He jerks his head to the left and I follow him into the stockroom. It's a chaotic mess. There are stacks of boxes everywhere, along with packs of dice, containers of paint, and tons of cardboard leaning against the walls. My eyes widen. "Does no one organize this?"

He glares at me. "Of course we organize it. It's very . . ." He looks at it and waves his hand. "There's a method to the madness. You'll figure it out eventually."

I shrug. "I'd rather not be here long enough to figure it out."

"Then why'd you take the job?"

His tone is too sharp for me to give him a real answer. "My parents wanted me to," I reply coolly.

"If you don't want to be here, then you should look for something else. Some of us actually like it here. And could use the hours rather than having them wasted on you."

I bristle. "You're working right now, aren't you? If you're desperate for more money, take it up with my dad."

He turns his back to me and picks up a box from the top of the nearest stack. "I don't think you appreciate how amazing it is to work at a place like this. The way you're sulking around makes it seem like it's a punishment or something."

My eyes flick to the back of his head. Nathan is more observant than I gave him credit for, but there's no way I'm getting into my punishment when he's already so judgmental.

"First off, why are you watching me? Second, the only real punishment here is working with you."

"Believe me, I was trying to ignore you, but your clothes are so loud you might as well be walking around with a bullhorn to announce your presence."

He glances at my outfit with a look of disgust. Today I'm wearing a red pleated skirt with an oversized pink and red polka-dot sweater vest over a bright blue button-up. Tasteful it is not, but I still look cute.

"At least I have a point of view with my clothes. You probably only own Spider-Man T-shirts."

Nathan scowls at me over his shoulder, and I match his narrowed eyes with a defiant smirk. He hands me a box cutter. "Here. We need to start by opening these. Careful, that's really sharp."

"Which end?"

His eyes widen slightly before he realizes I'm joking.

"That was a test, and now I know exactly how stupid you think I am."

He only grunts.

We work in silence, pulling down boxes, opening them, and carrying out the contents to the front of the store. The individual games aren't particularly heavy, but once you start stacking them, the weight adds up. Maybe all this heavy lifting will help when I'm (hopefully) building and moving set pieces for the musical that's back on schedule. Next, Nathan starts reorganizing the shelves, stacking the older games and making room for new things.

Just then, the door jingles with a new customer. We both turn to find a middle-aged man in a Captain America T-shirt walking in, followed by a pudgy white guy named Lucas from my school. Good Lord, does everyone come to the store on a daily basis? Lucas and his dad were here yesterday too.

Lucas waves at Nathan. "I thought you had tonight off. You aren't missing D&D, are you?"

"I'll be there. I'm just doing some stocking for Joel."

Lucas takes me in with a wide smile. His shaggy blond hair and open expression are welcoming, a bit like a fluffy golden retriever's.

"So it's true," he says. "The prodigal daughter really has returned to the nest."

"What?"

"Oh, nothing. Nathan and I were wondering if you'd ever come to the store and now you're here. I'm glad we haven't scared you off yet." He puts his hand out to me and I shake it. "I've been meaning to introduce myself. I'm Lucas Greenwald."

"Hi, Lucas. I'm Riley. Though I *do* know you from school."

"I know. But we've never talked."

"I wasn't wondering if you'd come to the store," Nathan says. "Lucas was wondering."

Lucas smirks at Nathan. "I want to talk more, Riley, but I need to get ready for the game. Come to the back and I'll introduce you to everyone." He leaves, and Nathan and I continue to work in silence for another ten minutes. I want this done as quickly as possible so I can get back to musical planning. Finally, the last products are on the shelves.

"I left a bag of peanut M&M's behind the counter," Nathan says as he walks away. "If I come looking for it later, don't call the cops."

I roll my eyes. "Haha, very funny."

The next hour and a half goes smoothly. Lots of people come in, but they all head directly for the Warhammer league Dad is running in the back room. I can hear them laughing and chatting with him. It's weird to experience this side of his life. Somehow, over the years, I'd gotten the impression he was lonely. Maybe I just wanted to believe he was struggling. That he regretted leaving Mom and me. But it's becoming apparent that, if anything, he's the opposite of lonely. He's got friends everywhere I turn, which means that every weekend he spent with me was a weekend he had to give up seeing all of them. I wonder if he was as irritated about those weekends as I was.

A middle-aged white man shoves a board game at me. "I need to return this. It's missing a piece."

I look at the board game and back up to him. I doubt it was missing a piece when he bought it. More likely he lost it and is trying to pretend it came like that. I put on my best customer service smile. "I'm sorry, sir, but we can't accept merchandise that has already been opened."

He frowns at me. "How was I supposed to know there was a piece missing unless I opened it?"

"I can offer you store credit." At least, I think I can . . . It's hard to keep all the rules straight.

"I want my money back."

"I'm sorry, I don't think I can do that."

"Maybe you can't, but someone can. Where's your manager?"

I try to keep my smile in place as I look toward the back room. I was hoping I wouldn't have to call Dad over tonight, but it looks like I'm overruled. "Just wait here, sir, and I'll get him."

I scurry through the shelves of merchandise and into the back room. As soon as I walk in, at least ten faces turn in my direction. There are only two other women in the room and they're both way older than me.

Dad glances over. "Riley? What's going on?"

"There's a customer in the front who wants a return on opened merchandise."

He sighs and puts down his iPad. "There always is. I'll take care of it." He looks to Nathan, who is sitting in the back corner with his friends. Nathan must be his right-hand man, because he comes over before Dad can say anything. "Sorry to keep doing this to you, but do you mind running this game for a few minutes while I deal with something?"

"Of course." Nathan grabs the iPad, and Lucas waves me over to their game table. I probably should follow Dad instead of hanging out back here, but I'd like to avoid that entitled customer if possible.

"Perfect timing! Now you can meet everyone," Lucas says when I approach. "This is John Turner." A skinny white kid with short brown hair and a polo shirt looks up just long enough to nod. Lucas points next to him at a Latino boy with light brown eyes and skin. "And this is Anthony Santos. Guys, this is Riley, Joel's daughter."

"My night just got better. It's good to meet you, Riley," Anthony says. He gives me a grin. "I'm happy to show you around if you want."

He actually winks at me then, but he's so carefree and relaxed that I can only laugh. This is certainly an interesting group of boys. "I've already gotten the tour, but thanks for the offer."

John sighs. "I was in the middle of casting Fireball."

"Fine, roll your damage," Lucas replies, and looks at me. "Sorry. John's single-minded when it comes to gaming."

"We're at a *game store*," John replies while simultaneously skimming a page in the thick book in front of him. "What do you expect me to do—flirt with every girl who walks in like Anthony? You should be lurking around that weird bar down the street instead of sitting back here with us."

"It's eighteen and over. I already checked," Anthony says with a laugh. He leans back and crosses his legs on the table. "And it's called *charm*, thank you very much."

"I'm just saying you could make polite conversation," Lucas tells John, both of them ignoring Anthony as he flashes another grin my way. "Obviously you shouldn't be flirting with anyone, unless you broke up with Jordan and failed to mention it."

John huffs. "Not likely. Jordan is perfect. He'd never give me crap for taking our campaign seriously. Can we get on with it now?"

"Hold up." Anthony sits up, his attention suddenly focused across the room. I spin, half expecting that angry customer to be storming back here. Instead, a willowy white girl walks in. She's stunning. She has long red hair—though it looks dyed—and is wearing a purple lace top and dragonfly-wing earrings. I haven't seen many people who stand out like her.

"I see she's deigned to make an appearance today," Lucas mutters.

"Late as always," John adds.

Nathan's entire expression changes when he sees her. His body lifts, his smile brightens, and he stops mid-instruction to say hello to her.

"Who is she?" I whisper to the guys.

"*That* would be Sophia. She goes to North with Jordan," Lucas says in an even tone.

Ah, that would explain why I've never seen her around school. We have two high schools in the area—Central Scottsville High School, where everyone who lives in town goes, and North Scottsville for the surrounding rural areas—and we don't mix much except for the occasional sports matchup.

"She's pretty," I reply to Lucas.

"You aren't the only one who thinks so."

She whispers in Nathan's ear and then comes over to us. "Hi, boys, happy to see me?"

They all wave half-heartedly. "I'd be happier if you were here at five o'clock when our game started instead of six-thirty," Lucas says.

Sophia sniffs. "You know I have a hard time getting here." She sits down and that's when I realize she's a gamer like the rest of them. She's part of their D&D group.

She eyes me warily. "I don't think we've met."

"We haven't." I wave. "I'm Riley. I work here."

"You do? I guess I've missed a lot."

"Yes, it would be helpful if you came in more than every fourth session," Lucas replies. "It's messing up the campaign."

"Just pretend I'm asleep at the tavern or something." She turns her focus back on me. "So, if you work here, why are you hanging out in the back room? Are you joining our game or something?"

"You should definitely join," Anthony says, and pats the empty chair next to him.

"I was just introducing Riley to everyone," Lucas says. "She's Joel's daughter, so she's going to be here a lot."

"Yeah, practically every night." I grimace in a way that I hope is funny. "You all are going to get sick of me. Some more than others." I nod in the direction of Nathan.

"Eh, don't worry about him. He'll come around to you eventually," Lucas says.

"What's going on between you and Nathan?" Sophia asks. Her tone is more suspicious than curious.

"Just some workplace bickering," I reply with a shrug. "I hope you're right about him, Lucas. Otherwise, I'll need to turn on my charm just so we aren't snapping at each other like overworked stagehands."

I say it as a joke, but Sophia's eyes narrow dangerously in my direction before flicking over to Nathan. Maybe I'm totally making things up, but she almost seems . . . jealous. I half smirk at the ridiculousness of the idea, but her expression only darkens more.

"I'm going to see if Nathan needs anything," she says to the group, and saunters back over to him. He gives her a sappy grin as soon as he sees her, and she leans close to read what's on the iPad. So close that her chest is pressed up against his arm. He starts chattering away, so different from how he acted around me earlier, and she meets my gaze with a little jut of her chin.

I take a step back. Um, what just happened? She might as well have peed on Nathan to mark her territory. Not that I'm sniffing around—she's welcome to him and everything else in this place—but that was still really weird. Thankfully, Dad calls me to the front and I'm spared from any further interaction.

I spend the rest of the night at the register, humming the *Waitress* soundtrack and taking notes on every musical I can find. As much as I love musical theater, there are a lot of variables I hadn't considered when putting on a production, like the number of male versus female leads, the level of dancing required, the licensing fees for each one . . . The list goes on and on. A weaker person might give up, but I'm determined to figure this out.

The store closes at nine, but it's not until eight-fifty

that people start leaving the back room. Lucas, John, and Anthony all come out huddled together.

"But the rule as written means that it should work against kobolds," John says. "Based on the spell description—"

"*Riley!*" Lucas calls. I get the impression that he's less excited about seeing me and more excited about getting away from John. "Did you have a good rest of the night?"

"Yes, very quiet. Exactly how I like it."

"Your night sounds better than watching Nathan stare at Sophia the whole time." Anthony rolls his eyes and leans against the counter. "I should have hung out up here."

Lucas gestures behind him to Nathan, who is at the doorway to the back room and glued to Sophia's side. "He's got to give it up."

"It's embarrassing," John says matter-of-factly. "And it's ruining the game."

Nathan is a manic ball of energy next to her, messing with his clothes, standing too close, smiling and nodding comically. Actually, I need to study this in case I'm ever directing an actor on how to behave like a lovesick fool. Sophia, on the other hand, is the exact opposite. She keeps looking at the door and checking her phone while he talks.

"It's pretty bad, huh?" I ask.

They all nod in unison.

"When did it start?"

Lucas and Anthony exchange a glance. "Beginning of the year," Anthony says. "Sophia came in looking for dice and Nathan was immediately hooked."

"It was hard to blame him at first," Lucas adds. "There aren't many girls our age who hang out here."

"Uh, no, it was easy to blame him, and I continue to do so," John says with zero hesitation. "He's acting like a fool."

"Nathan invited her to D&D when we started our latest campaign four months ago, and that's when it ramped up," Lucas says. "I wish he'd accept that it's never happening and move on instead of torturing himself."

"And the rest of us," John adds.

"You think she's *that* far out of his league?" I ask.

"It's just the way she is. Sophia only wants what she can't have. Which is why"—Nathan and Sophia walk up to us and Lucas switches midsentence—"I think the half orc cleric would be the best lawyer," he says with a flourish.

Anthony nods vigorously. "Can't argue with that."

"You're all the worst," John mutters.

I muffle a laugh. Mental note—if I manage to get this musical back on course, I'm definitely *not* asking these guys to audition for roles. They're horrible actors.

Chapter Four

Thursday night I get a reprieve from the store because Mom and I are having a girls' night. I was worried she might cancel this one as another form of punishment, but we both love them too much to give them up. I wish we could do them every night—so much candy, the softest pj's, and a musical that's bound to make me laugh and cry.

She walks out of the kitchen with a big bowl of buttery popcorn. "What should we watch tonight? Maybe *West Side Story?*"

I moan. Don't get me wrong, I love the original *West Side Story* movie. Mom let me watch it when I was eleven and fanatical about love stories, but unfortunately I didn't get the memo that it was a retelling of *Romeo and Juliet,* so the ending felt like someone was cutting out my heart with a dull spoon. After it finished, I distinctly remember walking out on our patio so I could cry alone in the rain. A small part of me loved how dramatic I was being, even then.

"I don't think I'm up for the emotional turmoil today. How about a comfort watch?"

"*My Fair Lady?*"

"Perfect."

Mom picks up the remote to pull it up. "So, you haven't said much about working at the store. How's it going?"

I shrug. "Fine, I guess."

"Is it pretty nice inside? It's been forever since I've been there."

"It looks like Dad designed it and runs it."

She laughs lightly. "Riley."

"It's okay. He seems to get pretty steady business. But it's not as nice inside as it would be if you'd done the interior."

"Well, thank you." She fiddles with the remote. "I'm sure it's great for your dad to have so much extra time with you now. He gets to see you right after school and hear about your day. . . ."

Mom's tone is weird, her eyes downcast, and it takes me a second to figure out what's going on. I think she's a little jealous of my new arrangement with Dad, which is *highly* ironic since she's the one who insisted on the grounding. I guess it makes sense, though. Mom and I have always gotten along so easily, and her interior design business is much more up my alley compared to gaming. It's not exactly theater set design, but she does have to think about the aesthetics of color and lighting in spaces and I've learned a lot by tagging along to job sites with her. And it's not just that—we genuinely like to hang out. She loves to get dressed up and play around with her makeup and hair color. It's not unusual for me to come home and find that she's suddenly a redhead instead of a blonde. We've had a lot of fun evenings, watching old musicals and trying out winged eyeliner.

"Mom, you know I'd be so much happier if I was working with you. And it's not like Dad and I are sitting around having heart-to-heart conversations while we check out customers. It's just a job."

She gives me a small smile. "I just hate to think that I'm missing anything from your life. But it's a busy season for me, so I'm bouncing all over to meet with contractors. Having you work at your dad's store makes more sense. It *is* supposed to be a punishment, after all."

I snort. "Oof, nice one. I won't repeat that to Dad."

"Please don't." She closes her eyes and rolls her shoulders back. "I'm sorry, I shouldn't have said that. That was petty. This whole situation feels so strange, though—I've never had to punish you before. And I want you to have a good relationship with your father, of course I do, but . . ."

She trails off and I reach out to squeeze her hand, unsure what to say, even though I know what she means. Particularly since the divorce, Mom and I have been more like friends than a parent and child. It's messed up, but the idea of being happy around Dad feels disloyal to her. Not that I'm expecting to have a lot of fun these next weeks at the store.

"Let's not talk about Dad or the store anymore." I grab a blanket and lay it over both our legs. "Thanks for not canceling tonight."

She clicks the play button and takes a handful of popcorn. "I need these nights as much as you do."

We sing "Wouldn't It Be Loverly?" along with Audrey Hepburn and then fall back into the couch laughing at our horrible accents. Once the scene continues, I pull out my phone and make a few notes about the musical. Maybe this would be a good choice to propose to Miss Sahni. It's not modern, but it is beloved, which could help with ticket sales. We should have some usable costumes from previous years that would cut down on costs. I'm not certain if—

"What's going on? You're never bored when we watch musicals."

I startle and put my phone down. With everything else that's been going on, I realize that I never told her about what happened in choir this week.

"Mom, the school wants to get rid of our spring musical! I know they've threatened it for years, but Mrs. Bordenkircher was always able to make it happen. But now we have Miss Sahni, and she's really nice and it sounds like she really wants to do it, but it might be too late, and everyone is so upset—"

"Whoa, hold on, you're talking so fast I can barely understand you. It's official, then, they're definitely cutting the musical?"

"Miss Sahni made it seem pretty official."

Mom sinks back into the couch. "That's horrible. What a loss for the school. Have you been holding this in all day so you wouldn't ruin our evening? I'm surprised you weren't screaming about it as soon as you got into the car."

A tinge of guilt pricks me as I realize that I haven't said anything about it to her, even though she's always been my fiercest theater supporter. Now that I spend most nights with Dad, things are starting to fall through the cracks. But after the conversation we just had, I'm not about to tell her that.

"I'm not giving up hope, though," I say, ignoring her question about when I got the news. "I'm going to talk to Miss Sahni about it more. I think if she and I work together, we could come up with a plan to convince the administration that—"

"Riley." Mom's voice has lost the soft, sad tone it had a moment before. "Despite all this"—she waves at the movie and popcorn—"you're still in trouble. Have you forgotten you're still grounded for your last theater-related choices?"

"No . . ."

"I'm very sorry about these budget cuts. It's shortsighted of them and will take a huge opportunity away from the student body. However, it's not your place to fix this. Right now, you need to be focused on winning back our trust, and then you can think about the musical."

I grit my teeth in annoyance. "But if I don't do something now, there won't *be* a musical!"

"Well, maybe that wouldn't be the worst thing in the world." She pinches the bridge of her nose in frustration. "I know I sounded reluctant about your father's store before, but I actually think it's a good thing for you. You've become entirely too obsessed with theater lately. I mean, you drove to Columbus without a license just to see a touring Broadway production! You could have gotten arrested or killed yourself and Hoshiko. You seem to lose all common sense when it comes to the theater. Without the musical, you'll have time next spring to explore other extracurriculars, join clubs, whatever. And there's always the community theater production next summer."

Next summer?! That's nine months away! And the community theater production isn't the same as our high school production. Those casts are filled with strangers and people double my age or more. I want to be with my friends on *our* stage at *our* school. And, most importantly, I want to vie for student director this year. It would be my first time in a directing role, and I need the experience if I ever want to be taken seriously after high school.

I start to argue, but her lips press into a firm line, and I realize any arguing will only hurt my chances further. Suddenly, Audrey Hepburn's voice isn't so magical to my ears. I don't care what Mom says, though—I'm not letting this go. I love musicals too much to let our school production slip through my fingers. Mom didn't explicitly say I couldn't research possible musicals in my spare time. Or have a casual conversation with my choir teacher about the future. By the time my probation is done, I'll definitely be back in my parents' good graces, and then I can get permission. I smile and take a handful of popcorn. No one needs to be the wiser until then.

When Dad and I arrive at the game store on Friday afternoon, he immediately gets pulled into a conversation with someone about donating for a nonprofit auction. Maybe this is the norm when you own a small business, but Dad is constantly being asked to donate to auctions or organizations or youth groups, and he says yes every time. I don't know why he agrees to sponsor so much stuff, but he clearly has a reputation because people keep asking him.

Nathan is nowhere to be seen, but Lucas is milling around the board games. "What are you up to tonight?" I ask him.

"D&D again. We play twice a week." Lucas shrugs. "It's a little intense, but I love it."

"So, I can look forward to seeing Sophia again?"

"Probably not. She almost never shows." He rolls his eyes. "Beyond the whole Nathan thing, it's a real pain, because it makes it hard to run the game when players are coming and going. I'd like to have at least four reliable people." His eyes flash in my direction. "Actually, you should join us! Would you want to? It's really fun."

"But I'm not here for fun." I spread my arms wide. "I'm here to work."

"I bet your dad wouldn't make you work if you were playing with us."

Hmm, well that *is* an interesting proposition.

Before I have time to think about it, a flash of a familiar smile at the entrance has me swallowing a primal scream.

It's Paul.

And he's not alone.

He strides into the store, handsome and smug, holding hands with Lainey Lewis. The silent scream intensifies. *Lainey?* She acted opposite him in *The Music Man*. Lainey is everything you'd want in a leading lady. Beautiful, tall, with an expressive face and a gorgeous voice. Even the alliteration of her name sounds like it was made for a Broadway marquee. I don't know her since she lives in the next town over, but I immediately noticed her eyeing Paul at the audition months ago. No wonder he was so quick to kick me to the curb after the cast list went up.

"Excuse me," I say to Lucas, and duck behind a shelf before they can see me. Lucas gives me a confused expression and leaves for the back game room.

Why are Paul and Lainey here? I know he couldn't care less about gaming, and I can't imagine Lainey spends her time painting tabletop models. But Paul knows I work here now after I stupidly blurted that out in the choir room. Would he really come here—all hand-holding and lovey-eyes with Lainey—just to rub it in? Paul might be a pompous jerk, but I never thought he was cruel.

"Riley?"

I bite back a string of curse words. I should have kept my eyes circling the store the way my thoughts are circling my mind.

I straighten to find Paul and Lainey in front of me, Paul with an uncertain look on his face. "You . . . busy?"

I shake my head and try to act as if it's a pleasant surprise to see them suddenly in front of me. Which I can totally do. I'm an actress. This is just like a play.

"Oh, hey! No, just looking over products here. You know, a little inventory."

He smiles indulgently. "Uh, right. Well, Lainey needs a present for her younger brother, so I suggested this place since I know you're working here now." He gestures to her. "You remember Lainey, right?"

The girl who was cast in the part I desperately wanted? The girl who obviously flirted with you when she knew we were together? Oh yes, Paul, I remember Lainey.

I turn my full-wattage smile on her. "Definitely! Good to see you."

She waves. "I'm so clueless about all this! It's kind of dumb, don't you think?" She lowers her voice and leans toward me. "Like, why are grown men still playing with this stuff?" She smiles as if we're sharing an inside joke. "But I need something for the party Saturday, so here I am."

"Yep. Here you are."

I'm seething. Which I know is totally hypocritical because it's not like I'm a big fan of gaming either, but does she have no idea that my father owns this store? And even if Paul didn't mention it, it seems like she should start with the assumption that I might like gaming if I'm working here. I don't know, maybe she's just oblivious, but either way I loathe her even more than before.

"Are you thinking board games? Because we have a lot over here." I point to the shelf behind her, and she randomly picks up a game box.

"*Sixty dollars?*" She exchanges a look with Paul. "For cardboard? I definitely can't afford that."

I pray to the theater gods that I don't lose my temper. *This is just another scene,* I repeat to myself.

"What about a card game instead? Magic is supposed to be popular."

She frowns and nods. "Yeah, that might work. I think I've seen some of those cards at our house before."

I lead her to that aisle. For a few moments, she and Paul stand together, heads tilted toward each other as they look through the options. Maybe I can slowly back away and disappear into the ether? But then he steps away and turns to me.

"So, how are you holding up, Riley?"

"What?" Please tell me he's not trying to talk about our breakup again.

"At the store? Is it horrible or are you liking it here?"

"Oh. Um, it could be worse."

He gives me one of his smiles. His patented, charming, made-me-want-to-kiss-him smiles. For a moment I'm flooded with memories of us together. Running lines, harmonizing to "It's De-Lovely," getting soft-serve ice cream cones and trying to eat them before they melted down our hands. And the look he gave me as I licked my ice cream cone, as if he was two seconds from knocking it out of my hand and kissing me until neither of us could breathe.

I take a deep breath. I can do this. Maybe he's trying to be friendly and normal again. If so, I can try as well. It would make life easier if I was on decent terms with Paul since we see each other in choir and around school.

"Did *Music Man* end up going well? I'm sorry I couldn't get to a show."

He brightens. "It went awesome. Our director knows her stuff, but she's also collaborative with the cast. I love her. And Lainey absolutely killed it."

I nod and focus on not letting my smile slip. I'm happy for him—or, at least, I *want* to be happy. He deserved the lead role. And maybe Lainey deserved her role as well. But all I can think is how much I wanted to be there with them. I could have spent my summer rehearsing and performing, and the pain of missing out is even worse knowing that there's a good chance I won't be part of a production this spring either. All I want is to review lines and memorize stage blocking and joke around with the cast. I miss being at my favorite place in the world—the stage.

Paul must notice some change in my expression because he tilts his head in concern and pats me on the arm. "Is this too much? Us coming here together?" He looks over his shoulder at Lainey, who is still busy searching through the different Magic card packs. "I wasn't trying to rub it in or anything, bringing her here. Don't worry, Riley. You're great. You'll find someone else, even if it takes you a while."

I step back. Any feelings of sadness or nostalgia I was entertaining flee at his words and righteous indignation takes their place.

"I know I'll find someone. I've already found him." The words are out before I can think, and I almost slap my hand over my mouth.

"You have?" He frowns. "I didn't know you were dating someone too." His face is skeptical, and it eats away at me.

"It's new."

"Who is it?"

"Just someone. It doesn't matter."

His frown deepens and then his lips twist in a small smile. "Oh, right. Sure."

Wait . . . is he insinuating that I'm making this up? That I'm some silly pathetic girl who is boyfriend-less and fabricating random relationships just to save face?

I mean, okay, yes, that's exactly what I'm doing, but *he*

isn't allowed to think that. Why is it so hard for him to believe I could have a new boyfriend?

"Are you insinuating he isn't real?"

He holds up his hands in surrender. "I'm just saying . . . either way it's totally fine."

My hands clench into fists. "He's real."

Lainey turns around to look at us. "What are you talking about? Who's real?"

"My boyfriend."

"Ooh, you have a new boyfriend? Do I know him?"

I have to stop myself from rolling my eyes. How am I supposed to know who Lainey knows when we've never spoken before? "I don't know. I doubt it. He's not a theater kid."

Paul's still looking skeptical, but also a little put out. The realization makes me want to do a victory dance.

"What's his name?" she asks.

"I already asked her, but she won't say."

I glance between Lainey and Paul, my heart racing double time and my mind as empty as a Broadway theater on a Monday night. I need to say something or they won't believe me. What are names? Um . . . Joel? Ahh, *NO*, that's my father's name! What are other names? *Why can't I think of human teen boys' names?!* One comes to me, and I practically scream it.

"Nathan!"

Paul blinks in shock. "Nathan? Wait . . ." He looks around the store. "You aren't talking about Nathan Wheeler, are you? He works here, right?"

Are you freaking kidding me? I was *sure* Paul wouldn't

know who Nathan is. Honestly, I'm not sure anyone at school knows who he is. He's basically a ghost there.

"How do you know that?" I ask.

"He sat in front of me in history last year. We did a project together."

Of course that'd be my luck.

"Is that him?" Lainey whispers, and I spin around. Nathan has suddenly appeared, the stockroom door swinging behind him as he walks toward me.

"Hey, your dad wants you in the back to help."

He couldn't sound less romantic or interested in me if he tried. Sweat beads on my forehead. I glance back at Paul, who is now looking extremely skeptical.

"Right," I reply faintly.

Why is this my life? I take a deep breath and stride toward Nathan, plastering a flirtatious smile on my face.

"Thanks so much for telling me," I say in as sultry a voice as I can muster. "I'll be right there."

"Um . . . okay?"

He stares at me like I've lost my whole mind, which I clearly have.

It feels like I should do something more—something that will make this look legitimate and not like the most ridiculous thing in the world—but it's not like I can throw myself into his arms and kiss him. Even the idea of trying to hold his hand is too much. He's liable to shake me off like I'm a rabid dog. But I have to do *something*.

My brain departs my body completely and I lean forward and kiss him on the upper arm. Except I can't quite get myself to move my lips so it's more like I press my closed mouth on his shirt and pull away.

I'm surprised my entire body doesn't shrivel and spontaneously combust into a bloom of dust from the embarrassment.

He stares down at me, open-mouthed, and I squeeze my eyes shut. "Please act cool," I whisper.

"Did you just—"

I spin around. "Lainey, looks like you found what you needed, yeah? Great! Curtis can check you out up front. I need to—" I mime walking into the stockroom and putting things on shelves. Now everyone is gaping at me.

"So . . . yep." I shuffle a few steps away. "Good to see you both. And I'll see *you* at school tomorrow, Paul! Or, I guess, we both will." I grab Nathan's arm and physically drag him behind me toward the stockroom. The door shuts behind him and he rips his arm from my grasp.

"*Riley*, have you lost your mind?"

Chapter Five

"Okay, okay, don't freak out. It's totally fine. I know that was weird, but—"

"Did you or did you not just kiss my *arm?*"

I drop my head into my hands, my cheeks erupting with heat. "I'm sorry. I shouldn't have done that. It's just that Paul came in with his new girlfriend—the girl who acted opposite him in the show that I didn't get into—and they were acting so cute and—"

"No."

"What?" I look up.

"I know what you're going to say next. And the answer is no."

I glare at him, my embarrassment shoved aside by his reaction. "You can't say no yet. I haven't asked you anything."

"All right, let's hear it, then."

I swallow. "Okay . . . so . . ." I'm having a hard time thinking of how to explain things. "So, Paul and Lainey came in and then Paul was acting all pitying about the fact that I wasn't dating anyone, and he had the nerve to tell me that I'd find someone *eventually*. I mean, seriously? Of course I'll find someone else. Someone better than him. I'm a freaking catch."

Nathan raises an eyebrow, but I push on.

"And I don't know what came over me, but I blurted out that I was already dating someone new. I just couldn't let him get the upper hand. But then they asked who it was, and I didn't have a name in mind, and yours was the first one I thought of and—"

"No."

"Nathan! You've got to stop saying that!"

"And *you've* got to stop saying my name when people ask who you're dating." He looks up at the ceiling and then takes off his glasses and rubs his eyes. "Why did you think you could pull me into this? In case you haven't noticed, I'm not a big fan of yours."

I gasp. "Now, wait a minute, there's no need to be rude."

"I'm just telling the truth. Something you might want to try sometime."

"Yeah, yeah, easy for you to say. You weren't standing in front of your ex making a total fool of yourself." I stop and stare at him. "Actually, wait a minute . . ."

"No."

"I'm not a dog and we're not in an obedience training class so you can stop saying that." I hold up a hand to keep him from bolting. *"Stay."* I pause for a moment. "Good job, buddy!"

I laugh and he practically growls at me, which only encourages me to make more dog obedience jokes, but I hold my tongue.

"This could work out for both of us," I say instead.

"I'm confident that no matter what you're thinking right now, it's not going to work out for me. So let's do this stocking and I'll try to forget any of this ever happened."

"We'll do the stocking in a second. First, let's talk about Sophia."

His eyes narrow. "*Definite* no." He turns and starts opening boxes. I swallow down my irritation and keep talking.

"Everyone knows you like Sophia. Even *Sophia* knows you like Sophia, and yet nothing has happened between you two."

"I'm ignoring you."

"Unlikely or you wouldn't be saying 'I'm ignoring you.'" I pace behind his back. "Lucas told me that Sophia only wants what she can't have. And the problem with you—"

"I have no problems."

"—is that you've made it too clear that you want her. You need to play hard to get. You need to make her come to you."

He keeps unboxing in silence, so I plow forward. "And if I'm a good judge of character, which I totally am, then it's clear that she's also the jealous type. You should have seen her when I casually mentioned that we'd be spending a lot of time together here. She went totally feral at the idea. And then she started . . . *pressing* herself against you." I shudder.

He stills and slowly turns around. "That's what happened? I couldn't figure it out."

"It was because of me." I grin and put my hands on my hips. "I didn't mean for it to happen, but it worked anyway. So, this is what I propose . . ." I pause, waiting for him to say no again, but he only studies me with wary eyes. "You play it cool with Paul. If he asks, you can say we're dating and if he sees us together at school, then we can pretend we're more than friends."

"When did we become friends?"

I roll my eyes. "Fine. More than mutually annoyed co-workers. And in exchange, I'll do the same with you at the store."

"And what exactly does that mean?"

"I'll make Sophia jealous. I'll . . . I don't know . . ." I have to push down a shiver of revulsion. "I'll flirt with you."

He lets out a laugh. "You'll *flirt* with me?" he repeats in an incredulous tone.

"I mean, not all the time. But when she's around, I can flirt and that'll make her jealous enough that she'll start paying more attention to you. What do you say? It's not a bad deal at all. And you'll save me the shame of having to admit to my ex that I made up a fake boyfriend."

"None of this is going to work the way you think it is."

"You don't think I can pull it off?"

"Um, no. Did you see yourself back there?"

"But you can?"

He shrugs and turns away. "I'd be fine. I'm good at playing characters. It's all my role-playing experience."

"*Excuse* me, I have plenty of acting experience. I'll have no problem doing this."

He looks over his shoulder. "Uh-huh." He gestures to

the boxes of Warhammer models. "Come on, we have to get these on the floor."

I sigh, pick up a stack, and follow him out. It isn't lost on me that he hasn't given a straight answer yet. But I can be determined—some might even say stubborn—and I'm not letting this go. This could work. It would solve both our problems. I just *cannot* explain to Paul that I made up a boyfriend. I won't be able to stomach the look on his face or the teeth-clenching pity in his voice. I have to convince Nathan.

We work in silence for a few minutes and I let him be, hoping he's turning this over in his mind and seeing how well this might work out.

"Going to get the rest," he mutters, and walks back into the stockroom. A minute later, Lucas pokes his head out from the back game room.

"Have you seen Nathan yet?"

"Yeah, he's in the stockroom. We should be done soon." I put another box on the shelf.

"Did you think more about joining the game? The offer still stands."

Thirty minutes ago I wasn't too sure, but now I hesitate. Join D&D? It's not something I have an inherent interest in, but it'd make sense if Nathan agrees to this scheme since it would give us a reason to be together in Sophia's presence. And I like the idea of getting a break from my shift, assuming Dad would agree to that. He has always wanted me to get involved at the store—showing some interest in D&D could be a great way to convince him to cut me some slack.

"Well, I'd have to run it by Dad," I tell Lucas. "I'm not sure if he'll want to let me off early."

Lucas shakes his head. "You don't know your dad very well." He turns back to the game room. "Hey, Joel?"

A moment later, Dad joins Lucas at the door. "What's up?" He sees me. "Riley, is everything okay up front?"

"Yeah, just finishing this stocking."

"Joel, don't you think it'd be a good idea to have Riley join our D&D campaign?"

Dad almost falls into the doorframe in shock.

"We could really use another reliable player and it would be so great to get to know her." Lucas is practically batting his eyes at Dad—laying it on a little thick in my opinion. "Plus, she doesn't know anything about D&D and this would be the best way for her to learn. It would make her a better salesperson."

"I don't know. . . ." Dad looks at me. "Was this your idea? I thought you had no interest in playing?"

"Um . . ." I look between Lucas, Dad, and the stockroom door that Nathan will be walking out of any second. I'm still conflicted. Having time off work would be awesome and Lucas and the other guys seem cool enough, though I wish I could use my time for musical prep. I'm almost positive that Nathan will hate the idea, which makes me want to do it more.

I shrug. "I mean, it would be good to try something new while I'm here?"

I don't sound particularly confident, but Lucas nods encouragingly.

"Well . . ." Dad frowns. "It's nice to have two people at the register on a Friday night . . . but Curtis has been handling it for months on his own, so I don't see why he can't keep doing it. And I *would* love to get you more involved here." He grins. "All right, sounds like a plan."

"Awesome!" Lucas high-fives Dad and they beckon me toward the back room, seemingly forgetting that I'm still in the middle of stocking shelves.

"You're going to love it, Riley," Dad says. "I don't know why I didn't think about this before, but D&D is perfect for you. Just think of it as acting practice."

"Acting?"

"Yes. You'll be playing your own character—deciding how they're going to speak, what they're going to wear, who they're going to kill. It's all up to you!" He beams at me. "I have a good feeling about this."

"What's going on?"

I turn to find Nathan, his face barely visible behind a stack of five board games.

"Riley is going to join your D&D game!" Dad exclaims. "Put those down. I'll take care of the rest so you all can start."

Nathan shoots daggers at me as we follow Dad and Lucas into the other room. "Seriously?" he whispers. "I leave for five minutes, and you weasel your way into my game? I never agreed to this plan of yours."

"I did not *weasel my way* into anything. If you're looking for someone to whine to, find Lucas. It was his idea."

As if to make my point for me, Lucas hurries over to the

table where the other guys are waiting. "Hey, guess what? Riley is going to start playing with us!"

John barely glances up before returning to his *D&D Player's Handbook,* but Anthony whips his head toward me. "What? Excellent!"

Nathan's face scrunches in annoyance and it brings me a perverse pleasure. I pull out a chair. "Yep. I thought it would be a fun way to practice my acting." I smile around at the table.

Dad grins bigger than I've seen in quite a while. "Great! Have fun!"

Nathan looks over his shoulder as Dad retreats before saying quietly, "Can I talk to you?"

"Sure." I spin and smile sweetly up at him. "What do you need?"

"In private," he growls.

I waggle my eyebrows suggestively at him. "Mmm, yes. Let's do that. In *private.*"

Nathan storms off and I stand. "We'll be right back."

I follow him to the corner of the room where the bathrooms are. We're partially hidden by a woven screen that Dad has erected in front of the bathroom doors, but it's hardly private.

"Way to be dramatic back there," I say.

He glares at me, then sighs. (Again, dramatically. Who says drama kids are always the dramatic ones?)

"Riley, what are you doing? You're in my D&D group now? Really? You hate D&D. Please don't ruin the game for me. You may think it's stupid, but I love it."

"I'm not going to ruin it. And it wasn't my idea. Lucas and Dad got excited about it, and I didn't want to turn them down, especially if you agree to my proposal. Plus, I get out of work during the games."

He rolls his eyes. "Of course that's your motivation."

"If you don't want to go along with my plan, then fine. Obviously I can't make you—although I stand firm in the belief that it would work. Sophia would be eating out of your hand if she realized you weren't interested anymore. But whatever. You do you. Let's just try to get through the game tonight without murdering each other."

Nathan takes the tiniest step toward me. "I didn't say I wasn't interested in the plan." His voice has lost the sharp edge it had a moment ago.

"Oh." I blink in surprise. After how angry he was, I figured that was definitely off the table. "Well, great. I figured you hated the idea."

He shrugs and steps even closer. He's definitely inside the invisible bubble of personal space around me and my heart thuds at his nearness. "I thought about it in the stockroom and decided you made a good point. Plus . . ." He reaches out and slowly brushes my hair away from my face. Goose bumps rise on my arms as he slides his thumb down the curve of my jaw until he's cradling my face in his hand. "I thought it might be fun to get to know you better."

Uh . . . *what?* I thought he liked Sophia? I try to swallow, but my throat is too dry.

"I . . . um . . . ," I choke out.

At my words (or lack thereof), he smirks and steps back. "That's what I thought." His voice has turned flat. "I told you, you won't make it one minute into this fake flirting thing."

"Wait, what?" Horror flies through me and I wrap my arms over my chest. "Were you just . . . was that . . ." I stare at him in shock. "Were you just *faking*?"

"Of course." He's laughing now, but it's an annoying, gloating sort of laugh that makes me want to push him into the nearest toilet. And I can guarantee the public toilets here don't get cleaned every day. "That's what you asked me to do. We're supposed to be fake flirting, aren't we?"

I throw my hands up in the air. "Well, it doesn't count right now! You have to warn me—I need to be prepared. I thought maybe you . . ."

He laughs again. "Yeah, no. I don't think so."

"Oh my God, you're horrible. *Why* did I have to blurt out your name?" I squeeze my eyes shut in frustration. And embarrassment. I can't believe I thought he might be serious there for a second—I'm such an idiot. Although I have to say, Nathan's a better actor than I gave him credit for. Maybe he'd be willing to audition for the spring musical once I bring it back—that is, if I don't kill him before that.

I pull in a long, calming breath and look him directly in the eye. "I'm a professional. Not literally, because I haven't made any money from my theater performances, but I consider myself one anyway. If you can pull off this fake flirting thing, then I absolutely can as well. And we only have to keep it up long enough for Sophia to get interested and for Paul to believe I wasn't lying. Then we break it off and go back to happily ignoring each other."

"If only I had a TARDIS so I could travel to the future now."

"Lovely." I roll my eyes. "So, we're good? You're not going to rat me out to Paul on Monday?"

We stare at each other. His lips are pressed into a thin line, but he doesn't look angry any longer. More like he's sizing me up.

"We're good. If you can pull this off."

"Don't worry about that."

He raises an eyebrow and then strides back to his friends, leaving me to follow. Sophia better wake up and notice him pronto, because I won't be able to take much more of Nathan Wheeler.

Chapter Six

Lucas, Anthony, and John stare at us expectantly when Nathan and I return to the table.

"Ready to play," I say in a falsely cheery voice. "What's first?"

Lucas looks between Nathan and me. "What's going on? What were you two talking about back there?"

"Nothing. Just a work thing," Nathan replies.

"A work thing?" Anthony raises his eyebrows. "A secret work thing?"

"Riley, first you need to make your character," Nathan says, ignoring him. "Here's your character sheet to fill out." He slides a paper over to me with a hard look in his eyes. I'm still getting to know his expressions, but I think he's trying to tell me that he doesn't want to talk about our deal with his friends. Which is fine by me, though they're definitely going to figure it out as soon as Sophia comes in and I have to lay on the charm.

The idea makes my stomach do a little flip. I've been so focused on trying to dig myself out of this mess with Paul that I haven't had two seconds to think about the consequences of Nathan saying yes. I can still feel the caress of his thumb across my jaw. Despite all my big talk, am I really going to be able to pull this off? I'm not sure I even know what to do around Sophia. Bat my eyelashes at him and say risqué things? Touch him? *Kiss* him someplace other than his arm? We might need a few more private discussions about this.

"Riley? You still with us?"

I shake my head to clear the thoughts and nod at Lucas. I scan the table, immediately overwhelmed despite Lucas's welcoming expression. He has a trifold divider in front of him to block our view from what he's looking at. There are piles of books on the table: *D&D Player's Handbook, Dungeon Master's Guide, Monster Manual,* and *Xanathar's Guide to Everything.* Everyone has dice—the fancy ones that Dad sells at the store, not the usual six-sided white and black dice that Mom and I use in Monopoly—along with iPads, notebooks, and figurines placed on a grid in the middle of the table.

I pick up Nathan's paper. There are a ton of boxes with labels like *Dexterity, Intelligence,* and *Charisma.* My imagination explodes at all the possible characters I could make. All the fun I could have acting—no, *role-playing.*

"Do I get to choose all of these characteristics? Because I definitely want high Intelligence, Wisdom, and Charisma. And maybe Dexterity just because."

"Okay, slow down," Nathan says, sighing. "The first thing you need to do is choose which race and class you want to be." He flips open a book and shows me the options. "And you can't just choose the highest scores in everything. It depends on the kind of character you're playing. If you're a fighter, then you would probably want to choose Strength and Constitution as your highest attributes. But if you want to be a wizard, then you would choose Intelligence."

"You can't play a wizard," John says. "I'm already the wizard of the party."

Now Lucas sighs. "It's fine if she wants to be a wizard. Maybe some people want to play wizards who do more than cast Fireball."

"But it wouldn't be helpful. We have a paladin, a rogue, a ranger, and a wizard. We don't need a second wizard. I think you should be a cleric."

"A cleric?" I read the description. "I have to serve a deity and heal people? I don't know, that doesn't sound very fun."

"Anyway," Nathan continues, "take a look at these and see which one you think you want to play."

I skim the *Player's Handbook*, reading over some terms I don't understand, like *tiefling* and *halfling*, and others I recognize, like *wizard* and *warlock*. Then my eye catches on a specific class of character. I point to it.

"Is this what I think it is?"

Nathan looks at it and deflates before nodding. "Yeah. Bards sing and tell stories together. They score highest in Charisma and Dexterity and can do some magic related to the music they play."

"Having a bard would be even less helpful than having a second wizard," John interjects.

But it's too late, I'm already grinning. "This! I *definitely* want to be a bard."

John groans and Nathan and Lucas exchange glances. "I'm not surprised," Nathan mutters.

My worries about the deal with Nathan and playing in this game disappear as I read more about bards. I get to sing! And I'll get musical instruments and my character can dance and perform! Dad was right when he said this would be good practice for me.

"Can I have a guitar as my instrument? I always wanted to learn to play guitar."

"It's called a lute, but sure. But you haven't chosen your race. There's all these—"

"I want to be a human."

"A human bard. So you want to play a character that's as close to you in real life as possible?"

I shrug. "It's just too perfect to not go for it."

"All right," he says with yet another sigh. "That was easy enough."

I fill out the character sheet, then quickly text Hoshiko to tell her that I've joined the game. I miss her and wish she could hang out here every evening with me like the guys do. If only I could see her expression when she realizes I'm becoming a D&D player. I leave out my new arrangement with Nathan, though. That's something that definitely needs to be explained in person.

I'm coming up with a tortured backstory for my character—something to do with being abandoned in the forest and surviving through my singing—when Lucas calls us to attention.

"Let's get going. So, as usual, you three have left Sophia behind at a tavern to sleep off her latest night of debauchery."

Nathan groans. "Do you have to do that? Can't it just be that Sophia is staying behind to help orphaned children for once?"

"No. When you're the DM, you can have Sophia do that. For me, she's sleeping off her ill-timed hangover. Now, when we left off last time, the party had decided to go hunt for a magical sword you overheard talk of in town. Rumors swirl that the sword is hidden away in the vault of an ancient king. His kingdom was on the eastern shore. Are you going to travel there immediately or explore this area more?"

The guys look at each other for confirmation.

"We should move on," John replies, his voice slightly lower and more commanding than usual. I'm guessing this is the voice he uses for his character. "We can't hope to defeat the hydra otherwise."

"A day's walk around the forests wouldn't be a bad idea, though," Nathan replies. "And I'm sure Spruce would appreciate the time in nature before we get on the open roads."

Anthony glowers at Nathan. "Don't use my ranger affinities as an excuse to stick around here so Sophia can quickly catch up to the party next time. If she didn't want her character left behind, then she'd come to the session."

I look between them, excitement growing in me. I'm not totally sure what's happening, but I'm surrounded by people playing characters and doing voices and following story lines, and I already love it. It's like improv meets choose-your-own-adventure theater. Why haven't we been running these games between musical rehearsals for years? I can't wait to tell Hoshiko everything.

"Let's stay in character, please," Lucas replies. "Then it's decided that you'll continue the quest. As you do, you come across a young woman on the side of the road." He gives me a small smile of encouragement.

I sit up straight and try to channel my best bard. "Good day, sirs! Where are you off to on this fine morn? May I offer you a song in exchange for coin?"

Anthony chuckles lightly and everyone else exchanges glances.

"Uh, *what* is that voice?" Nathan blurts out.

"I'm getting into character!"

He looks at the other guys in mock confusion. "I'm sorry, are we in a Charles Dickens novel? Good day, guv'nor! Need your chimney swept?" He mimes tipping his hat to me.

I bristle and roll my eyes. Honestly, I was pulling the voice from Eliza's father in the movie version of *My Fair Lady*. I love doing a Cockney accent. "I thought this was my character and I could play her how I want?"

Lucas nods seriously. "It is."

"I think it's really great, Riley," John says. "I'm glad you're getting into it. Or do you have a character name we should be using?"

I consider for a second and then put my hands out. "I am Elphaba," I announce, thinking of the famous lead character from *Wicked*.

"Good morning to you, Elphaba," John replies. "I am Vafir, an evocation wizard."

"I'm a dwarf ranger by the name of Spruce Wayne." Anthony bows deeply and grins. "Don't let the term *dwarf* confuse you, though. I may be short in stature, but I'm larger than life in heart. And other things."

Nathan and John groan. I laugh and nod approvingly. "Wow, good to know. And I love the name." I turn to Nathan, who says, "I'm a half-elf paladin. I go by Sol Juur."

I squint at him. "Soldier? What kind of name is that?"

"An amazing name, thank you very much. And it's not Soldier, it's Sol Juur." He points down to where he's written his character's name. "First name Sol, last name Juur. As a paladin, I'm a warrior of the sun deity. Sun, Sol—get it? But I also fight and protect the party, so I'm a soldier—Sol Juur." He grins widely, much too pleased with himself.

"Uh . . . cool." I still don't really know what paladins are, but at least I can appreciate the attention to detail.

Lucas clears his throat to get our attention. "You all realize that this girl is friendly and could add new energy to the group. You need to decide if you're going to invite her to join your party."

John—Vafir—turns to me with a discerning gaze. "We don't need a song right now, Elphaba, but we could use help with a quest. Are you up for it?"

"Will there be singing and dancing?" I ask.

"I'm always up for a song," Anthony replies. "And I'm eager to get out of this town and away from the crowds. Your singing can keep me company in the evenings." He flashes me a grin.

"I'm not convinced," Nathan says, his voice harder than usual. "The smaller our party is, the stealthier we can be. A bard could announce our presence to others if she's singing all the time." He cuts his eyes to me. "Particularly one who doesn't seem to recognize the gravity of the quest we're on. This isn't a game."

I narrow my eyes at him. "Isn't everything in life a game?"

Lucas and Anthony both laugh.

"Maybe to you, but not to me."

"Be reasonable, Sol," John says. "A bard could be useful when we get to the ancient city. The sword is most likely under lock and key and her powers could help us with that. Especially since we can't rely on our rogue to do it."

Nathan frowns but doesn't give in. Well, fine. I look down at my character sheet—I'll make him relent.

I turn to Lucas. "I'd like to use my persuasive powers to convince Nathan. I mean, Sol Juur."

His eyes widen. "Um . . . you can try using one of your spells on him."

"Try to calm his emotions," Anthony says with a wink, and points to a spell in the book.

Nathan shakes his head. "Hold on, you're not supposed to cast spells on your own party members."

"Well, I'm *not* a party member yet because you're being stubborn. So I'm using a spell. How do I do it?" I lift my chin defiantly, glad that Sophia isn't here tonight so I don't have to pretend to like Nathan when he's being annoying.

"Technically, you would speak and gesture to cast the spell, but it's also fine to just say you're casting it," Lucas explains.

"Actually . . . I have a better idea," I reply.

Nathan puts out a hand to Lucas as if to say, *Come on, man*.

Lucas ignores him. "Go ahead, Elphaba."

I clear my throat and stand, turning slightly toward Nathan. Fear flickers across his features and it makes me grin. Oh yes, I'm already liking this very much. I clear my throat and begin singing the first verse of "Say My Name." Not the Destiny's Child song—the song I'm singing is the one Beetlejuice sings to Lydia Deetz in the Broadway show. I've listened to the soundtrack enough to have it memorized.

Everyone in the back room stops and swivels to stare at me. I project just a bit more and push away from the table so I can sway and do coordinating hand motions in Nathan's direction. I even do the gravelly, slightly creepy voice that the actor uses. Nathan's whole face goes red, and he slowly slides under the table, which makes the whole thing glorious.

I'm tempted to keep going, but the song is a duet and without Hoshiko—my eternal duet partner—it's just not as much fun, so I finish and sit down with a flourish. To my surprise, multiple strangers in the back begin clapping in delight along with Anthony, John, and Lucas (possibly because of Nathan's mortification). Fred and Arthur, the retired men Dad introduced me to on my first day, call for encores. And Dad must have snuck through the doorway to the back room while I was singing because he's clapping and his eyes look a little wet. I didn't think he'd care.

"Now, *that's* how you play a bard, people!" Lucas yells to the room at large.

"You really don't have to sing," Nathan whispers.

"Oh, I know I don't have to. But I want to."

"Well, good luck trying to persuade me with my bonus." He sits up and grabs one of the dice. "Rolling a Charisma-saving throw."

The die comes up as a five. His eyes go wide, and the other guys break out into raucous laughter. I guess that means he didn't get the number he needed.

"Elphaba's song *did* persuade Sol and now she's officially in the party," Lucas announces. The other guys whoop and I beam at Nathan.

Dad was right. This *is* fun.

Chapter Seven

I take a deep breath and squeeze the straps of my book bag. It's Monday afternoon after last bell, and I've spent the whole weekend amping myself up to talk to Miss Sahni after choir today. I was at Dad's for the weekend, which was no better than all the previous weekends together, but it did mean I got plenty of alone time in my room to get ready.

Hoshiko waves at me from the choir door—she has to get to her dance classes so I won't have her for moral support—and I wave back. She mimes texting and I nod. As soon as this is over, I'll let her know how it went, though she won't see the texts until later tonight when she's out of class.

"Miss Sahni?" I ask as she walks into her tiny office right off the choir room. My voice croaks and my cheeks heat. I've got to sound more confident. I try again. "Miss Sahni, do you have a minute?"

Her office is like a glorified closet with a big glass window into the choir room. It's clear she hasn't had much time to decorate it. She does have a few framed photos that must be of her large South Asian family and one of her in costume, hugging another girl. They're standing on a stage as if they've finished a performance right before the picture was taken. It gives me a bit of confidence to remember that she's also a performer. She'll be on our side.

"Riley, have a seat. Is something wrong? Are you feeling okay about your solo?"

I sit and force myself to smile. "Yes, absolutely. Thank you again for the opportunity."

"You earned it. You have a lovely singing voice." She looks me up and down. "What can I help with?"

"I wanted to talk about the spring musical." Her face falls and I push on before she can interrupt. "It's so important to me and Hoshiko and so many of us. We can't let the school defund it."

"I know how hard this is on everyone. Several students have already told me—I'm so sorry."

She does sound sincerely sympathetic, but in that way when everyone knows the outcome is inevitable and all that's left is to commiserate about the unfairness of it all. I'm not ready for commiserating. I'm ready for action.

"There's still time to change the administration's mind."

Her eyes widen. "I don't think that's possible."

"You mentioned that they're looking to save money and chose to cut the musical because of waning interest. Well, I'm positive that we can show them just how popular the musical can be. It's all about choosing the right musical to pull in interest and having a new director that everyone can rally behind." I gesture to her. "And that's you. And I would be happy to help in every way I can—I could run auditions and rehearsals, help with sets and pulling together costumes, whatever it takes."

A small voice in my mind reminds me that Mom and Dad might have something to say about these promises. That, in fact, Mom told me I can't do any of that until my grounding is over. But hopefully that will all be in the past by the time Miss Sahni would need me. And, either way, I can't worry about that now. This is definitely a better-to-ask-forgiveness-than-permission situation.

Miss Sahni's expression softens at my words. She leans across her desk toward me. "Oh, Riley, that's really sweet. But I think you're getting ahead of yourself. Convincing the administration to reverse course is"—she shakes her head—"well, that would be a massive undertaking. I wouldn't even know where to begin."

"I do." I smile and pull out my phone. "I've been re-searching possible musicals we could do and taking notes. I know we should probably consider something low-budget, like *You're a Good Man, Charlie Brown*, but . . . I don't know, in my opinion it's more important to choose a musical that the students will get excited about so we get more buy-in. Actually, I bet people would love to do something fresh like *Six* or *Hadestown*, but I don't think we can get licensing and then there's the question of casting and—"

Miss Sahni laughs lightly and I break off.

"I love your passion. If you want to make it in the arts, then you're going to need a lot of that. And this is a good start." She points to my phone and smiles gently, but my shoulders sag. Her tone isn't what I was hoping for. "But it's *a lot* of work. And even if I agreed to direct the musical, you'd need to convince the rest of the administration, the Music Boosters, not to mention the rest of the student body and community. We'd need people onstage, sure, but we also need more people behind the stage and in the audience buying tickets." She runs a hand through her long black hair, looking more tired than she should for being in her mid-twenties. "Are you really serious about this? *Really* serious?"

I had stopped breathing toward the end there, anticipating her telling me to give it up, but I perk up at her question.

"Yes. Incredibly serious. I'll do whatever it takes to convince whoever it takes. Please, Miss Sahni. I need this. The whole school needs this."

She takes me in for a moment and then sighs. "I do agree it's a tragedy to cut the arts like this. And I've always wanted to direct a musical—I did theater all through high school and college." Joy floods me and I bounce in my chair—I can't help it—but she puts up a hand to stop me. "Don't get too excited. I'm only agreeing that the musical is worth the work, not that it'll actually happen. I'll talk to Principal Holloway about the possibility of scheduling a meeting to discuss it further. But I'm already pushed to the breaking point, so if you're as serious as you sound, then you're going to need to be the one pulling together all the details to convince him and the others. A few notes on your phone won't be enough—you will need a serious presentation if you hope to impress everyone. I'll shoot for next month after homecoming. I'm overseeing that committee as well and I can't think of taking on anything else until that's behind me."

My elation from a second ago dissipates. A big presentation with administrators? That sounds seriously intimidating.

"I'm not saying to give up hope," she says quietly. "It's not impossible—it's just going to be an uphill battle."

I nod and try to look more confident than I feel. "Thanks. I'll keep working."

I walk out of the school, my mind reeling. The good news is she didn't say no. And she sounded like she was on my side. I'm not giving up. I whip out my phone and start texting Hoshiko to tell her everything.

Her response comes immediately. *This is going to happen! I'll help you as much as I can—do you think your mom will let me come over sometime?*

I purse my lips. *No, I'm still grounded*

☹ *What about your dad? Would he mind?*

I'm supposed to work Sat morning because he's coming in late. Could you get there as soon as it opens? We could work together before he gets in

☺ ☺ *I'll be there!*

Chapter Eight

When Nathan walks into the store Friday evening for the D&D game, he strides directly to me, takes my arm, and pulls me to the back corner. It's cool for mid-September, and he's wearing an oversized navy sweatshirt with the hood pulled up to shield his face, like he's hiding. His eyes bulge behind his black glasses.

"I can't do this. Deal is off." He tries to walk away, but I jerk him back toward me.

"Wait a minute, what's going on? Why are you freaking out?"

I can't stop myself from glancing over at the aisle where I stood with Paul and Lainey last week and made a complete fool of myself. Paul's pitying face is still so vivid. I don't want this thing with Nathan falling through until I've convinced Paul he was dead wrong about me, and so far there haven't been any opportunities for Paul to see us together.

"I'm not freaking out."

"You absolutely are. Calm down."

He sighs and pushes the hood back. His hair is disheveled now, but he doesn't notice. "She's outside. I saw her pull into the parking lot as I was walking in."

"Okay . . ."

"She's going to see right through this. Or she's going to be annoyed that I'm hanging out with you and then I'll lose the small chance I still have with her."

I put my hands on my hips. "Well, this is an interesting change. Weren't you saying that *I'd* be the one who could never pull this off?"

"Riley—"

"Fine, fine. Listen, there's nothing to worry about. None of that's going to happen. People talk and flirt all the time. Even if she's annoyed, she'll only be annoyed with me, and I don't care what she thinks."

The bell chimes as the door opens and Nathan eagerly swivels toward it like one of Pavlov's dogs looking for a treat.

"No." I take his arm and physically turn him so his back is to the door. "No searching for her as soon as she walks in the door. No waving. No running to her side." I narrow my eyes at him.

"I'm not going to be rude to her."

"That's not being rude. You're only treating her like you'd treat anyone else. If you do that, it'll make her think you're losing interest. She needs to work for *your* attention for once."

"As if that would happen." His gaze strays from me, as if unconsciously looking for her.

"Nathan." I lay my hand on his chest, and he jumps slightly. His eyes lock on mine. "Trust me, it's going to work. Just try tonight and if it blows up in our faces, then the deal is off."

"You're here for another game!" Anthony calls, and I quickly pull my hand from Nathan's chest. "Look, Nathan, Riley's already a better player than Sophia."

Nathan rolls his eyes.

I do a little spin. "I'd like to think I add an element of entertainment to the game."

"Yeah, you do. You're my new favorite part of D&D nights." He gives me one of his wide, charming smiles. "Particularly when you're embarrassing Nathan. That's the best part."

I sneak a glance at Nathan, who is now glowering at us both. It's fun trolling him, but how are we going to pull off this ruse when we can't stop glaring at each other for two seconds?

We follow Anthony into the game room. Fred and Arthur wave me over to the corner where they always play. We've become friendly lately. I think they've begun thinking of me like another granddaughter.

"I've got something for you," Fred says, and holds out a small sack filled with tomatoes. "From my garden. I don't know why I plant so much when it's just me at the house, but I need to do something in my retirement. You take 'em. You know your father won't eat anything unless it's fried or covered in cheese."

"Or both," Arthur adds.

"Right. So can you and your mother use those?" Fred

asks. He has a kind face with lots of smile lines around his eyes and mouth.

I nod immediately. "I'm sure Mom will be thrilled. We don't have a garden."

"I don't have food to bribe you with," Arthur says, "but you better be planning to sing again tonight."

I laugh. "You don't mind me interrupting your games?"

"Mind? Hearing you reminds me of my niece. She's older but she was in choir all through school."

"Then I'll see if I can get another song in." I thank Fred for the tomatoes and head toward the D&D table.

"Hey," Arthur calls after me. "You tell me if those boys aren't treating you right! We'll show them a thing or two."

I give him a thumbs-up, happily surprised that the retirees have decided to befriend me. And now if Nathan annoys me too much, I can sic Fred and Arthur on him. I laugh at the idea but know I need to turn on the charm before Sophia gets to the table. I take a deep breath. *Okay, showtime.*

I walk to Nathan's side and smile up at him. A real smile that reaches my eyes, not the exasperated or sarcastic ones I've given him so far. For just a flash, he looks confused. Then he swallows and smiles back at me.

My stomach does a tiny flip. He's much cuter and less annoying when he's not scowling.

"You should do that more often," I whisper.

"Do what?"

"Smile. It makes it easier for me to look at your face. Otherwise, it's pretty painful."

His eyes narrow. He's having to work to keep up that pleasant expression and I can't help it—my smile widens.

"Is this really your idea of flirting?" he whispers.

"Mildly insulting you and watching you try to hide your annoyance? Actually, yeah. It might not work for everyone, but with you it's a winning combination." I lift my chin defiantly. "We're standing close together, aren't we? And I'm studying your expressions as if I can't pull my eyes from you." I nod. "Yes, this will work very well."

"Until someone hears us."

I lean in. "Then I'll just whisper the insults in your ear."

Someone sniffs behind us and we turn in unison to find Sophia. "What's up?" she asks.

"Glad you could join us," Lucas says with a voice that sounds the exact opposite. "We have a new player in our party. Riley's joined."

"What? Why?" she asks.

I grit my teeth. Way to be welcoming.

"Because we need reliable players and Riley wanted to."

"Like I said, I'm here a lot now. I'd like to make better friends with everyone." I glance around the group, letting my eyes linger on Nathan for a second longer than necessary. Sophia's eyes flash. Good. At least she's a quick study.

John arrives at the table next, carrying a plastic shopping bag similar to the one I was just given. I point at it. "Oh, did you get tomatoes too?"

He glances at me in confusion. "Is this a new inside joke? I can't keep up."

"No, they're real." I hold up a tomato to show the table and the others glance around with smirks. "But they aren't rotten, so nobody better throw them at me when I sing."

"Um, okay. Well, good job eating healthy or whatever,

but Jordan and I were out buying fabric." John opens the bag to show the group. "Fake fur to line my new cloak."

"Wow, you two are serious about your LARPing," Nathan says, and pulls out a chair at the table.

This conversation is beyond me. I know John is dating Jordan, but I have no idea what LARPing is and I can only keep up with so much. Right now I need to focus on tonight being a success with Sophia.

I dart to the chair next to Nathan before Sophia can get there. Sophia walks around so that she sits opposite him. I smile at him again and try to tamp down a thrill of nerves. I still can't believe the position I've gotten myself into. I should have run into the back room as soon as Paul and Lainey walked in. Or given Paul whatever weird name came into my head instead of Nathan's. Or, of course, been the bigger person and ignored his comments altogether. But let's be real.

"So, Sophia, what kind of character do you play?" I ask her.

"I'm a half-elf rogue."

"Cool, cool." I don't know why I asked. It's obvious I have no idea what a rogue is.

"Rogues are nimble and stealthy." Her tone has turned patronizing, and she cuts a glance over to Nathan like they're in on the joke. To my relief, Nathan doesn't say anything to egg her on. I don't think I could pretend to be into him if he was actively being a jerk to me. "We can get in and out of places undetected and we have high Charisma and Persuasion," she continues. "I'm like a spy for the group."

"Time to get started," Lucas says with a more authoritative voice than usual. He reminds us that we're still traveling to find the ancient civilization where a magical sword is supposedly hidden. "As you scan the area, you see some stone ruins to your left. To your right is a well-traveled road. There are fresh tracks from wagon wheels in the mud."

"Sounds like that way could be a town. We could replenish our food and trade for weapons," John says to the group.

"Meh, we just came from a town," Sophia replies. She turns to Lucas. "I'm more interested in the ruins. What kind are they?"

He looks displeased and a bit thrown off. "Um . . . they're . . . dwarven ruins. Set in the base of a giant rock cliff."

She sits up. "They are? Okay, I want to go there."

John sighs. "We don't need to explore more ruins. We need food and to gather more information about this sword."

"But they're dwarven, so there might be gems. Right, Spruce?"

Anthony shakes his head. "I don't know, I'm not that kind of dwarf."

She bats her eyes at Nathan. "What do you say, Sol? You're up for the adventure, right?"

I try to get Nathan's attention, but it's too late. He nods. "Yeah. Let's explore."

The other guys exchange glances. "Fine. Callista, you're going first."

"Of course." Sophia sits up, clearly happy to get her way, and I decide that I really don't understand what Nathan sees in her. She's pretty, sure, and she knows about D&D, but she doesn't seem to care about doing what's best for the party.

I nudge Nathan's foot under the table and raise my eyebrows at him. "Get it together," I whisper. He grimaces.

"Callista," Lucas says, "as you get closer to the ruins, you hear shuffling and then a rock flies into one of the buildings, cracking it."

She frowns. "I roll a stealth check." She rolls and groans.

"Three ogres come out from the ruins and spot you. One raises its arm, ready to toss a boulder in your direction."

At this, John's shoulders slump and Anthony falls back into his chair. "I knew we should have gone to the town instead."

"What do you want to do next?" Lucas asks her.

"I run back to the group!"

"Not so stealthy now," I mutter under my breath. "Is there anything I can do? Could I lull them to sleep by singing or something?" I ask.

Lucas shakes his head. "It's the ogres' round first." He looks at something behind his paper screen and then back to the group. "All right, all three ogres are attacking the party— the first two toward Elphaba and Callista, the last toward Spruce Wayne."

Nathan sits up, adjusting his glasses and pushing up the sleeves of his sweatshirt. "I'll use my protection reaction to guard Elphaba."

The whole table freezes. The guys gawk at him, then at me, and back to him. From their looks of shock, I assume this must be like Nathan telling them he's going to become a professional ballroom dancer. Or try out for lacrosse.

"*What?*" Lucas asks.

"I'll protect Riley." He turns and gives me a small, nervous smile.

This is more like it. I put my hand on his arm. "Thanks, Nath—uh, Sol."

"Are you kidding me, Nathan?" Sophia asks incredulously. "You're supposed to be my paladin. You protect me."

"I'm not actually *your* paladin. I'm supposed to protect the party—especially our most valuable player."

"You're not protecting me," John grumbles to himself.

Lucas rolls his dice. "The first ogre attacks Elphaba with disadvantage and . . . it's a miss." He gives me a small grin. "The next ogre attacks Callista and . . . it's a critical hit."

Sophia throws her hands up in the air. "Great, now I'm taking a dirt nap. Somebody better protect me next time." She turns to Nathan. "Do you have change I can use for a Diet Coke?"

"Sorry, I used my last change on these." He holds up a pack of M&M's. Sophia gets up from the table, but not without a lingering glance at Nathan. Lucas moves on to Anthony's character.

"What's your favorite color?" Nathan asks me in a hushed tone. His eyes trail down my body. "Or is that a silly question given what you're wearing tonight?"

I look down self-consciously. The chilly fall weather means I got to wear one of my favorite sweaters—rainbow polka dots—along with my bright red jeans. I don't see why I need to limit myself to wearing one color when I can wear them all.

"First, well done a moment ago. You're catching on," I

whisper. "And second, you're not allowed to make fun of my clothes anymore. You have to be nice now."

"I think we already established that mild insults are acceptable if delivered in the right way. Which is why I'm staring at your very bright red jeans as if I can't pull my eyes away." To prove his point, he drags his gaze slowly up to my face and raises his eyebrows. "Is she still paying attention?"

I look over my shoulder and catch her staring at us from across the room. "Yes."

"Perfect. Maybe you weren't completely wrong about this." He leans a touch closer. The guys are still talking—something about a wizard spell—and I'm assuming it's rude to ignore them, but it's hard to divide my attention between the game, monitoring Sophia, and talking to Nathan. Especially when his glasses have slipped down his nose again.

"You didn't tell me your favorite color yet."

I reach out and gently slide his glasses back onto the bridge of his nose. He blinks in surprise. It feels weirdly intimate to have my hands so close to his face.

"Your glasses do that a lot. You should probably get them refitted. And if I had to pick, I guess I would go with red. It's so vibrant."

His gaze falls back to my red jeans and I cross my legs, trying desperately to come across as nonchalant. It's so weird to have Nathan looking at me like this, but I have to remember why we're doing it. And that I'm the one who convinced him.

"Red is my favorite color too." He smiles and picks out two red M&M's for me.

"Uh, *hello*? Sol and Elphaba? Are you two still with us?" Lucas gapes at us from across the table.

"Yep," I say quickly. "Ready for fighting. Or singing. Whatever the group needs."

Anthony coughs out a laugh.

At 8:45, Dad comes over and lays a hand on my shoulder. "Great singing earlier. If you keep this up, I'm going to need to build a little stage back here for you."

My eyes pop and I turn around to look at him. "You heard?" Of course, I knew that anyone playing in the back room would hear me, but I hadn't seen Dad back here like last time.

"I snuck in as soon as I realized." His hand squeezes my shoulder. "I never miss a chance to hear you sing. Your mom will be jealous she's missing out."

There's a flutter in my chest to know that Dad was listening. He's never been actively *unsupportive* of my theater and singing in the past. He came to my recitals and shows, even remembering to bring flowers a few times, but he seemed to be there only out of obligation. He always sat in the back instead of center front like Mom and he snuck out as soon as he'd said congratulations after the performance. I figured it was always pretty boring to him. I have to admit, it feels good to know he was listening. I just hope he went back to the registers before he noticed any flirting between Nathan and me.

"I hate to break up a great session," Dad continues. "But

it's time to close up for the night. Riley, do you mind helping with the register?"

"Um, sure," I say, and stand up.

Nathan looks between Sophia and me, clearly pulled between staying to talk to her before she has to leave and making her more jealous. After a moment, he stands and walks to the front with me. I glance over my shoulder.

"She's looking at you," I say in an *I told you so* tone.

He shakes his head and follows me behind the register counter. "Fine, go ahead and gloat. You were right. I can't believe how well this is working."

"You're welcome."

"I was thinking we should talk a little more about this, though. Maybe—"

"Incoming," I interrupt. I nod toward the back of the store where Lucas is marching toward us. Clearly Sophia isn't the only one to notice something different between us tonight.

"What's the plan?" I ask Nathan. "Are we telling the others about this?"

He hesitates and then Lucas is upon us. "What is going on with you two tonight?"

Nathan shrugs at him. "Uh . . . listen . . ."

But Nathan is too busy with Lucas to notice Sophia is heading our way now. If I don't stop him, she's going to hear everything and there's no coming back from that.

"Just having fun at the game," I say. I lay my head on Nathan's shoulder. "And his paladin character is really cute."

"You don't know that," Lucas argues, and leans across the counter. "Maybe he has a snaggletooth."

"Who has a snaggletooth?" Sophia asks.

"Nathan's paladin," Lucas replies with exasperation.

"No, he doesn't. My character would never date someone with a snaggletooth."

Nathan swivels toward her. "I didn't know our characters were dating."

"Maybe not right now," Sophia says with a wink. "But she's always wanted to."

Nathan steps away from me and I have to catch myself before I fall over. *Seriously, man?* I swallow my annoyance. Way to lose your cool at the slightest moment of interest.

"Nathan, if you're done, will you walk me out to my car?" Sophia asks. "I don't want to be alone after dark."

Nathan barely gives me a backward glance as he scurries out the door with her. I sigh. If he drops me every time she gives him a bit of attention, then she'll realize there's nothing to be jealous of and this will all be for nothing. I need Nathan to keep up with this plan until we've convinced Paul I'm off the market.

John and Anthony come up on either side of Lucas, all three of them staring intently at me.

"Are you into Nathan now?" John asks. "Because this is too much change for our group. How are we supposed to defeat the hydra with all this drama going on?"

"I . . ." I look out the glass door into the dim parking lot, but I can't see Nathan or Sophia. Is he going to keep his friends in the dark or not?

"Sorry, guys, Dad wants to lock up, so I need to count this register. We'll talk about it later."

"No way," Anthony replies. "You two were definitely flirting tonight, and it was super uncomfortable to watch." He cocks his head at me. "I'm going to give you some advice— don't crush on a guy who is caught up on someone else. If you're looking to flirt with somebody, I'm right here and I'm not hung up on any redheaded rogues." He raises his eyebrows mischievously.

I shake my head. "I'll keep that in mind."

Dad comes out of the stockroom and pauses when he sees the four of us huddled around the counter. "Riley is never going to finish if you all keep chatting. Time to head out, boys." He gestures to the front entrance.

Lucas scowls, obviously wanting to argue but knowing he can't. "We'll talk more later," he whispers as he leaves. The others trail behind him, looking both intrigued and dis- gruntled.

Chapter Nine

Mom drops me off at the store early Saturday with a hurried wave. She and her interior design partner are off to a country flea market to look for treasures. Nathan must have a key because he's the only one inside when I walk in.

I sit down next to him at the front counter, where he's painting tabletop game models. The store is quiet this morning, but I've been working here for two weeks now and know it'll start to ramp up by noon. That's why Dad has the high school students cover the morning hours—so he can sleep in.

I pull out my laptop. Hoshiko should be here soon, but until she comes, I'm going to work on my history paper.

"Thanks again for last night," Nathan says.

"You're welcome."

"Do you think it went well? I'm not making that up, right?"

"She practically flipped the table over when you helped my character instead of hers. And she asked you to walk her out to her car." I arch an eyebrow. "That has to be a good sign."

"She kissed me on the cheek before she got into the car." His eyes are glued to his painting, but I can hear the excitement in his voice.

"Well, it's no awkward upper-arm kiss, but I guess it's progress."

He laughs, and I have to admit that the sound fills me with a thrill of success. Nathan doesn't laugh much, or at least he doesn't around me. I can tell he keeps a very tight circle of people around him and it's hard to break in. But somehow, I might be.

He puts his paintbrush down and turns so he's facing me. "So. You really thought I was a thief that first day, huh? Just walking around and stealing in front of the owner's daughter?"

My eyes fly wide. He's still thinking about that? "You have to admit it was a weird way to meet you. And I didn't realize then that you knew I was Dad's daughter. How did you even guess that—do we look similar or something?"

"I mean, a little around the eyes, but I've known about you for years. Since I first started coming around here."

This knowledge sends a flutter through my stomach. "You have? How?"

"Don't worry, I'm not infatuated with you or anything. Your dad sometimes shows us photos of you on his phone. And he likes to talk about your recitals and stuff."

He *does*? I scoot forward on my chair and give Nathan an incredulous look. "Are you serious? Dad never talks to *me* about my performances."

"Oh yeah, I've heard a lot about your singing and acting skills over the last few years." He rolls his eyes, but in a lighthearted teasing way to show he's not actually annoyed. "All the regulars know about it. We could probably list off your past theater roles if we pushed ourselves. Why do you think the old guys like hearing you sing during D&D so much?"

I stare, not caring that my mouth has dropped open. I'm struggling to comprehend anything he's saying. Dad talks about me? And shows people pictures? Suddenly, my throat is tight. I had no idea he cared enough to do that.

Nathan rubs the back of his neck, looking uncomfortable. "I can't remember most of your roles, so don't quiz me on them. But I think last year it was . . ." He squeezes his eyes shut for a second. "Uh . . . Edith or something? In that pirates musical?"

My hand goes to my mouth. "Yeah," I whisper. *"Pirates of Penzance."*

He looks pleased. "My aunt is named Edith, so that one was easier to remember than most. Anyway . . ." He bobs his head like he's not sure what more to say. "I would have recognized you no matter what, though. You know how to stand out at school." He waves at my oversized neon-green sweater.

I try to shake myself from thoughts of Dad. I need to process this new info, but I can tell Nathan is trying to cut the tension of this conversation. I sit up and point to his black T-shirt with Spider-Man throwing dice. "It's better than that—I *knew* you owned a ton of Spider-Man shirts. What's that even supposed to mean?"

"If you're not cool enough to know, then I'm not telling you."

I snort and gesture around us. "Oh yes, we're both spending our Saturday in a *super* cool way."

"Speak for yourself. There's nowhere else I'd rather be right now." He stills, as if realizing how his comment could be interpreted—as a compliment toward me—but he doesn't take it back.

We sit for a few moments in silence and my thoughts slide back to what we were just talking about. "So, you must be at the store a lot, then? For Dad to talk to you so much?"

"Yeah. We've joked about me getting a cot for the back room."

"And your parents don't mind?"

His expression darkens. "No. They don't mind." Before I can say more, he clears his throat and stands, pointing to a note on the counter. "Your dad wants us to inventory the Games Workshop paints this morning."

Now it's my turn to distract him from whatever emotions are underlying his words. It's nice to be on good terms with Nathan this morning, and I don't want to jeopardize that by bringing up anything that could upset him.

"To double-check if anyone's stealing?" I ask with a raised eyebrow.

He laughs. "Exactly. You can't trust anyone around here."

"Oh, *that* I know all too well."

As we start to work, I'm pleased to notice that I don't have to search for products like I used to a couple weeks ago. I might not know how to play all these games, but at least I've learned enough to recognize their names and boxes.

I elbow him. "Hey, I guess it's a little late for this, but I *am* sorry for accusing you of stealing. It wasn't personal."

"Eh, it was my fault. I could have said something to you when I saw you behind the counter—I just figured it'd be fun to mess with you." He adjusts his glasses sheepishly. "But then, I also figured you wouldn't immediately try to rat me out to your father."

"Well, now you know not to test me."

"I didn't know you were such a rule follower."

I laugh. "Oh, believe me, I'm definitely not. Which is why I'm here with you on a Saturday morning."

"Wait, I *knew* there was more to this story. Why are you working here? Really?" He must see my hesitation because he shakes his head. "As your pretend boyfriend, I deserve real answers."

I purse my lips, wondering if there's a way to get out of this, but he seems very intent. "Fine." I sigh. "So, my best friend, Hoshiko, and I had tickets to see *Waitress* in Columbus and we were both so excited. We'd been waiting months for the show."

"That's the title of the show? What's next—*Cook*? Or, wait, maybe *Butcher*? Actually, that one has promise . . ."

I groan. "Remind me to show you *Sweeney Todd,* then. Are you finished?"

"Never. But I'm intrigued, so please continue."

"So, the day of the show, Hoshiko's car broke down. Mom couldn't drive me, but we had to find some way to get there."

"Did you ask your dad?"

I blink. Even though he lives close by, it never crossed my mind to ask him.

"No, I didn't," I reply slowly. "I drove. In my mom's car. Without telling her. And, um . . . I don't have my license yet."

He falls back like somebody shoved him. "Are you serious?"

"When they found out, I got majorly grounded, and now I'm here almost every day because they don't trust me at home alone."

He throws his head back to laugh. "Okay, this makes *way* more sense. Honestly, I'm almost impressed. Was it worth it?"

"Yeah. Totally," I say with a chuckle.

"Nice."

The door opens and for a moment I'm upset that a customer is interrupting us. Then I realize it's Hoshiko. "Yay, you made it!"

"Hi!" She looks around, ducking her head shyly when she sees Nathan. "Am I the only customer here?"

"Yeah, mornings are slow. You know Nathan from school." I gesture to him, and they both give a small wave.

"Is it cool if Hoshiko and I hang out in the stockroom for a bit? We were going to work on stuff before Dad gets in."

"Sure, I'll be painting my models."

I hesitate. I feel a little guilty leaving him alone now that we aren't flinging snarky comments at each other constantly.

"Don't worry," he says, "I'm fine out here on my own. And I'm sure I have zero interest in whatever it is you're working on."

I roll my eyes and lead Hoshiko to the stockroom. It's still incredibly messy, but Dad does have a small desk and a few folding chairs shoved in one corner. I pull the chairs to the center and push a stack of broken-down cardboard boxes to the side so we'll have some space.

Hoshiko surveys the room skeptically. Today her hair is braided to mimic a crown and she's wearing a long-sleeved *Sound of Music* shirt from our freshman year musical. I really hope we get a new musical shirt this year too.

She hands me a mug of something, and I take a sip. Hot chocolate. "Mmm, thanks."

"I figured we'd need something warm for our early morning meeting, but I'm too poor to buy us both pumpkin spice lattes."

"Hot chocolate from home is perfect." I pull out a notebook and sit next to her. "Are we ready?"

"Uh, I don't think so. *First,* I need to know more about what's happening with Nathan. You told me how annoying he is, but then you joined his D&D group and now you two are looking awfully chatty. What's going on?"

I sigh. Part of me can't believe she noticed, and part of me would be sad if she hadn't. That's the best (and worst) thing about having a best friend—they know you really, *really* well.

I doodle a flower in the notebook and avert eye contact. This whole scheme is pretty embarrassing when I have to say it out loud. "How about we focus on theater for now and I tell you later?"

She raises an eyebrow. "Yeah, I don't think so. This is even better than I originally thought. Do you like him now? Or are you getting vibes from him? I need to know everything." She rests her chin on her fists like she's readying herself to watch a movie.

I heave another sigh. "Don't forget you're my best friend,

which means you can't judge me too harshly. Or at all. I was desperate, Hoshiko!"

"Stop stalling."

"Fine." I launch into my deal with Nathan.

She falls back against her chair. "Omigod."

I sing the next few lines from the *Legally Blonde* song without batting an eye. It's an unwritten rule that one of us can't say "omigod" without the other singing the rest.

"You're in one of those fake relationships like in the movies?" she asks.

"It's not a relationship. It's not like we're officially dating. If we were, then he couldn't flirt with Sophia without cheating on me."

"That sentence is really weird." She stares at me, blinking slowly, a smile spreading across her face. "So, are you two, like, making out now? Just for show, of course." She winks.

"No! Everything's been totally PG. I'm just thinking of it as acting practice."

She laughs. "Mmm, yes, you're very dedicated to your craft. And luckily there's no possibility of more happening since actors *never* fall for each other." She lifts a knowing eyebrow.

"Shhh, these walls might be thin!" I whisper. "Can we please move on to more important things now? Miss Sahni was not particularly reassuring about our possibilities for bringing back the musical, but she did confirm a meeting with Principal Holloway in three weeks, as soon as she's done with homecoming prep. There's so much to do before then that my brain freezes when I think about it. I haven't done *anything* yet."

Hoshiko mimes taking a slow, deep breath and then points to my travel mug. "First, drink more cocoa. Then we'll start by working on a timeline. When the license application is due, auditions, cast list, rehearsal schedule, possible show dates." She ticks off the items on her fingers. "Once you have it all laid out, I bet you'll feel way better."

I take a deep drink of my hot chocolate and smile at her over the mug. Thank goodness for best friends.

At eleven-forty-five, I pop my head out to the front to see how things are going. Dad will be here soon, and I don't want to get caught hanging out in the back with Hoshiko. Thankfully she was right—having a tentative timeline calmed me down.

Nathan is still sitting at the counter painting. "All finished?"

"Well, taking a little break at least. Is everything fine out here?"

"Quiet as always."

The door opens and Lucas walks in with his dad, who waves to us and heads for the back game room. Lucas rushes over to Nathan and me. "All right, don't try to distract me. What was going on last—" He pauses midsentence as Hoshiko comes to my side.

"I thought I might be missing out on all the fun," she whispers.

"Oh, hi, Hoshiko. I'm, er, Lucas. If you didn't already know that." His cheeks have gone adorably red.

"I knew. Hi, Lucas."

Hoshiko is calm but quiet, and I watch her furtively. It's amazing how different she can be in different settings. She's incredibly powerful and confident when she's dancing or acting, but she often shies away from attention in everyday life. In fact, multiple times classmates haven't recognized her onstage because she's nothing like her usual humble self.

"You were saying?" Nathan asks Lucas with a grin.

"I . . ." He falters. Hoshiko's appearance has sucked away all of Lucas's thunder. "What was going on with you last night? Are you two—"

"No," Nathan says.

I let out a breath. I'm really glad Nathan doesn't want to lie to his friends about this.

"*Definitely* not," I add. "We're just trying to make Sophia jealous. And I think it's working."

Lucas gapes at us. "Wait, so that was all an act? Are you serious?"

I share a look with Nathan and then quickly explain the deal again, brushing over the details about Paul.

"Isn't it the craziest thing you've ever heard?" Hoshiko asks Lucas when I finish. "As if this isn't going to blow up in their faces."

Nathan and I roll our eyes. It's not that big of a deal.

Lucas nods emphatically at her, clearly excited that she's talking to him. "Right? That's exactly what I was thinking! Dude, even if this works, she'll lose interest as soon as she realizes that she 'has' you. And who even wants to be with someone if you have to trick them into liking you? You're setting yourself up for failure."

"You don't know that," Nathan argues. "I think as soon as Sophia and I start talking more, she'll realize just how much we have in common and the rest will be history. This is going to be a funny origin story we tell everybody when we're old and gray."

The three of us groan in unison.

"That was sad," Lucas says. "Like, I'm legitimately depressed hearing you say that."

"So glad to have your support."

"I'm a supportive friend who thinks you deserve better than Sophia. I can't believe you agreed to this, Riley. I thought you had a better read on her."

Secretly, I agree with Lucas, but I can't risk having Nathan drop the deal before Paul is fully convinced. I raise my hands in surrender. "I'm a neutral player over here."

"And I'm the casual observer who's bummed she won't get to see this craziness unfurl firsthand," Hoshiko adds.

"You can *totally* come and watch it implode," Lucas says immediately. "I'll even bring popcorn. Come to our next game, you're always welcome."

"Yes!" I exclaim. "Hoshiko, come, please? You could even make a character—we could be bards together!" I turn to the guys. "That'll be fine, right? We can't have too many people."

Nathan shakes his head. "Actually, we can—"

"We can *never* have too many people." Lucas gives Nathan a sharp glare. "Consider yourself the newest member of the party."

Chapter Ten

I should have been paying more attention. If I had been, then I might have seen Paul coming my way in the cafeteria during lunch on Monday. I could have casually turned without him realizing I was avoiding him. Or even rushed into the bathroom if necessary. Instead, I'm buried in my phone when I hear it.

"Riley?"

My head snaps up and I almost groan out loud. *Why* is he still talking to me? There's nothing more to say.

"Uh, hey." I look around for Hoshiko so I have an excuse to bolt, but remember she stayed behind to talk to our French teacher about the upcoming test.

"So . . . I've been thinking about what happened at your dad's store and I want to clear the air." He slides his hands into his pockets, looking relaxed and self-assured.

My stomach locks into knots, but I force a calm expression

on my face. "There's no air to clear. It's perfectly breathable right now."

What am I even saying? I've got to stop blurting out mortifying stuff around him.

"Listen, I should have given you more time after the breakup to . . . you know, feel better or whatever, instead of bringing Lainey there with me. That wasn't cool."

He's right, it wasn't cool, but that doesn't mean I want to talk about it. Plus, I can never tell what his motives are. Is he really worried about my feelings or is he just trying to clear his own conscience? Probably the latter. I'm tempted to tell him off, but I don't want to get into a fight in the middle of the cafeteria. "Don't worry about it."

"Yeah? Cool. And we'll just forget about that whole Nathan thing." He winks, then mimes locking his lips and throwing away the key. It's like he's dumped a bucket of ice water on me. I have to stop myself from picking up that imaginary key and shoving it somewhere else on his person.

"What Nathan thing?" My voice is barely above a whisper.

He leans in like we're sharing secrets. "You know . . . where you pretended he was your boyfriend? Don't worry, I won't say anything about it."

Anger races through my body so fast I'm surprised my favorite floral dress doesn't burst into flame and leave me naked like I'm in one of my classic nightmares. I don't care that he's 100 percent correct. He shouldn't just *assume* that.

If there was even the tiniest possibility before of me telling him the truth, he's just blown that to smithereens. I'm *never* coming clean now. Not when he's acting like he's doing me some big favor or keeping a shameful secret for me. I'm digging my heels in until the soles of my shoes melt from the magma in the core of the earth.

"I wasn't pretending."

He scoffs. "Riley, come on. It was pretty obvious."

My nerves skitter and I glance around the cafeteria, even though I have no idea where Nathan could be right now or what period he eats lunch. Suddenly, I'm desperate for him by my side. If he were here, we could smack that expression off Paul's face. That's all I want in the world—to watch Paul realize he's wrong.

And then I see Nathan striding toward me, seeming to appear out of nowhere. His face holds a small reassuring smile as if he knows exactly what I'm thinking and is saying, *We've got this.*

"Hey." His voice is warm. "I've been looking for you."

I'm so grateful that I don't think; I just wrap my arms around his stomach and pull him tight. He stiffens for the slightest moment before returning the gesture. I take a deep breath. His T-shirt smells good.

I pull away and Nathan keeps his arm around my waist. He looks up at Paul. "What's up, man?"

Paul's gaze flicks back and forth between us. "I . . ." He trails off, his eyebrows furrowing as he takes us in. "Uh, just talking with Riley."

"Yeah, I can see that."

Nathan's fingers gently press into the skin at my waist. My heart thumps faster and I'm distracted by the fact that he's touching me. The lengths of our bodies press together so I can feel the rough seam of his jeans through my dress.

I turn to Nathan. His eyes are a glittery green behind his

glasses. "We were just talking about you." I turn back to Paul and smile. "Weren't we?"

Paul looks so shaken by this turn of events that his mouth has gone slack. I want to soak in this moment like it's the most luxurious bubble bath in the world. It's *glorious*.

"Um, well . . ." Paul shuffles his feet.

"We were talking about you and me dating," I continue on, unwilling to let Paul off the hook just yet.

"You don't say," Nathan replies. "That's my favorite topic of conversation." He shifts closer and his hand moves slightly, leaving five warm spots where his fingertips had been.

"Mine too."

He turns to Paul. "Are you okay? You look kind of queasy." Nathan's voice is even and calm, almost tinged with concern, but there's also the hint of a challenge. His performance is a beautiful thing to behold. Tony-worthy, for sure.

Paul shakes his head. "I'm fine. Just . . . you know, catching up with Riley. I'm happy for you guys." He takes a step back, but his eyes are flipping back and forth between us like we're a riddle he can't solve.

"Thanks. Though you can't be as happy as I am." Nathan squeezes my side again. "I was going to grab some pizza. Do you want a slice, babe?"

Babe? Okay, we need to work on nicknames, but I'm too grateful to care right now. I nod eagerly. "Yes, I'm starving. Later, Paul."

We don't wait for him to respond. Nathan releases me, but only so he can slide his hand into mine. Our fingers intertwine and it feels odd. The last person to hold my hand was Paul and his hand was wide and soft. Nathan's hand is cool and slim, his fingers longer than Paul's.

We walk toward the pizza station, not saying a word until we've put a good amount of distance between us and Paul.

"Okay, I have to admit, that was pretty fun." Nathan chuckles. "Was that okay?"

My heart is about to thump out of my chest, but in the same way as when the curtain has just fallen after a show and I know I nailed the performance. "That was amazing. You're amazing. *Thank you.*"

"No problem." His grip on my hand loosens. "Do you want to stop holding hands? Or will that look suspicious if Paul's still watching?"

I glance around. I can't see him, but I'm not taking any chances after what we just pulled off. "Let's keep going for a little longer. If you don't mind."

"I don't. I'm not actually in second grade anymore— I know you don't have cooties." He points ahead of us. "I *was* going to grab a slice of pizza. Do you want one?"

I nod. "Sure." I'm still too dumbfounded to think clearly.

He glances at me, his face worried. "So . . . it was okay that I came over like that? I saw Paul talking to you and I figured it was my call to action."

"It was perfect." I shake my head, my whole body tensing as I remember what Paul said. "He'd just accused me of making up the whole thing with you."

Nathan gasps sarcastically. "He's smarter than he looks."

"It doesn't matter if he's right or not. It's the principle of the thing," I say under my breath. "You don't just outright accuse someone of that! Not unless the whole purpose is to make them sweat and admit to being a total fool. And the way he did it too . . . as if he's such a good guy, checking on me. Ugh." I spin to face Nathan, making him stop. "You'll keep this up with me, right? For a while?"

"I'm here, aren't I?"

"You are. That's a good point. How *are* you here?"

"We have the same lunch period, Riley," he replies, like it's the most obvious thing in the world.

"We do?"

"Yeah. We've had the same lunch for the last two years. I sit over there." He points across the cafeteria, and I find Anthony, John, and Lucas all openly staring at us.

I gape at him and back at the table. "Huh."

I can't believe I've never noticed them before. Hoshiko and I do tend to be in our own world when we're together, though.

We step up to the counter and each get a slice of pizza. Then we look at each other, as if realizing at the same time that we don't know what to do next. Flirting at the game shop is one thing, but being at school is something totally different. I hadn't thought about the implications. Do we need to eat at the same table now? Should we be walking the halls hand in hand? Giving each other longing looks and kissing when the teachers aren't around? At least we don't have any classes together so we don't need to worry about how that's going to work.

"Actually, let's sit here for a second." He motions to the end of an empty long table. "I wanted to talk about something before, but then we got interrupted at the store."

We both sit and I pick at my pizza.

"So, if we're going to keep this up for a bit, maybe we should talk about the . . . um, rules of it all. Like, what's okay and what's not okay to do."

I shake my head. "What do you mean?"

"Like when we held hands. And when I had my arm around your waist. We never talked about whether that kind of stuff was cool or not."

I lean back in surprise at his thoughtfulness. "Nathan, if I didn't know you better, I'd think you were being considerate."

He rolls his eyes. "Oh, don't worry, you still annoy me, but I'm not a jerk. I don't want to do anything that's going to make you uncomfortable."

"You didn't."

He looks relieved. "What about in the future? If we keep doing this, then things might come up—things we didn't plan on. We should know where the line is. Or have a code or something so we know when the other person isn't comfortable."

My cheeks flush. "Like . . . a safe word?"

He chokes on his bite of pizza. Our eyes lock and we start laughing.

"Whoa, that escalated quickly," he says, and coughs out another laugh. "Not a word, that would be too obvious. And weird."

"How about we pinch each other?" I grin and reach over and pinch his forearm.

"Oww! Not that hard!" He rubs his arm. "I'm already regretting this, but fine. As long as you don't pinch hard enough to draw blood."

Chapter Eleven

To my surprise, Mom is in the parking lot Tuesday to pick me up, looking like she's just walked off a fall photo shoot. Her hair now has a reddish tinge and she's only wearing makeup and clothes with a "warm autumn palette" until December. If she could walk around holding a pumpkin, she would.

"Where's Dad?" I ask as I climb into the SUV.

"He got caught up at the store and asked if I could swing by. How was school?"

"It was fine." I pause and then smile at the music filling the car. "Back to listening to this again?"

"Time doesn't diminish quality."

Mom and I spent a good six months listening to the *Hamilton* soundtrack on a loop when I was in elementary school. In fact, we almost always have a soundtrack playing when we drive places. I try to remember if we did that when

Dad was in the car with us, but I don't think so. It was always a special thing we saved for the two of us.

The knowledge gives me a twinge of guilt, which is weird. I've never felt guilty about leaving Dad out before.

I glance over at Mom. "Did you know Dad has been telling people at the store about my theater performances?"

She raises an eyebrow. "How could I possibly know that?"

"Right. It's just . . . isn't that weird? I didn't think he cared."

"Well"—she hesitates—"he doesn't love theater the way we do, but he does love you. Maybe he wanted to show off a bit about his talented daughter. I know I do." She pats my leg fondly.

I take a breath, thinking of how happy he's been at the store. You'd think I wasn't there as a punishment at all, the way he smiles at me and bustles around checking on me and asking how I am. It's not that he's unhappy when I stay with him on weekends, but there's always underlying tension, like we don't know how to be around each other. Being at the store with him is the first time we've been together doing something he actually likes and knows about.

"Maybe you should ask him," Mom continues. "You should have a good relationship with your dad. I know we haven't always made things easy on you since the divorce . . . that *I* haven't made it easy. It's hard to share you." She looks over and gives me a smile. "But maybe this time at the store will give you the chance to get to know him better."

"Okay. Maybe I will."

"But I'm not giving up our musical movie nights. We're

due for another this Thursday. Maybe a *Hamilton* rewatch is in order?"

"Yes!" I agree, and turn up the volume. We sing along to "Wait for It" and then I think of something else I've been meaning to bring up. "Soooo, homecoming is the first weekend in October."

She raises an eyebrow. "What an interesting and random fact to mention out of the blue."

"Mom," I plead. "Do you think there's any way I can still go? I know I'm in trouble, but you wouldn't want to deprive me of such a time-honored American tradition, would you?"

She shakes her head and groans. "You can do better than that."

"Hoshiko and I always go together. It's just one night."

"I don't know, Riley. You're supposed to be learning a lesson with this punishment. If we give you everything you want, then what's the point?"

"But I am learning my lesson. I've already learned it." I lean my head against her arm, which is maybe dangerous since she's driving, but I need to suck up to her. "Will you at least think about it?"

She's silent for a few moments and I think I've lost her, but then she quickly kisses the top of my head. "We'll see. Don't get your hopes up."

I grin and sit up straight. "I promise."

When I walk into the store, Sophia is standing at the register in the middle of what looks like an intimate conversation with Nathan.

I cluck my tongue. He's clearly useless without me. I roll my shoulders back and walk behind the counter. "Hi, Sophia. Nathan."

"Hey." He barely looks my way, then does a double take. "Oh, I mean, *hey*."

Good Lord, he isn't selling this at all.

"What are you guys talking about?" I ask.

"Just gamer stuff." Sophia looks me up and down. "That's quite the outfit."

"Thanks," I say, even though I know it wasn't a compliment. "You too."

Both of us would stand out in a crowd. Sophia looks like she's about to go live her best cottagecore life in a billowy flowered dress cut low enough to pull all eyes to her chest. Meanwhile I'm sporting my favorite black and white checkerboard pants, a chunky orange sweater, and yellow smiley face earrings. Elegant and demure I am not.

I glance significantly at Nathan, waiting for him to compliment me. Instead, his eyes linger on Sophia. I push down a sigh. He's clearly forgotten all about the plan in the presence of her dress.

I lay a hand on his arm. "Lunch was fun today."

I say it to remind him that I'm standing there, but it's also the truth. The guys have started sitting with Hoshiko and me, and at first I wasn't sure if she'd like adding anyone else into our tight twosome, but she's been cool with it. This afternoon we all got into a weirdly hysterical debate over whether frosted Pop-Tarts are better than unfrosted ones. I stand firm that frosted are superior because more sugar is *always* better, but Lucas and Anthony strongly disagree. Something about getting more filling in the unfrosted ones. We were practically in food fight territory by the end of lunch.

"Team Frosted forever," he replies, and high-fives me.

"Forever." I chuckle. "If I had a car, I'd run to the store and get a few boxes just so we could slowly eat them during the game to troll the others."

"We should do that! I can drive."

I blink in surprise. I was only kidding, but he seems totally serious. "Um, I mean, I doubt my dad will let me go, but I love your enthusiasm."

I glance at Sophia, who is frowning, clearly confused by our inside joke. I almost feel bad about the way I'm trying to exclude her—and the fact that we're trying to make her jealous in the first place—but then I remember how dismissive she's been to Nathan (and me) and my sympathy fades.

Nathan looks at the time on his phone. "The game is going to start soon, but there's a grocery store down the street. I bet we can make it. Want to?"

"Sure, if we can get Dad to agree. I call strawberry."

"You better share." He grabs his keys. "I'll go talk to your dad."

He dashes off for the stockroom and Sophia and I eye each other uncomfortably. After a moment she walks off without another word. I wander over to Fred and Arthur and chat for a few minutes about their kids and grandkids.

Nathan comes back out looking triumphant. I follow him out the door rather than ask questions.

"We have to pick up diet soda for the store. Don't let me forget."

"I can't believe you got Dad to agree to this," I say as I click my seat belt and try to find a comfortable place to put my feet where they won't be directly on top of discarded fast-food bags. At least the car doesn't smell bad. "I thought I wasn't allowed to ride with anyone but him and Mom."

"Well, you might not want to mention this to your mom just to be on the safe side. But your dad trusts me implicitly."

"Yeah, clearly. And Dad wants diet soda? He hates that stuff."

"I know," Nathan says with a shrug. "But his doctor told him to start exercising and cut his sugar, and this is the closest he's gotten. At least he's trying to be healthier."

I bite my lip and nod. I didn't know anything about that. Dad is under doctor's orders to change his diet? And he's telling Nathan about it, of all people? Maybe the better question is why he isn't telling me. I guess Mom is right about trying to build a better relationship with him.

Nathan starts the car and a song blasts my eardrums, startling me. He quickly shuts it off, but I've heard enough to recognize the music.

"You listen to oldies music?" I ask with a grin.

"Not exactly."

I scoff. "Um, I'm pretty sure that was Michael Jackson you were just blasting through the speakers."

"Oh, yeah?" He turns up the volume and backs out of the parking lot. The song begins to play again, and it's "Beat It" by Michael Jackson . . . but it's also not. I squint and listen to the lyrics. Is he saying *eat* it? What kind of weird song is this?

Nathan laughs when he sees my confused expression. "It's Weird Al Yankovic. He made parody songs back in the day. Lucas's dad introduced us to his music when we were kids."

"And you're still listening to it now. Very cool."

"I thought you'd already realized I *am* the coolest."

"Well . . ." I pat his dashboard. "It's pretty cool having your own car. I wish I had one, but I don't think that's ever going to happen now."

His smile slips. "You need your own car when your parents aren't around to drive you places. I got my license the moment I could."

I blink, surprised by his change in tone. Nathan never acts this way around his D&D friends. He's never melancholy or bitter—but then he never brings up his parents or home life. I wonder if it's possible I'm seeing a side of him most people aren't privy to. It makes me even more curious, but I'm not sure I should be the one asking questions. Maybe he should be the one who chooses to share.

"I guess I should've gotten my license, too, huh?" I ask lightly instead.

He chuckles. "That probably would've saved you some trouble."

"And saved *you* a ton of trouble." I gesture around the car. "Imagine how easy your life would be if I hadn't gotten caught coming home from *Waitress*. You'd be hanging out with your friends instead of fake flirting and buying frosted Pop-Tarts."

"Actually . . . this timeline is growing on me."

He looks away from the road long enough for our eyes to meet, but it's enough time for my stomach to jump like we're on a roller coaster that just dropped.

We split up at the grocery store—him running for the soda while I grab the Pop-Tarts—then we hurry back into the car and to the game store. We probably aren't gone more than fifteen minutes, but I feel different when I walk back through the door to Sword and Board Games, strawberry goodness in hand. I smile at Nathan, and he smiles back without the slightest bit of animosity.

I think we're actual friends now.

Chapter Twelve

I link my arm with his as we walk back into the store. "Here we go. And remember, you're not thinking about her. You're too caught up talking to me."

He raises his eyebrows. "Don't you mean teasing you about your pants?"

"You love my pants," I say, not missing a beat. "They're amazing."

"I could play chess on them."

I grin at him. "Who said fashion can't be practical?" I push open the door to the back room and we head to the D&D table, the others eyeing us as we approach. Nathan shakes the grocery bag at them. "Guess what we got?"

"I don't get it. What's the big deal with Pop-Tarts?" Sophia says with a pout as Nathan pulls out a box and waves it in the air.

"Wait, you brought us Pop-Tarts? Sweet!" Anthony exclaims.

"You do realize which kind they got, right?" John asks him, and then glances at me for confirmation. I smile wickedly.

"All the frosted ones you can eat," I reply.

Anthony groans.

"Nathan?" Sophia's voice is low, and I fight my urge to look her way. "I just finished the first Wheel of Time, and I loved it. Especially the ending."

"Wow, that's so cool that you read it," he replies. "What'd you think of that last fight scene with Ba'alzamon?"

I bite my lip, unsure whether I'm supposed to be pulling his attention back toward me or letting them talk. After a moment I slide my arm out from his and turn away from them. I don't want to distract from a real conversation since that's the whole point of this deal. Although this fake dating is so convoluted that it's hard to keep it straight.

Luckily Hoshiko walks in at that moment, glancing around nervously, and I hurry over to her. "You made it!"

To our left, a group of middle-aged guys erupt in raucous laughter over their board game and she jumps. "What are you getting me into?" she whispers.

"We're going to have so much fun together!" I beckon her to the table. Lucas sits up straighter and John and Anthony look more awake as well.

"Hi," she says with a little wave.

"I'm so glad you could come," Lucas says, practically vibrating with excitement, and introduces her to everyone else. Sophia barely looks over, she's so busy talking about books with Nathan.

"So . . . how does all this work?" Hoshiko asks, looking at me for help.

I hesitate and then shake my head. "Lucas is the expert. He'll help you make a character."

She sits down and he scoots his chair closer to her.

"I do know what class you should be," I add. "A bard!"

"Sure." She turns to Lucas. "I want to be the same thing as Riley."

"Yay! Maybe we can sing duets!"

"Is that a thing in D&D?" she asks. "Why haven't we been playing this?"

"Um, no, that's not a usual thing. But . . . I mean—"

"Now we have two bards?" John interrupts. "This is getting ridiculous. Why are we adding to our party so much when they're not contributing?"

"Dude, shut up," Anthony says, and grins at Hoshiko and me. "This is way better than before."

John rolls his eyes and shrugs.

I realize I've been ignoring Nathan, so I turn around. He looks perfectly happy chatting with Sophia. This is such a weird line to be walking. Am I supposed to break into their conversation and start flirting? But the whole point is to help him talk to her. What if he wants me to stay away so they can talk longer?

Hoshiko quickly builds her character with Lucas's help and then we jump back into the quest. We've trekked to the eastern shore to find the sword for Nathan's paladin, but now we've learned it's guarded by a troll. Unsurprisingly, that leads to another battle.

"What can I do? Don't bards just sing and tell stories?" Hoshiko asks Lucas.

"You could use your inspire ability to buff me," Anthony says, and scoots his chair closer to her. I guess he's turning his flirting on her since I'm too caught up with Nathan to reciprocate. I wait for Lucas's reaction.

Hoshiko frowns. "*Buff* you?"

"Anthony, cool it," Lucas says, and glares at Anthony.

There it is. Lucas is clearly into Hoshiko.

"He means your ability will strengthen his attack," I explain to her. "This is officially my favorite part of the game. Just watch." I turn to Lucas. "I'm using my inspire ability to buff Sol."

"And what will you be singing for us this time?" Lucas asks.

"I'm in the mood for a classic." I turn to Nathan. "Sound good?"

Rather than glare or slink under the table like our first game together, Nathan nods. "I'm prepared to be duly inspired."

I give him a playful smile and then launch into "People Will Say We're in Love" from *Oklahoma!* A few guys on the other side of the room chuckle—they're getting used to my singing—and Nathan rubs a hand over his mouth to cover his laughter. I've been waiting for my chance to sing this one.

I can't believe I'm allowed to break out into song and actually have it be useful to the campaign. And Nathan's reaction is night and day from before. Of course, that might be because his character is stronger after I use my amazing singing abilities to inspire him. Or maybe he's only pretending to enjoy it for Sophia's benefit. Either way, I'll take what

I can get. I beckon Hoshiko to join me and she takes over Curly's part, the two of us trying out a little harmony as we finish the chorus.

Lucas claps more than a DM probably should. "Amazing."

In my peripheral vision, I see Dad slip back to the storefront. I guess he was listening to me again. He must have a sixth sense for when I'm going to sing. Or his ears are attuned to my voice. It's still hard to reconcile this with the way he acted in the past.

"Hear, hear!" Fred calls out. He's become a particular fan of mine. I'm pretty sure Sophia rolls her eyes, but I don't pay much attention.

"See!" I tell Hoshiko. "We're going to have so much fun."

As soon as John starts his turn, Sophia slides her hand up Nathan's arm. "I need some new dice for the game. Can you help me look?"

"Sure."

They get up and disappear through the door to the front. The group turns to me as soon as they're gone.

"I still don't understand why you're *helping* Nathan get closer to Sophia," Anthony asks.

"We're just . . . doing each other a favor."

John shakes his head. "If you're doing him a favor, then you should be keeping her away from him. He'll thank you later."

"You know she's going to come back with new dice that Nathan bought for her, right?" Lucas asks.

"Does she pay him back?"

"Uh, *no*. She's always using him to get stuff. That's the

only reason she gave him any attention to begin with—his employee discount and willingness to pull out cash whenever she's around. She's probably worried you're going to take away her gamer bank account."

"Are you serious?" Revulsion boils up in me, and I peek over my shoulder to double-check they haven't come back in. She's using Nathan for his money? Not that he has a lot of it, as far as I can tell, but that's even worse. "I didn't know she does that. That's horrible."

Anthony nods slowly like I'm a little kid who can't understand difficult concepts. "Uh-huh. Which is why the last thing we want is the two of them getting closer."

I bite my lip, worry gnawing at me. Suddenly I see my plan with Nathan in a whole new light. I don't want to give her more opportunities to take advantage of him.

"Maybe I should go interrupt them. . . ."

"Please." Lucas shoos me away. "Otherwise she'll keep Nathan there all night and we'll never get anything done."

I swallow my nerves and walk to the front display case of fancy dice that Dad has by the registers. "Hey, we need you guys for the game."

"Just a second, deciding between these two," Sophia says over her shoulder.

I come to Nathan's other side and tug him away. "Don't buy those dice for her," I whisper.

He blinks in surprise. "Why not? I don't mind."

An idea comes to me suddenly. "Actually, you should buy *me* something instead."

"No way. You have your own employee discount."

"I'll pay you back later, but if you really want her to think

I've taken her place as your new crush, then you can't buy her anything."

I'm only half sure what I'm saying makes sense. I don't have time to analyze it; I just know I can't let him buy anything for her tonight. It'll weigh too heavy on my conscience otherwise.

He nods slowly, so I must not be saying total nonsense. "Smart." He looks back at the huge display where Sophia is pretending to look at dice but is really watching us. "What kind do you want?"

"Doesn't matter. Knock yourself out." I give him a flirty smile, kiss him on the cheek, and stride back into the game room before I can fully comprehend what I did.

I bring my fingertips to my lips. I just kissed Nathan. I mean, not *kissed*-kissed him, but my lips were on his skin. I can't believe I just did that.

Lucas and Hoshiko are chatting when I return to the table. Lucas is speaking animatedly, with a look of adoration on his face. It's pretty cute, actually. But I don't have time to think about them. I'm still stuck on the fact that I kissed Nathan. My heart speeds at the thought.

They break off and wait expectantly for a report from me.

"Mission accomplished," I tell the table, taking a seat. "I think."

Nathan and Sophia are back by the time Anthony has finished his next turn. "Sorry it took so long. It was hard to choose," Nathan says as he sits down.

"What'd you get?" Anthony asks Sophia.

She shrugs. "I decided not to get anything. The store is overpriced anyway. I'll order online."

I never thought I'd be loyal to this store, but I ball my hands into fists at the words.

"Here." Nathan drops a little fabric bag in front of me. I pick it up and pour out a set of seven dice. A little gasp escapes me as I take them in. I've never thought of dice as something that could be beautiful or personal, but these are. I pick them up, one by one, turning them so the facets catch and glimmer in the overhead light. They have swirls of brightly colored jewel tones—cobalt blue, jade green, chartreuse, maroon— all my favorite colors in the world, with sparkly gold numbers imprinted on the sides. I shake my head softly. "They're . . ."

Nathan chuckles. "They're *you*."

I look up in shock. He's right. They are me. These might as well be stamped with the letters of my name rather than numbers. Lucas is now describing the ancient vault where the sword is being kept, but I'm too distracted to hear everything. My heart beats faster knowing that Nathan picked these. I thought he'd grab the cheapest thing possible for the sake of the ruse.

"These are . . . wow. Like little gemstones."

"Do they make you more excited to play?" Nathan whispers.

I nod fervently.

"Then they've already done their job."

I'm still not sure what to say, so I study the dice again. I've been around Dad enough to know that the large, ball-shaped one is called a d20. And, of course, I recognize the normal six-sided dice. But I don't know the others.

"Honestly, I'm still not sure what these all do."

He leans close, so that our shoulders touch, and picks up

the d20. "You use this one the most—for skill checks, initiative, lots of stuff. This one is a d4. You use it for low-level spells. And these others will depend on the situation. You'll figure it out if you stick around. And, in the meantime, I'll help you."

"Thank you," I whisper, and impulsively lay my head on his shoulder. It's part of the act, sure, but right now I'm not doing it for Sophia's benefit.

I'm doing it because I like the feel of my head on Nathan's shoulder.

Chapter Thirteen

I wait after choir on Thursday to speak to Miss Sahni again. She's at her music stand at the front of the room but beckons me over as the rest of the class streams out.

"I've been making good progress on my plans for the musical and I wanted to run them by you," I tell her.

She nods. "Of course, I'd love to hear what you've been working on."

"So, I decided on three potential musicals that would work best and pulled the licensure fees, a list of possible costumes and sets, and what we'd need for cast numbers. I also wrote up a possible budget for each, but I wasn't sure about some of the numbers, so I think I'll need help tweaking those." I hand her a stapled packet that I printed at home last night.

"This is really impressive, Riley," she says, flipping through the pages. "I wasn't expecting you to do so much."

"Do you think it'll be enough to convince them?" I ask.

Her shoulders sag. "I don't want you to get your hopes up. This is great and I can tell how much work you've done, but . . ."

I wait impatiently, wondering what I'm missing. Do I need to add more detail? Would a personal essay on the importance of theater sway them?

"You're just one person," she says finally, her voice resigned.

I frown. "I don't understand."

"It's true that budget is a big concern, but the reason they chose to cut the musical instead of something else was because of flagging interest from the student body and community. I know you're enthusiastic, but they want to see everyone share that excitement. And, unfortunately, that's not something you can control."

I blink, trying to process this. She's losing hope. I can't let that happen—I need at least one adult at the school on my side.

"Okay . . . okay, we can make this work. I'll figure something out."

She chuckles. "You're going to be a great theater director someday, I can already tell. Unflagging belief and resilience will get you far."

"Thank you. I will come up with something. Don't cancel the meeting with Principal Holloway."

"No, of course I won't do that. If anyone can figure out a solution, it's you."

I sigh deeply and head out toward the parking lot. Nothing is going the way I hoped with the musical, but Miss Sahni is right about one thing: I am determined.

Unfortunately, I'm also out of ideas.

To my surprise, Nathan is also walking toward the door, and I'm grateful to see him. I come up beside him and nudge his shoulder. "Hey, boyfriend," I whisper.

He jumps and looks around us. "Hey. Is Paul here?"

"No. Or, at least, I haven't seen him." I push open the double doors to the parking lot. "Were you leaving your locker just now? I never realized ours are in the same hallway."

"Yeah, it seems you were completely oblivious to me before you told Paul we were dating. No wonder he didn't believe you."

I scowl. Nathan squints at the sudden sunlight and scans the area.

"Who are you looking for?"

"Lucas. He rides with me to the store some days, but I guess he already left. I can't keep track of him. He's been weird the last few days."

"What do you mean weird?"

"Just . . . distant. I think he's got his mind elsewhere." He raises an eyebrow at me.

"He's totally into Hoshiko, isn't he?"

Nathan laughs. "Yep. He thinks he's keeping it under wraps, but it's obvious."

"Well, I don't think you have a lot of room to judge in that department."

"Touché."

We grin at each other. I glance out at the parking lot for Dad's car, but I don't see it. I know I should walk out there to wait for him. It's not like I won't see Nathan again in

5.8 minutes at the store, but it's nice talking to him without anyone else around—particularly Sophia.

I lean against the tall partition wall that separates the main sidewalk from the yard. A few girls from choir walk out the front doors and wave at me, but their eyes linger on Nathan.

"I think people are starting to notice us together. Hope you're okay with that." I nod at their backs.

"Yeah, sure," he says. "Rumors about us will be a big upgrade from what people are saying about me now."

I straighten in alarm. "What's that?"

"Nothing. No one even knows I go to the school. Including you."

I laugh and jostle his arm. "I don't think that's my fault. Maybe if you actually got involved, that wouldn't be the case."

He shrugs. "Except I don't care about these people. No offense, I know you're into this stuff, but in ten years, am I going to remember any of their names? Will I care about being on the junior varsity blah blah team? Not in the least."

"You'll remember Lucas. And Anthony and John."

"Of course, but that won't be because we had bio together."

"And maybe you'll remember my name?"

He looks back at the school entrance for a moment and then steps so close I take a quick breath in surprise. Suddenly my entire view is taken up by Nathan. His floppy dark hair, his sparkling green eyes, his wide-rimmed glasses. My heart thumps wildly even though I tell my body not to react like that to him. His head tilts slightly and I swear he's about to kiss me. I should step away—I should pinch him so he knows not to go too far—but this doesn't feel too far. It feels like exactly what I want. The realization makes me dizzy, and I lean harder into the wall.

His palms press against the wall on either side of me and he leans a fraction closer. His lips twist in a small smile as if he's reading my thoughts.

"Maybe I'll remember." His voice is a whisper. "But no promises."

My jaw drops in shock and his eyes light with delight.

"What are you doing?" I whisper back.

"I'm following your directions. Your ex is coming."

Oh.

Right.

Of course that's why he's suddenly pretending he wants to kiss me. What other reason would there be? And more importantly, why is his presence sending my body into overdrive?

I shift to look for Paul, but Nathan puts a finger under my chin and turns my face back to him. "Keep your eyes on me. Pretend I'm saying something romantic."

His face—his *lips*—is still shockingly close to mine. I have to swallow before I can think of something intelligible to say. "Like how you have an unopened box of strawberry Pop-Tarts sitting in your car with my name on it?"

"The box is open and half eaten, but they're yours if you want them."

"I'm literally swooning."

A honk sounds and we both turn at the same time. Dad waves his hand out the window at us. Nathan jumps away from me as if Dad had pulled a sawed-off shotgun from the backseat. Now my heart is flying for an entirely different reason. How much of that did Dad see?

He sticks his head out the window. "Nathan, are you having car trouble?"

Nathan shakes his head. His cheeks look a lot redder than they did a few seconds ago. "No, I'm okay," he calls.

"We'll see you at the store, then. Riley, let's go."

Nathan and I share a nervous look before I walk away. Dad's eyes are sharp and his expression knowing when I climb into the passenger seat. "*So* . . . looks like you and Nathan are friends now?"

"Yeah." I mess with my seat belt rather than make eye contact. "I guess."

"You guess? Hmm." He laughs to himself, and I scoot a little farther down in the seat. Clearly, he saw *something* and I really don't want to talk about it with him. I can barely work it out in my own head. What was going on back there? When did I go from loathing Nathan to tolerating him to being disappointed he didn't kiss me? There wasn't supposed to be any kissing. There wasn't supposed to be anything *real* at all—just enough acting to keep up the facade.

I squeeze my eyes shut and wish Dad would drop me off at Mom's house rather than take me to the store. I need time to process everything before I'm with Nathan again. If I told Dad I wasn't feeling well, then he'd probably agree to take me home, but he'd also call Mom.

To his credit, Dad isn't grumbling about me and Nathan or asking pointed questions like Mom probably would. Maybe now is the time to bring up other topics before he gets any ideas.

"Dad?" My voice is quiet and a little shaky. I'm surprised how nervous I am to talk to him about something serious.

He turns off the radio. "What's up?"

"Do you . . . Have you been telling people at the store about my theater performances?"

"Well, yeah. Was I not supposed to?"

"No. I mean, I don't mind. It's only that Nathan mentioned something, and I was surprised." I play with the edge of my sweater.

"You're never happier than when you're performing," Dad says. "And you're so talented. Of course I'm going to shout it from the rooftops."

My heart thumps at his words, but I'm also confused and a little bitter. If this is how he felt, why hadn't he said those things to me before? I almost ask, but I'm scared of getting into a fight.

"Did you have a favorite role of mine?" I ask instead.

He fiddles with the radio. "That's like asking me about my favorite D&D campaign—I love them all. But if I had to choose . . . I guess I'd say when you played that little girl in *Mary Poppins* in seventh grade. You were just perfect."

I swallow hard. I'd been so nervous to play Jane Banks in that show. It was my first performance in a lead role and I was scared I'd forget my lines or accidentally drop my British accent halfway through a scene. Mom brought such a huge bouquet of flowers after that I could barely hold them, and everyone was coming up to congratulate me or give me hugs that . . . well, I'm not sure I remember Dad being there at all. Did he come up to talk to me after? Or maybe he only talks to other people about me.

I debate telling him about the musical being canceled this year, and my plans to bring it back. Mom wasn't pleased when I told her, but I wonder if Dad would be more supportive since he just said how much he loves my theater roles. But I can't rule out the possibility he'd turn around and tell Mom. They don't speak much, but they did talk about the *Waitress* incident, so it could happen again.

I bite the inside of my cheek, deliberating.

"Riley," Dad says, pulling me from my thoughts. "I just want you to know how happy I am that you're working at the store. I love getting to see you more during the week and the customers love it too. Fred and Arthur won't stop raving about you! I think they like you more than me." He chuckles as he pulls into the parking lot. "Who knows, maybe after these eight weeks are up you'll decide you like it at the store so much you'll want to stay on."

Any thoughts of coming clean about the musical fade away. Because if I do convince the school to bring back the musical, and I'm allowed to return to theater after probation, there's no way I can have a part-time job and also be student director of the show. More importantly, there's no way I'd want to. But Dad is smiling at me with such thinly veiled hope that I can't find it in myself to say any of that.

Chapter Fourteen

Minutes later we're walking into the store and somehow Nathan has beat us here again. Dad looks between Nathan and me with a little too much interest.

"I'm going to work on payroll in the back. Call me if you need me," he says, casting one last glance over his shoulder.

I sit down behind the counter, next to Nathan, and tell myself to chill out. There are way too many emotions rolling around inside me right now between that conversation with Dad and what happened with Nathan outside school. Everything is okay, I remind myself. It's just Nathan. It's just the store.

"How do you always get here so fast?" I ask him.

He looks over the top of his glasses at me. "That's a secret."

I snort. "You're obnoxious."

"Did you already forget? You're only allowed to insult me if you're using that quiet voice you have when you're pretending to flirt with me."

My heart spikes. I use a special voice? I decide to ignore that comment and pull out my English homework instead.

"Sophia texted that she might come by tonight."

I look up. "But it's not a D&D night."

"I know." He shrugs, but I can tell from his expression that he's pleased.

"Oh. Cool." I fight to control my tone. They're texting each other? Whatever this weird feeling is that I'm having around Nathan, I can push that aside. But it's hard to forget how she acted last time—trying to use him for free stuff. Which reminds me . . . I pull out twenty-five dollars and slide it across the counter to him. That's way more money than I would have paid for dice, but they're undeniably gorgeous, so I can understand the price.

"For the dice."

He frowns and pushes the money back toward me. "No, it's not a big deal. Keep your money."

"You're not buying things for me. I'm giving you this money even if I have to shove it in your mouth and tape it closed." I hold it out to him.

"Wow, calm down. I'll take the freaking money." He reaches for it and pauses. "Wait, did you paint your nails to match the dice?"

I close my hands into fists, embarrassed. I'd come up with the idea late last night. I have all the polish colors that are in the dice, and I was curious about whether I could swirl them together on my nails the same way they did with the dice. It's definitely not professional-looking, but I think I did a decent job.

"Let me see." He puts out his hand, palm up.

I hesitate and then place my hand in his, ignoring the fact that my heart speeds at his touch. My heart would speed up no matter who was holding my hand.

"You did a great job. Maybe you should help me paint my Warhammer models sometime."

"The old polish was chipping."

"Hey, guys, I could use some help with—" Dad's voice breaks off when he sees Nathan holding my hand. He looks between the two of us and we rip our hands away.

"Back here." Dad points to the office/stockroom. "Now." He calls for Curtis in the back room to watch the register.

Nathan and I share a horror-struck look before following him. My thoughts swirl a thousand miles a minute trying to decide what we're going to tell him. Technically, I don't think I've broken any rules from my grounding. My parents only said I needed an after-school job, not that I couldn't make friends or date someone at said job.

Not that Nathan and I are actually dating.

Dad gestures to a few folding chairs. "Sit down."

We both sit and put our hands in our laps.

He paces in front of us. "I have to say, I already had my suspicions as soon as you all started playing D&D together. In my experience, that game brings people together like nothing else. And then I saw whatever was going on between you two at school today, and now—" He shakes his head. "I wish you would've told me rather than having me learn this way."

"Dad—"

He holds up a hand. "This job is supposed to be a punishment, Riley. And this is a workplace. It's not exactly appropriate to have employees dating each other."

My eyes flick over to Nathan, but he's staring down at his hands.

"*But* I can't deny how happy I am at the idea of you two being together. I can't think of a better couple."

The words jolt me, and in my peripheral vision Nathan sits up straighter. Dad rests his hands on his round stomach with such a joyous expression I can barely comprehend it.

"Riley, it's always been one of my greatest dreams that you would come around to gaming. And now, to see you making friends and playing here . . ."

Oh my God, his eyes are actually shining with tears. Is he about to *cry* because I'm hanging out with Nathan?

"And, Nathan . . . ," Dad continues.

Nathan freezes.

"I've watched you grow up at the store these last few years, and I know I can trust you with anything. Including my daughter's life."

"Dad, no!"

He chuckles and puts up a hand again to stop me. He's clearly enjoying messing with us, but I'm so overwhelmed with stress that my body is tying itself in knots. I have no idea how Nathan is holding it together. I'm surprised he's still upright in his chair, but he's likely in too much shock to respond yet.

"I'm sorry, I'm sorry!" Dad continues. "I know I'm not about to walk you down the aisle or anything—I'm just excited! Though I'm not sure your mother will feel the same, Riley. I'll see if I can bring her around."

"Oh my God," I whisper, and cover my face with my hands. I peek through them at Nathan. He's so pale you'd think he just donated enough blood to take care of all of Ohio. "Dad, please, you've got to calm down. It's *really* not like that. Nathan and I are only friends."

Dad holds up his hands in surrender. "Okay, fine, whatever you kids are calling it these days." He winks like we're all in on a big joke. "All right, I guess I've tortured you enough. Get back out there. Just be professional around the customers." He waves us toward the door.

Gingerly, I stand. I'm so rattled I can barely walk. We both go back to the checkout counter in silence. I'm relieved that he didn't just chew us out, but I feel weirdly . . . *guilty* about the whole exchange. It's no secret that Dad likes Nathan a lot, and now Nathan and I feel like one more piece of my life that makes Dad proud while also being a huge lie.

"What . . . just . . . happened?" Nathan whispers after a moment.

I shake my head.

"Your dad was about two seconds away from securing a church for our wedding."

We stare at each other with a dumbfounded look, and then a manic laugh bubbles up in me. "No, no, a church would be too conventional. He'll want the wedding here. And we'll have the reception in the back room."

"Ha, good point." Nathan's shoulders relax slightly from

their position up by his ears. "Soda and chips as appetizers. And we can push the game tables out of the way for dancing." He grins and the sight makes me laugh again.

"Ooh, we're dancing? I didn't think you'd be up for it. Which song should we choose for our first dance?"

He doesn't even hesitate. "Anything by Weird Al, of course."

"Obviously. Oh, and a Pop-Tart cake!" I clap with excitement. "We can stack them in a pyramid like people do with playing cards."

"You're a freaking genius."

I bow and we both simultaneously crack up and shake our heads at how ridiculous this situation has become. It's easy to push away the guilt of letting down Dad when I'm laughing with Nathan.

"Are you okay, though?" I ask him. "You looked like you were about to pass out."

The smile falls from his face. "I don't like lying to your father."

"I don't either. Though I *did* tell him the truth—that we're only friends. Unless we're still mutually annoyed co-workers."

That lifts the corner of his mouth into another small smile. "If we're discussing Pop-Tart wedding cakes, then I think we've officially moved beyond that."

An irrational thrill rolls through me at his words.

"We could go back and tell him the truth—the full story?"

Nathan shivers. "Oof, that would be embarrassing. Hey, Mr. Morris? The girl I like isn't interested in me, so your daughter is pity-flirting with me to get her attention." He grimaces and runs a hand through his hair. "That sounds even more pathetic out loud than it did in my head."

I can't help laughing. "It's . . . not the best."

He glares at me. "Don't pretend your part in this isn't embarrassing too. You're the one person who can't judge me."

"I'm not judging you. I need you."

His eyes flash up at me and I mentally kick myself. I can't blurt things out like that around him.

"You know what I mean. I need you to throw Paul's condescension back in his face." I mess with my nails in order to avoid making eye contact. "So we're not telling my dad everything?"

"Unless you want to. I don't want to cause any problems between you two."

"It's fine. And . . . we're good? Still flirting partners in crime?"

"Yeah. If you think you can handle it," he says with a small mischievous grin.

"I can," I reply confidently, even though that grin is melting my insides into goo.

Chapter Fifteen

"How'd it go?" Hoshiko asks as I sit down at the cafeteria table on Friday.

She's wearing an old Columbus Children's Theater shirt and her hair is in double French braids. I'm a little more tame than usual in a black and taupe plaid dress and ankle boots. It's less colorful than usual, but I can't resist an autumn moment.

"Well, I got five more names, so that's something," I reply. "They *all* want us to choose a different musical if it happens this year—but I convinced them to audition no matter what."

I skim over the names again. With these five, and the four people Hoshiko was able to convince, I'm up to almost forty students who say they'd be interested in auditioning for a speaking role or being in the chorus of a future musical. I've been pitching the idea to everyone I see for the last week in the hopes that I can show the administration we have a lot of buy-in from the student body this year. I have two and a half weeks until the big presentation and I'm still not sure I'll have enough to convince them.

"You're doing awesome," Hoshiko says.

"But not everyone who is signing this sheet is going to audition." I shake my head. "I don't know if this will be enough."

"You can only do so much, Riley. Don't beat yourself up about it."

"Only do so much of what?" Lucas asks as he sits down at our table.

"I'm trying to rally support for the musical." I shrug and steal a chip from Hoshiko.

"She needs to convince Principal Holloway that there's enough interest to keep the musical this year," Hoshiko explains to him.

"Why don't you put together a show or something?" he says while dunking a chicken nugget in ketchup.

"A show? What do you mean?"

He waves his nugget at me. "You know, like you guys do at the store. Could you gather up the people on that list and sing something in front of the principal? Maybe that'll show how much interest there is?"

Hoshiko gasps. "Lucas, that's brilliant!" She turns to me. "You could choose a song, or maybe even more than one, and put together a performance. I bet Miss Sahni would let us use some of the old theater costumes." She takes my list and scans it, pointing at names. "You have enough people here that you could cast a few as leads with more for a chorus. This would be amazing, Riley!"

I look between Lucas, Hoshiko, and Anthony, who left

the group of girls he was chatting with to sit down at our table. "Do you think I have time?"

"Absolutely. You have three weeks. You can do anything in three weeks."

I look back down at the interest list, my heart beating quickly. This would be a *huge* undertaking, and I'd have to find the time to stay after for rehearsal without my parents catching on . . . but it could be really amazing if we can pull it off. In fact, the more I think about it, the more I realize there's no better way to convince the administration to keep the musical. It's one thing to talk about theater hypothetically. It's a totally different thing to experience it. To *feel* it. That's what we need to do.

I squeal and Hoshiko starts dancing in her seat. Lucas bows over his nuggets and fries.

"My evenings are too busy to add anything else," Nathan says to John as they approach the table. "But thanks for the offer."

"I swear you'll have fun," John argues.

"What's going on over here?" Nathan asks, and sits down next to me. "I saw dancing."

"Lucas had the great idea that we should put together a performance to convince the principal to keep the musical," I explain. "What are you two talking about?"

"I'm making a last-ditch effort to convince Nathan to join my LARPing group," John says. He meticulously pulls out a sandwich from his TMNT lunchbox and takes a bite. "I was hoping he would since the others turned me down."

Hoshiko squints at me in confusion. "What's LARPing again?"

"Live-action role-playing," John says.

"Oh, right!" I grin. "Don't people get dressed up in costumes for that?"

"Yeah. It's a little like D&D but in real life."

"Wait," Hoshiko says. "So, like, you carry swords and wear armor?"

"Well, we try to make it as realistic as possible, but we all have a pretty strict budget." He shrugs. "I love it."

"Sorry to change the subject, but we have something else extremely important we need to discuss," Lucas announces. He puts his palms on the table and leans forward. "I had an epiphany—we need to introduce the girls to Monty Python."

"That's an *excellent* idea," Anthony says.

Nathan nods from my left, where he sits every day now. "Required watching."

"Actually," I say, "we already know about Monty Python. We *are* certified theater geeks and they're the ones who inspired *Spamalot*."

The guys exchange glances. "Have you seen that show?" Nathan asks.

"Well, no," Hoshiko admits.

"And have you seen any of the Monty Python movies?"

"Not exactly," I say with narrowed eyes.

"That's what I thought. We have to start with *Holy Grail*," Lucas says, not missing a beat. "If they see only one movie, then it should be that one."

"But that's the best one," Anthony argues. "It'll be downhill from there."

John gasps. "Sacrilege! Everything they made is a classic!"

"How old *are* these movies?" I ask.

"Excuse me," Nathan replies, "weren't you just extolling the virtues of *Hello, Dolly!* and Barbra Streisand yesterday at work?"

"That movie is a classic," I protest.

"*Anyway.* I vote for *Holy Grail*," Nathan continues. "Who else?"

John and Lucas raise their hands. Anthony huffs but does the same.

"Do we get a vote?" I ask.

"Oh sure, of course," Nathan replies. "We wouldn't want to leave you out. Just go ahead and tell us the other Monty Python movies you want to put in the running and we'll vote." He puts his chin on his hand and innocently bats his eyes at me. I shove at his arm and he cackles in triumph. I want to be annoyed, but instead I flush with heat and pull my gaze from him.

"Don't worry, you're both going to love it," Lucas says.

"Is there singing and dancing?"

"A bit. And there are the knights who say 'Ni!'" Nathan says.

"Ni! Ni!" John says, and cracks up.

Hoshiko and I give each other an exasperated look. These boys are such dorks. "If we're going to sit through this, you guys need to watch one of our movies," she says.

That wipes the smiles off their faces, and I love seeing it. "Yes, Hoshiko!" I tap my chin. "Something like *Oklahoma!* or . . . *Hello, Dolly!*"

"*Grease* could be fun."

"Oh yeah, they'd love that." Now it's my turn to cackle. "Oooooh, I have it. Have you guys seen *Sound of Music*?"

Nathan frowns. "The one with the lady twirling on the mountain and all the nuns?"

"One and the same. You haven't seen it? Now *that's* sacrilege. How have you survived so long in the world?"

Nathan snorts and eats a chip. "Uh, just fine."

"That's debatable."

Lucas clears his throat. "Aren't you still grounded?"

My gaze flicks to Nathan quickly. Given what Dad said in the stockroom yesterday, it sounds like he'd make an exception for almost anything if it means Nathan and me spending time together.

"He might make an exception for this," I say casually. "I'm supposed to stay with him next weekend. Maybe I could ask if we could watch it at his place? If it's all right that the space is tight?"

Everybody nods. "I'd love to see Joel's place," John says. "I heard he's got some amazing Warhammer 40K armies."

"Yes, definitely ask him," Lucas says with an eager grin, his eyes flicking to Hoshiko.

Suddenly, Nathan is inches from me. "He's coming this way," he whispers. I turn to him just as he curls his fingers through mine and pulls my hand close to his mouth. His eyes find mine and he tilts his head as if to ask permission. I nod faintly. I don't know what is going on with me, but when he looks at me like that, he might as well be a magnet tugging me to him. He presses his lips to my skin and my body explodes at the gentle pressure. I know it's stupid—the gesture is so innocuous—the lightest kiss on the top of my hand. It means nothing. But that's not what my body thinks—not my tight chest or the electric tingles running down my spine and legs. I've got to get ahold of myself.

I'm grateful for the chorus of groans around the table because it gives me an excuse to look away. Anthony and John are shaking their heads in disgust. I hadn't wanted to tell them about how Paul factored in to my arrangement with Nathan, but it was impossible to keep it a secret when my ex shares a lunch period with us. I'm pretty sure their respect for me dropped a few notches, but honestly that's fair.

Nathan doesn't let go of my hand as he glares around the table. "You're going to give us away."

"It'll just look like we're annoyed by your cuteness," Hoshiko says. Her eyes are twinkling in a mischievous way that doesn't bode well for me. The boys might not be able to read my expressions, but I'm guessing Hoshiko's figured out what's going on in my brain.

"This whole thing is so stupid," Lucas says.

"Seriously, what's the deal with you two? How far does all this go?" Anthony asks. "Are you going to homecoming together now too?"

I look at Nathan in surprise. We *definitely* haven't talked about that . . . though I highly doubt we need to. The dance is only two weeks away, and Mom hasn't said anything more about letting me go. I'm about to say as much when Nathan shakes his head vehemently and lets go of my hand. "Is homecoming an extracurricular school function? With uncomfortable clothes and bad pictures and worse music? Then no way. Just tell Paul you have to work."

Anthony snorts. "Good luck getting Nathan to do anything school-related that's not absolutely required."

"Are you going with someone?" I ask Anthony to change the subject and take my mind off the sting of Nathan's response. I might not be allowed to go, but he didn't need to be so horrified at the idea.

"Yeah, I asked Kenzie Hunter last week," he replies nonchalantly.

I shouldn't be surprised by that. In fact, I probably should have said Anthony's name during that fateful meeting with Paul. Anthony is such a flirt, he would've loved it and I bet we wouldn't have all this weirdness I'm feeling with Nathan.

"I'm out. That's my LARPing night and I'm not missing it," John replies.

"Has your mom softened about the dance?" Hoshiko asks me.

I shake my head. "Well . . . she didn't say absolutely no, but when she says 'we'll see,' it usually means that a no will be coming before long."

Her whole body deflates. "You've got to work on her, then. What will I do without you there? We never miss a chance to get dressed up and go dancing."

"I will," I say, but my attention is caught elsewhere. "What about you, Lucas?" I ask. "Any interest in school dances?"

"Uh, I don't know. Maybe."

His eyes flick to Hoshiko long enough to make me smile shrewdly. She squeezes my leg under the table and I stand up. "We're going to the bathroom."

"Have fun talking about us!" Anthony calls as we hurry away. I practically squeal.

"What's going on?" I ask as soon as we're far enough away from them. "I'm definitely getting vibes between you and Lucas!"

Her cheeks are pink. "He hasn't asked me yet, but I think he wants to. Maybe he's just scared?"

"Oh my God, that's too cute. Do you want to go with him?"

We push open the bathroom door and stand in front of the mirrors. She bites her lip and nods. "Yeah, I think I do."

I squeal again. Honestly, I'm a bit surprised. Lucas is a nice guy, but he isn't someone I would have seen with Hoshiko. For the last year she's talked about finding a tall hot dancer so they could perform together and do all the viral TikTok dances. I can't imagine Lucas doing intricate choreography, but if she's happy, then I'm all for it.

"Am I crazy?" she asks.

"No! If you like him, then you should do it! I think you'd have a good time."

She checks her hair and looks up at the ceiling. "Yeah? Except I don't even know if he's going to ask me. There's not much time left."

I laugh. "You could always ask him if you're worried. But he definitely wants to ask you. He's clearly besotted with you."

"Ooh, nice use of *besotted*. What about you, though?" She turns to me with an arched eyebrow.

"What? There's nothing going on."

"Oh really, Miss About Fell Over When Nathan Kissed Her Hand?"

"Hoshiko!" I bend over to make sure no one is inside

the stalls. When I'm sure we're alone, I drop my face into my hands. "Was I really that obvious?"

"You wear your emotions on your face. Though I don't think Nathan has learned to read them yet."

"At least I have that." I groan. "Ugh, I don't know what's going on. I can't keep up with my own reactions. We hate each other . . . we're friends . . . we flirt . . . it's all fake . . . I have no idea." I start laughing at the ridiculousness and she does the same.

"He's probably just hiding what he feels. If you press him, he'll go to homecoming with you. I'm sure of it."

"*If* my mom even lets me go. And either way, I've already pressed him enough. I only started this with him to prove a point to Paul and we've done that. It doesn't need to keep going."

"I don't see you telling Nathan that."

I squeeze my eyes shut in embarrassment. "I just . . . I don't know. Promise you won't say anything to Lucas?"

"I would never!" She looks scandalized at the idea. "And if Nathan is too stubborn to ask, then you'll be there with me." She links her arm with mine. "Your mom *will* let you come, and we'll dance until we've sweated off our makeup. Do you think there's any way I'd go without you?"

She grins at me and I grin back, trying to push away the faint disappointment I'm feeling. Thirty minutes ago, homecoming wasn't on my mind, but now I'm wounded at Nathan's reaction to the idea. Things were supposed to be so different this year. At one point, I'd imagined going to homecoming with Paul. It would've been the first time I'd gone to a dance with a real boyfriend, and I was looking forward to having my *person* by my side—someone who got me and liked me and gave me goose bumps when he held my hand. But there's no point in thinking about that possibility anymore. Even if I was allowed to attend, I'd never go with Paul. And Nathan . . . well, he's not my boyfriend anyway, so it doesn't matter.

Chapter Sixteen

"All right, everyone, settle down!" I call to the students milling around onstage. "We need to get started—we don't have a lot of time."

I stand back and put my hands on my hips, hoping that I don't have to yell again. In front of me are twenty-five students who've all agreed to be a part of this musical preview. After Lucas gave me the idea Friday, I spent the weekend messaging everyone and getting organized. Luckily, Miss Sahni was excited about the plan and agreed to reserve the auditorium for us for the next two weeks, although she doesn't have time to help with rehearsals. We only have it two days a week for forty-five minutes, which isn't much, but I'm staying positive.

After lots of internal debate, I ultimately chose "Big Bright Beautiful World" and "Story of My Life" from *Shrek the Musical* as our songs for the musical preview. They can showcase many different people in singing roles; there's minimal dancing, which will make it easier to rehearse given our limited time; and there are small roles for townspeople so we can include everyone. I want the administration to see all the talent and excitement we have. Unfortunately, not everyone is excited about my choice.

"*Shrek,* though?" Kelly says again. "I mean, I wouldn't mind playing Fiona, but you didn't choose one of her songs. Can't we do 'Defying Gravity' instead?"

I vehemently shake my head. "No, that song is a duet and it'll be better if we can show off as much talent as possible. As I already explained."

"What if we did something from *Dear Evan Hansen?*" Jeremy asks from the back.

"Guys, listen. Do you want to have a musical this year?"

They all nod.

"Then we need to work together. This isn't about one of us; it's about all of us. And just because we're doing *Shrek* for this performance doesn't mean we're doing it for the actual show. But if we can't pull this off, then maybe we don't deserve to have a musical this year." I narrow my eyes and survey them. A few people look sulky, but no one fights back. I've been in a lot of musicals, and I've helped run bits of rehearsals in the past, but I've never been in charge before. I roll my shoulders and give off an air of confidence.

"Okay, for the sake of simplicity, I've gone ahead and cast the major parts." I start calling out names. Hoshiko will be Mama Ogre for the showcase, which means she kicks off our performance, along with Terrance playing Papa Ogre. The majority of students will be playing fairy-tale creatures for the second song, and everyone else will be in the chorus as townspeople who are scared of Shrek.

I catch Paul's gaze as I call out the last of the names for chorus. His eyes are wide and he's standing extra tall. He doesn't need to say anything for me to know exactly what's on his mind. He wants to know if I've cast him as the lead. I wondered if he'd be too busy or important to show up today, but I should have known that Paul would never miss an opportunity to perform.

I force myself to smile and make eye contact with him. "And, Paul, I have you singing as Shrek."

A few girls, who are clearly still charmed by his good looks, squeal and applaud him. He smiles indulgently and bows his head slightly in my direction. I'm going to get a headache from clenching my jaw so tight.

This is all practice for the future, I remind myself. If I'm going to direct anything, from high school theater all the way up to a professional production, I'm going to be working with a range of people, some of whom will be unlikeable. But I need to stay professional no matter what. And the truth is, I need Paul here. He's the best male performer we have in the school, and I want to make sure the principal sees what we have to offer. So, yeah, I gave him Shrek. But against my will.

"Okay, everyone, I think the first thing we should do is listen to a cast recording of the songs so we know what we're aiming for." I scan the stage. "After that, we'll rehearse each song as a full group so that everyone is clear which parts they're singing. Then we'll break up into smaller groups to practice. When we come back on Wednesday, we'll work on blocking, and Hoshiko has kindly agreed to put together some simple choreography for the townspeople and fairy-tale creatures."

I pull out a stack of papers with printed lyrics since I don't expect everyone to have the songs memorized. A moment later, Paul is by my side.

"Here, I'll help pass them out."

He puts out a hand, standing next to me like he's become my assistant director along with lead actor. I'd much rather have Hoshiko helping me, but everyone is watching us, and I don't want to make a scene, so I smile politely and hand him half the stack.

"I've labeled them by role," I explain, and point to the top of the page. I spent last evening prepping these so that each person only has the lyrics they need.

"You're doing a great job, by the way," Paul says quietly. "Don't let anyone make you second-guess yourself. They don't know how hard this is."

He turns away to pass out the papers and I stare at his back, my eyes narrowing at his words. Who's making me second-guess myself? Are people saying I can't do this? Or am I letting Paul's words get to me way too much like usual?

I take a deep breath. I don't know where Paul's head is at, and it doesn't matter. The only thing that's important is pulling everyone together to produce the best showcase we can. I wish I didn't have to deal with him along with everything else, though. Maybe I should try convincing Nathan to stay after and play the supportive boyfriend during rehearsals. The idea floods me with giddy joy, but I push it away. That would be so much fun, but having Nathan by my side would distract me even more than Paul.

Chapter Seventeen

The next few days go by smoothly, most likely because I'm becoming a skilled liar. In order to have an excuse to stay after school for rehearsals, I told my parents Miss Sahni had called additional choir practice to prep for the winter recital. They didn't question it, and I *am* staying for a type of singing rehearsal that is supported by Miss Sahni, but there's no question I'm pushing my luck with this. I hope it'll all be worth it in the end. And, because I have *no* shame, I'm still pestering them to give me a final answer about homecoming. They won't say yes, but they're hedging enough that they might be secretly considering it.

Nathan's judging a Pokémon tournament in the game room on Thursday, so I don't see him for most of my shift. I'm sure he's busy, but he's probably also caught up with Sophia, who came in halfway through the tournament and went directly to the back room. I want to go back as well, but there's no way I can since Dad needs me at the register.

Maybe it's good to give them some time to talk so he can get to know her better and win her over.

Or, you know, so he can realize she's the worst and give it up. Either way.

Finally the tournament ends, and players start to slowly file out from the back room. Quite a few stop to chat with Dad. He seems to know almost everyone by name. I've noticed some of them don't buy anything but instead come in carrying satchels and boxes of game supplies. It's a weird business strategy to encourage people to use the space without requiring them to spend money in the store, but it certainly makes for a jovial atmosphere.

Many of the players wave goodbye to me, and one jokes that I should've been back there singing show tunes to give him good luck. It's strange that many of them knew about me long before I showed my face in this store, but I appreciate that they've all been nice.

Nathan comes through the game room door alone and agitated.

"What's wrong?" I ask. My thoughts immediately jump to Sophia. Maybe they got in an argument?

"Lucas texted that he had to catch up on homework, but I don't know. It's not like him to blow off Pokémon like that."

"I'm sorry. Maybe he really did have a lot of work?" I frown. "Or he's with Hoshiko . . ."

"And didn't tell me? Do you think so?"

"I'm not sure. She hasn't said anything to me about it either." I shrug. "Though I have to say, I'm surprised you're thinking about Lucas with Sophia around." I try to give a small innocent smile, as if I'm not digging for dirt.

He shrugs. "It's cool that she came by to hang out."

"Where is she? Did I miss her leaving?"

"She went to the bathroom, but she'll be back out in a second."

"Cool."

Sigh. I guess things are still going well between them. Just then my phone rings with a call from Mom.

"Hold on." I answer the phone. "Hey, Mom. Are you on your way already?" Most days Mom picks me up from the store after I finish my shift.

"I'm caught up here at the Davidson's house. The kitchen cabinets were installed upside down and the husband is having a fit. It's going to be a late night."

"Ugh, I'm sorry. I'll ask Dad instead."

"Okay. And, while I have you . . . your father called me today."

"Yeah?" Hope bubbles up in me. Maybe Dad called her to say he thinks I should be allowed to go to homecoming?

"He told me you're dating one of the boys who works at the store? Someone named Nathan?"

I yelp. Nathan turns to me in concern, but I wave him away and walk to the other side of the store.

"No! We're not dating."

"He sounded pretty certain. Are you sure there's nothing to tell me?"

"I'm sorry Dad called and told you that, but Nathan and I are just friends."

"He also told me you'd say that."

I heave a huge sigh. "I promise we're not actually dating."

There's a moment of silence on the phone and I assume

she's deliberating. "I believe you." She chuckles. "Joel's en-amored with the guy, though."

"Yeah, I know. It's over the top." I roll my eyes.

"He wants Nathan to start driving you to the store after school. He said it's a waste of gas for him to pick you up when this boy is driving to the same place—which I guess is true—but I don't know, Riley. Did you put your father up to this?"

I stumble and catch myself on the nearest shelf. Dad wants me to ride with Nathan? A trill of joy runs through me at the idea of more opportunities to hang out and make fun of his music choices, though I'm surprised Dad suggested it. I thought he liked the extra time together. I can't imagine a few miles a day would use that much gas.

"I definitely didn't ask him," I tell her fervently. "I had no idea he was even thinking about that."

"So your father is playing matchmaker over there," she replies dryly. "It figures that I'd agree to have you work there so he can keep an eye on you and instead he tries setting you up with an employee."

I hesitate. I don't want to explain why Dad thinks we're dating, but I also don't want to throw Dad under the bus and pretend like this situation is all in his head. I'll admit that in the past, if Mom made an annoyed or passive-aggressive comment about Dad, then I was always quick to agree with her . . . but that doesn't feel right anymore. And I certainly can't blame Dad for his assumptions given how Nathan and I are acting around each other.

"In Dad's defense, Nathan is a pretty great guy. I can see why he'd be happy if I was dating him."

She sniffs.

"What if we give it a trial run tonight? I could ask Nathan to drive me home and we'll see how it goes? If you still feel comfortable after tonight, we could talk about him driving me here after school too." I try not to sound desperate or overly excited about the idea. If she knows how much I want to ride with Nathan, then she definitely won't agree. Of course, assuming Nathan agrees to this at all.

"Can I trust him? Teenage boys are notoriously bad drivers."

"He's very responsible." Although he does somehow get to the store before Dad and me every day, which probably involves some level of speeding. But he gets here in one piece.

Voices shout in the background on her end. "I need to go." She sighs. "All right, you can ride with Nathan tonight if your dad thinks it's okay. I don't love it, but you *have* done a good job at the store so far. Maybe it's time to start giving you more flexibility."

"Yeah? Great!"

"But *be safe*. And make sure you're home no later than nine-thirty."

"Okay. Thanks, Mom! See you tonight!"

I end the call. My pulse quickens at the idea of spending more time with Nathan, but then I remember that Sophia is still chatting with him. I press my lips together. I don't know if he'll be up for this if it means leaving her.

Although, on the other hand, I *am* supposed to be flirting with him and I've done a horrible job of it today. This might be the perfect way to show her I'm still in the picture.

I take a deep breath and walk back to Nathan. "Hey."

Both Sophia and Nathan stop talking and turn to me. Sophia looks none too pleased that I'm interrupting, but I can't read Nathan's expression.

"Sorry, that was my mom. She can't drive me home today and she mentioned that maybe you could drive me. If that's all right?"

He blinks. He's probably trying to figure out if this is real or another weird way to flirt with him.

"I guess Dad mentioned something to her," I add. I give him a meaningful look to hopefully get across the idea about what Dad told Mom.

Nathan's eyes widen. Still, he hesitates, and I don't want to admit that it hurts. I've got to do a better job of reminding myself why we're doing this to begin with. I agreed to flirt with Nathan to help him get Sophia, *not* me.

I shake my head. "Actually, never mi—"

"I can do it," he interrupts. He turns to Sophia. "Sorry, maybe we can get ice cream next time?"

Her eyes narrow slightly but she smiles. "Of course. Can't wait."

She walks off without a backward glance. After she's gone, Nathan looks at me with a cynical expression. "Well, that certainly got her attention."

"I'm sorry if I ruined something there—this isn't part of the flirting. Mom can't come tonight and I convinced her it would be okay for you to drop me off. Unless it's too much? I'm sure Dad can do it."

"Seriously? Of course I'll drive you if you need a ride."

"Awesome, thank you."

We head to the back room to tell Dad. He's talking with Lucas's dad and a few of the older guys who come in after work. They all wave and say hello like I'm family.

Dad nods when we ask about driving together. "Sure. I'm glad your mom came around."

I study him. He's red in the face and his expression is pinched like he's in pain. "Are you okay, Dad?"

He waves me off. "I'm fine. Just tried to pick up too many boxes at once, so I'm taking a break. I'm getting old."

Nathan and I look at each other. "Do you want us to help with it?" he asks.

"No, no. You two can take off. I've got it."

"But the store isn't closed yet," I say. "We still need to clean up the back room and everything."

"It's all right. There's not much to do—I can take care of it."

A few of the guys smirk. I don't know who Dad's trying to fool. He's clearly using this as a way to push me and Nathan together and it's all so embarrassing I want to melt into the floor. But Nathan doesn't hesitate.

"Thanks, Joel. See you tomorrow."

"Yep." Dad points a finger at him. "Drive safely."

"Of course, sir."

I'm hesitant to leave Dad if he's in pain, especially now that I know his doctor is concerned for his health, but he shoos me away. We grab our book bags from the front counter and head out to Nathan's car. The sun set hours ago, so the only light comes from the store windows and a flickering streetlight.

"Sir?" I ask him with a raised eyebrow.

"It never hurts to be polite."

"Unless you're talking to me?"

Nathan walks over to the passenger side, opens the door for me, and bows deeply at the waist. *"Madam."*

I groan. "I should have had Dad drive me." I put my book bag in the backseat, which is covered with sweatshirts, old receipts, and fast-food bags.

He climbs into the driver's seat, still smirking, and turns on a Madonna parody song. "Okay, where to?"

I give him directions to my house, and he pulls out of the parking lot with a thoughtful expression on his face. His gaze flicks to me and back to the road.

"What?"

"When is your mom expecting you home?"

"Um . . ." I glance at the clock on his dashboard, which says eight-forty-five. "Not until nine-thirty. Why?"

He smiles but rubs a hand over his mouth to cover it. "I have an idea for a little detour. If you're up for it."

A kernel of excitement lodges in my chest, and suddenly there's nothing I'd rather do than learn what's making him smile like that.

"Sure. Although I should tell you that Mom is considering this a trial run. If I get home on time, then she might let me ride with you to the store after school. Assuming you don't mind driving me."

"Of course I don't mind, Riley." His voice is quiet. "I'll get you home by curfew."

He makes a right turn when he should make a left and winks at me. A spark of electricity rolls up my spine. I press my back into the seat and focus out the window. I don't know this road, but most of the country roads in Ohio look the same. Rolling hills, corn or soybean fields, occasional houses set back from the road. We're the only car out here.

It makes me realize that I'm alone with Nathan . . . in close quarters . . . in the dark. Electricity zips through me again. It feels very different from our other times together. Sure, we're together a lot, but we're always surrounded by other people. I don't think I've ever been *alone* like this with him. I run my palms down my legs and take a breath.

He props his left elbow on the driver's side door, a small smile playing on his lips as he drives. He looks so content it's hard to pull my eyes from him.

"Why are you looking at me?" he asks without taking his eyes off the road.

I snap my attention to the windshield. "You just seem so . . . happy."

"This is one of my favorite things to do—driving at night with my weird eighties parodies. Sometimes, if I can't sleep, I'll get in the car and drive for hours." The corner of his mouth lifts. "It's why most of my money goes to gas."

"I bet."

He accelerates over a small rise in the road and then we drop down on the other side so fast my stomach lifts to my throat. I squeal in surprise and we both laugh.

"This road is really fun to drive. Don't worry—I know every inch of it."

"I'm not worried." I swallow. "So, is this what you wanted to show me? The road?"

"No. We'll be there soon. You haven't been out this way before, have you?"

"Uh, no." I shake my head. "Weirdly, I don't do a lot of driving."

"Good," he says with a laugh. "It'll be way more fun if you've never seen it before."

I frown, still having no idea what he's talking about. But I'm okay waiting.

"So how are you allowed to go out driving in the middle of the night? Don't your parents freak out?"

He laughs again, but the sound is hollow this time. "They don't know. My parents aren't around much." He sits up from the relaxed position he'd been in. His right hand grips the steering wheel tight enough that his knuckles turn white. "Dad's a nurse at the local hospital and he works a ton of night shifts. Mom used to be a bank teller, but she got laid off a few years ago, so she took a second-shift job at the manufacturing plant outside town. She got promoted to shift manager last year, which I guess is a pretty big deal." He shrugs. "It's good money and benefits. But, especially now that I can take care of myself, they tend to be working or asleep when I'm home."

"So . . . do you have to cook for yourself and stuff like that too?"

"Yeah." He smirks. "Don't get the wrong impression— it's mostly cereal, microwave popcorn, and frozen pizza. Or fast food." He waves vaguely at the bags littering the car.

I sit for a second, letting the information sink in. The fact that he's at the game shop every night is making a lot more sense.

"I'm surprised you like driving alone at night, then. I'd think it would be too solitary."

"I'd rather have someone else in the car, but my friends aren't allowed to leave the house at three a.m." He smiles over at me. "And it's not all bad. I can do stuff like this."

He jacks up the volume and yells the chorus of Weird Al's "Smells Like Nirvana" at the top of his lungs. I clamp my hands over my ears even as I burst into laughter. Night Nathan is different from Day Nathan. And I like it.

Eventually he turns the music back down. "I'm totally losing my hearing by the time I'm thirty, but I love it."

"If I can throw some *Les Mis* into the mix, then you'll have yourself a singing partner."

"Text me the titles and I'll have them ready next time."

Next time. The words send a jolt through me. I hope there's a next time.

"So . . . is that why you like being at the game shop so much? Because otherwise you'd be home alone?"

I bite the inside of my cheek, hoping he won't be put off by the question. But he nods easily.

"Yeah. It's a second home to me. Or really, it's like a first home. I sleep at my house, but I don't do much more than that there. I'm really grateful to your dad for letting me hang out every night even though I don't have the money to buy much. He didn't have to do that, but I think he sees it as community service." He chuckles lightly. "And he's good friends with Lucas's dad, so it made sense for all of us to be there together."

I'm silent for a moment, staring out into the night and thinking about the store. I've always thought Dad ran it be-cause it made him happy. It never occurred to me how the store impacted his customers or the outside community. I can see now that it does—how Dad treats everybody who comes in the door as friends instead of walking credit cards. A small part of me wishes he would have put that much effort into our relationship, but I know that's not totally fair.

Nathan flips on his turn signal and pulls onto a narrow road. This is the kind of road where two cars can technically pass each other but it's going to be tight. Luckily, it's quiet.

"All right, are you ready? I present to you . . . *the Holiday House*." He slows down and pulls off to the side, then leans his seat back so I have a good view out his driver's side window.

I gasp. What in the . . .

Every single square inch of this house's large front yard is covered with Halloween decorations. Not in a beautiful or tasteful way, but more like the owner was determined to hide every blade of grass with a decoration. There are fake pumpkins as tall as me, inflatable ghosts, and a ridiculous number of skeletons. Massive fuzzy spiders crawl around the yard and up the house.

But the part that makes me shiver in horror are the mannequins.

So. Many. Mannequins.

Some have been dressed as mummies and vampires, others as pirates and knights, along with princesses, witches, and a seriously messed up Elmo.

I burst out laughing. "*Nathan*, where did you bring me?"

I edge in front of him to get a better look, craning my neck to the right and left to see everything. It's both bizarre and hysterical.

"Wow . . . what do you think the thought process was here?" I ask. "A mannequin world record?"

"No idea. The creepiest costume party the world has ever seen?"

"Ooh, good point—do you think they rotate the costumes every year? Maybe we could sneak a few off and use them for our show. We have a bunch of fairy-tale creatures to clothe, and these would work nicely."

"Of course that's where your mind would go."

"When you're a musical fanatic, costumes become a big part of your thought process."

He laughs and his T-shirt brushes up against my left arm. It's only then that I realize how close I've gotten to him as I tried to see more and more of the yard. I'm practically lying across his lap now. I look up at him and take a quick breath. If I lifted my face another inch, our mouths would be perfectly aligned.

Orange lights flash on in the yard. We both turn, eyes trained on the front door.

"Do you think anyone is home?" I whisper.

"I don't see a car in the driveway and the windows are dark. Those are probably just security ligh—"

A large silhouette suddenly fills the doorway to the house and I jump, falling directly into Nathan's chest. I pop up and scoot over to my seat before this becomes any more awkward.

"Do you think he can see us?" I ask.

But the man answers my question by waving at our car. There's something in his hand I can't make out. Then he steps out onto the lawn and I bite back a shriek.

"Is that . . ."

"Yep. That's Michael Myers coming toward us in the middle of nowhere." The man strides quickly toward our car, and Nathan pulls his seat upright and turns the key in the ignition. "Aaaaaand he's holding a knife."

"*Nathan!* Is it fake?"

He slams the car into drive, and we zoom down the road. "I'm not waiting to ask him."

"Go, go, go!" I yell as I scurry to refasten my seat belt.

Nathan bursts out in frantic laughter once the house is in the rearview mirror, and I do the same despite how fast my heart is racing.

"Oh my God, that was freaky! I'll be up all night with that image in my mind!"

"I swear no one came outside last time I was here." Nathan lays a hand lightly on my knee. "Are you okay?"

Heat radiates through me, but I try to ignore it. "Yes, I'm fine." I glance over my shoulder. "No famous horror movie murderers are following us. Do other people know about this place?"

"I've never heard anyone talk about it. It might be our secret." He looks in his rearview mirror. "The owners switch it out for every holiday. You should see the Easter bunnies."

"Creepier than the princess mannequins?"

"A hundred times worse. I'll show you in the spring if you're still up for it."

He glances at me with a small smile. It's such a simple statement, but it shakes me. Spring is half a year away. Will we still be friends then? Will we still want to spend time together?

More and more, I'm really hoping so.

Chapter Eighteen

I'm able to secure the auditorium for a short rehearsal Friday afternoon before the D&D game. There are a few grumbles about extra rehearsals, but everyone knows we need as much practice as possible.

"Okay, that was better, townspeople." I wave to a cluster of six students. "But you're still too far upstage when young Shrek comes up to you. I need you to get *here* by the time Henry has finished the next part of the narration." I walk to the center of the stage and tap on the location with my foot. "Can we run that from the top one more time? And when he roars at you, really let go and screech with fright. I want to bring some humor to this scene so you can be a bit silly with it."

I nod encouragingly and Meera—the youngest of the group—does a little jump of excitement that brings a smile to my face. I'm really loving the underclassmen who signed up to help with this showcase. I don't know them well yet, but they're so enthusiastic and almost wide-eyed on the stage. A few of them have never done anything like this before.

I gesture to Henry to start his narration from the top. Seeing their excitement only pushes me harder to make this performance perfect. They need the musical as much as the upperclassmen do. I can already see Meera being the perfect lead her senior year. Since she's on the shorter side, I bet she could pull off playing Annie.

After they finish a second run-through, Hoshiko steps up with the sixteen students who are playing fairy-tale characters. "We just finished reviewing the choreography for 'Story of My Life.'"

"Perfect!" I say to everyone onstage. "Take a break. And great work." I wave the newest group up. "Okay, I'm excited! Let's see what we have."

Hoshiko comes to my side as I'm cueing up the instrumental version of the song on my phone. Many wisps of hair have come out of her braids to frame her face in a frizzy halo, and that's all I need to know she's stressed. She's used to working with trained dancers at her studio, and our group is the exact opposite.

"It's, uh, not quite there yet," she whispers. "I tried putting in a few shuffle steps to liven it up, but Eileen and Jack kept literally falling into each other."

"Thank you anyway," I reply. "You're an angel."

We step back and my eyes widen as I watch it unfold. Thankfully, I've got Jeremy playing Pinocchio and he's terrific. But I can't hear half the characters when they sing their lines about how hard it is to be a fairy-tale creature, and a few practically stand behind someone else so I can't see them either.

I keep a mental tally of all the things we need to work on, but I start losing track. And then there's the costumes. I figured one of the good things about doing this song is that we could rely on miscellaneous Halloween costumes to fill in for the Mad Hatter, White Rabbit, and others. For some roles we can get away with part of a costume—a pair of fairy wings for the Tooth Fairy, and pink shirts and pig ears for the Three Little Pigs, that sort of thing. But who knows if everyone will be able to source their own. I was joking at the Holiday House with Nathan, but I seriously wish I could go back and strip those mannequins. All those beautiful costumes in the wind and rain. What a tragedy.

The group ends up successfully moving into a line(ish) at the front of the stage for the final bars of the song. And we do have a few really beautiful singers in the group, despite some projection issues. I nod. This is workable. Meaning it'll take *work*, but it'll be impressive if we can clean it up.

Paul steps into my peripheral vision, but I don't pull my attention away to acknowledge him. If I know Paul, he has an opinion about the performance, but there's no time for that.

The song ends and I clap loudly despite the dejected looks and grimaces on the faces of many of the actors.

"That was a great start," I tell them.

"You either don't know the meaning of great or you're an *amazing* actress," Papa Ogre—that is, Terrance—mutters from a seat in the audience.

I spin to him and narrow my eyes. "We have rehearsals for a reason. And we *all* need help with things." I turn back and take in the entire group. "We still have a week and a half of rehearsal and we can get a lot done in that time. For now, the big thing I want everyone to remember is to project when they sing. We need the administration to be blown away. Pretend you're singing to your hard-of-hearing grandma sitting in that back row." I point to the very back of the auditorium. "If needed, we can simplify the choreography even more. But you need to memorize your lyrics and play it up. Be fun! Be dramatic! You're pissed-off fairy-tale characters—it's okay to be over the top for this!"

I sing the chorus, doing extra dramatic sulking as I do. There's a few chuckles in the group. A small part of me misses this part of theater—being onstage, learning lines and perfecting characters. But being the director, watching and helping with it all, is exhilarating. I love it. And it makes me want to bring back the musical all the more.

Hoshiko points to her phone with raised eyebrows.

"Okay, we're out of time. Thanks, everyone. Keep practicing and we'll work on it next week!"

They head off, waving and thanking me. It's hard to pull myself from the auditorium. I'd stay here all night rehearsing if we were allowed.

"It's progress," Hoshiko says. But I can hear the question mark in her voice.

"It absolutely is. We'll get there. You already helped them so much today. Thank you again."

She shrugs and swings her book bag onto her shoulder. "I did what I could."

"I don't know what I'd do without you." I hug her.

"Are you sure I can't give you a ride to the store?" she asks. "It's not fair that you got to ride with Nathan last night but you can't ride with me."

I texted her as soon as I got home last night to update her on things with Nathan, and she promptly sent me a playlist of love songs that I'm supposed to send him for our next late-night drive. I'm so *not* doing that.

"I bet they'll let us drive together soon—they're clearly getting sick of driving me around everyplace."

She pouts. "I'll see you at the store in a few minutes."

I wave goodbye and turn, only to find that Paul hasn't left with the others. I almost groan aloud.

"What's up?" I ask as I gather my things.

"I got my Shrek mask." He pulls a green latex mask out of his book bag. Did I purposely choose *Shrek* because I knew the lead would need a mask that covers his face and gives him mask hair? No. Do I love that outcome anyway? Unequivocally, yes.

"It's going to need some work," he says, and pulls it over his head. I can't help it—I start laughing.

"Um . . . wow."

"Yeah. It's a little big." His laugh is muffled.

My smile turns to a frown. We can get away with covering his face, but his voice needs to be on full display. "Can you sing something to make sure I can hear you?"

"Sure." He belts out the first few lines and I'm annoyed that it gives me goose bumps. He even nails the accent. But it's definitely harder to hear him with the mask on.

"Do you think you could try cutting a bigger hole in the

mouth?" I ask him. "Otherwise you're going to *really* have to project, and I already know you're doing that."

He pulls the mask off and his hair flies everywhere with static. I try not to laugh again.

"That latex is hot too. I'm glad I don't need to wear this for long. We'll need another solution if we do the full musical in the spring."

I zip up my book bag and head to the auditorium door, Paul following along. Outside, a cool breeze whips through my hair and I pull my sweater tighter around me. I tilt my head up to take in the maple leaves that are beginning to turn rust-orange. It's not quite October yet, but I'm reminded of why I love this time of year. Crunching leaves, bright sunshine, and all the colorful sweaters I can wear.

"Fingers crossed we'll be worried about spring musical logistics soon," I say softly.

"I think it'll happen."

I turn to him, surprised. "Yeah?" I hesitate, but he seems genuine. "Thanks."

"Of course. So, I noticed Nathan doesn't stay for rehearsals."

I bite back a sigh. Things were teetering on the edge of pleasant for a moment there, but then he had to keep talking.

"He has to work."

"Right." He speeds up to stay at my side. "I just wondered if, you know, maybe things weren't working out so well."

"Things are working out perfectly."

"You don't need to be defensive."

I practically growl but force myself to take a breath. "I'm

not being defensive. I'm telling the truth. Nathan and I have a great time together. How are you and Lainey?"

"Perfect."

There's a moment of hesitation before he says it, but I'm not going to prod. There's no need for us to know about each other's relationships.

"Glad to hear it. Well, I've got to go to work. See you."

"Hey. Riley?"

Despite my better judgment, I turn. "Yeah?"

"Do you want me to take you to work on rehearsal days? I have to go past the store anyway."

I'm so surprised by the suggestion that it takes me a few moments to form a coherent thought. "I already have a ride. My parents pick me up when Nathan can't drive me. And I shouldn't be driving with my ex-boyfriend either way."

He rocks back on his heels. "Right. Just wanted to help."

"Well . . . thank you. But I'm good."

He lingers, but thankfully Miss Sahni comes walking our way down the sidewalk.

"Done with rehearsal, Riley?" she calls.

"Yep!" I reply, and jog toward her, grateful for the excuse to leave Paul, his nosy questions, and his weird vibe behind. "We have a ways to go, but it's getting better."

"If you have a second, I wanted to talk to you about something."

"Okay." I pull my book bag higher on my shoulder and try to relax even though nervous thoughts skitter through my mind. She wouldn't want to pull the plug on our show-case after all the work we've put in, right?

"I don't think you've noticed because you've been so

focused during rehearsals, but I've been peeking in here and there this week to see how it's going. And I have to say, I'm very impressed."

"Oh?" There's not much to be impressed with yet. She chuckles like she knows exactly what I'm thinking.

"I know the numbers need work. And I'm sure you'll get there. But I'm impressed with *you*. It's not easy to direct your peers. Many students would get distracted with friends or short-tempered or overwhelmed. But you seem so at ease. And you have a good way with everyone—serious without being harsh."

"Wow, thank you," I reply, my tension evaporating at her kind words.

"Of course, I'll make it clear to the administration at the meeting that I support bringing back the musical. But I have something else to run past you. Would you be at all interested in helping me after school with choir rehearsals? The junior high show choir is scheduled to perform for the Rotary Club in town, and we're nowhere near where we need to be. I couldn't pay you—this would be strictly volunteer-based—but I can already imagine the effect you could have with them."

"So . . ." I pause, my thoughts running slow and then very fast as I process her words. "So, you mean like . . . you're asking if I'd be your assistant?"

"Exactly." She beams at me. "But there's no pressure if it doesn't sound interesting."

I shake my head. It sounds *extremely* interesting. Just the idea of working with Miss Sahni, of spending my afternoons and evenings running rehearsals, fills me with joy. However,

I don't know how I'd balance that and still work at the store every night.

"Well, it sounds exciting. Let me, um, talk to my parents."

"Yes, of course. I hope they'll be on board!"

My insides shrivel. It's easy to get your parents on board if you never tell them anything.

Chapter Nineteen

I meet Mom in the parking lot, my head still spinning with Miss Sahni's words. Today, of all days, I really wish Nathan was able to drive me. Then I could think in peace or possibly talk this out with him. He did get me home on time, and Mom agreed to let him drive me again in the future, but she wanted to pick me up this afternoon. I'm staying at Dad's apartment this weekend, so if Mom doesn't see me now, then she won't get another chance until Sunday evening.

"You have everything for your dad's?" she asks as we make our way down Main Street. Flags with our high school mascot hang from the light posts, and each corner is decorated with big pots of mums and pumpkins. Scottsville has extra charm in autumn.

"Yep." I don't want to come across overly happy or sad to be staying with Dad—but it's hard to keep the excitement from my voice. Dad agreed to let everyone come over Sunday afternoon to watch the Monty Python movie. It turns out he loves them, which shouldn't surprise me, and his face practically lit up the store when I mentioned I was interested in watching one.

"I guess you two are getting along better? I used to have to drag you to his apartment."

She isn't wrong. This weekend feels different. I'm excited to spend Sunday with everyone, but it's not just that. All this time at the store with Dad has made spending weekends together significantly more fun. We talk about the customers or the newest products—we even had a conversation about D&D a few days ago. I *never* thought we'd be able to do that.

"We are. I'll miss you this weekend, though," I reply quietly.

She cuts me a glance. "It's okay for you to want to spend time with him. I think it's a good thing."

I survey her skeptically. I don't want her thinking that I love her less or am less loyal to her just because I'm spending more time with Dad.

"Thanks for agreeing to let me have people over at Dad's."

Her lips press into a thin line. "Well, I wasn't in love with the idea. But I *am* proud of how you've acted throughout your grounding. I was worried this was going to be a constant battle, but you've held up your end of the deal so far."

Her words make me itchy. Mom and Dad still have no idea that my after-school rehearsals are for the musical showcase. They think Miss Sahni is just a taskmaster who keeps calling for more chamber choir rehearsals after school. Every time the guilt grows too strong—like now—I remind myself that it's not like I'm making truly irresponsible choices. I'm still (barely) keeping up with my homework and working at the store . . . and the only reason I'm lying is so I can sing show tunes. But as much as I say that, I'm still going against their wishes and I don't feel good about it.

"In fact," she continues as she parks in front of the store, "I have something to tell you." She unbuckles and turns to me, grinning widely. "I was talking to your father about how well you've handled this and your work ethic at the store, and he agreed you've been a big asset. I'm seriously impressed with your attitude change, Riley."

I shift in my seat, the guilt gnawing at me. It would be way easier to rationalize all this if my parents were being horrible.

"*So* . . ." Mom pauses dramatically, and I'm reminded that I'm not the only one in the family who loves a little theatrical drama. "I know we said eight weeks minimum at the store, but I suggested that we end your grounding after next week and your father didn't argue!"

I gape at her. "Three weeks early?"

"What do you think? You can get your life back."

She looks so pleased that I automatically return the smile. Inside, though, I suddenly feel cold. No more game store? Five weeks ago, I would have done anything to hear those words, but now my first thought is that if I leave the store, I won't be spending my evenings with Nathan and the guys anymore. But . . . the things I could do with all that free time. My thoughts return to Miss Sahni's offer to become her choir assistant. That's not exactly the same as student directing the musical, but that doesn't mean I wouldn't have a blast doing it. And the meeting with the administration is less than two weeks away. If that meeting goes well—I mean, *when* it goes well—there will be so much to organize. Deciding on the musical, applying for the license, setting up and running auditions. My afternoons would fill up immediately.

Her expression flickers with confusion, probably because I'm not bouncing out of my seat at the news.

"And . . . ," she says with more hesitation, "your father and I also talked about homecoming. I know it's only a week away and you don't have a dress so maybe you aren't still interested in going but—"

"I can go?" I screech.

She laughs and throws her hands in the air. "That's the enthusiasm I was expecting! Yes, you can go. We can swing by the mall and look for dresses this week if you'd like."

With just a week until homecoming, the only dresses left in town will be the ones no one wanted. It'll be like trying to get a decent plate of food right after the high school football team has demolished the local Chinese buffet (true story). But whatever, I don't care. I'll wear a gray poncho and clogs if it means I get to go to hoco.

"Mom, I love you!" I lunge forward and pull her into a hug.

"*Now* you love me," she complains, but her voice is teasing and her arms are tight around me.

I'm going to homecoming! I don't know how I'll handle the rest, but that'll be for future-Riley to figure out.

Dad and I work at the store on Saturday, but he schedules us to both get off early. I expect him to mention something about the end of my probation, but he doesn't bring it up so I don't say anything either. Every time I think about it, my chest tightens with anxiety and conflict. How can I say no to Miss Sahni? It's an amazing opportunity. But how could I tell Nathan I'm quitting the store? How could I tell Dad? I'm not even sure I want to quit. It's all too confusing.

To my surprise, Dad suggests we drive out to one of the local farms after our shift to pick up pumpkins for store decorations. Given Mom's love of all things design, I've been to many fall festivals over the years to get fancy heirloom pumpkins, but it's not something I've done with Dad. I take charge of the pumpkin choosing and then we eat spiced donuts from a picnic bench while sugared-up kids race around us. It's all so charming that I can't stop grinning across the table at Dad. I feel like we're in an old-timey sitcom.

When we get home, he suggests breaking out Ticket to Ride and, for the first time ever, I don't refuse him. I can tell from his expression that he's surprised but trying not to act like it. And the game is pretty fun. It's not going to overtake theater as my favorite pastime, but maybe Dad wasn't *completely* wrong about all this game stuff.

I sleep in late on Sunday because Dad loves to sleep and never gives me a hard time about it. When I finally poke my head out of my room around eleven, Dad chuckles and waves me into the "dining room," which he long ago converted into a painting space for his Warhammer models. I don't think we've ever eaten a meal there. We just take our plates and sit on the couch.

"There she is!" he exclaims. "Ready to watch one of the best movies ever created?"

"Ooh, are we watching *Les Mis* today?"

He chuckles. He's got a soda and a bag of potato chips next to him, and it makes me think back to Nathan's comment about how Dad's supposed to be watching what he eats. I hope for Dad's sake that Nathan was confused because his kitchen might as well be the junk food aisle at the grocery store. But Dad is so happy that I hate to bring it up. If something serious was going on, I hope he'd have already told me.

"You are your mother's daughter through and through. Except for the sleeping in. But you wait until you've seen *Holy Grail*."

A knock on the front door alerts me that Hoshiko is here. Her eyes open wide as she steps in. She's only been to my mom's house before and this apartment couldn't be more different from Mom's gorgeously decorated home. There, every corner, shelf, and end table has been thoughtfully decorated with color-coordinated knickknacks. There are themed rooms and artistic lighting, and you don't leave a cup on a table unless you have a coaster under it.

At Dad's, there's stuff everywhere. It's very college dorm. In the kitchen there's cereal and frozen chicken tenders and way too many bags of chips. The living room is nothing but a black leather couch, a recliner, and a TV that's so big it might as well be a movie theater screen. Dad's bookshelves are filled with sci-fi novels, D&D books from before I was born, and tabletop games. Honestly, I can't imagine two people more different than my parents. I'm shocked they lasted as long as they did.

"Hoshiko!" Dad walks in from the other room. "It's good to see you again."

"Hi, Mr. Morris." She waves and rocks back on her heels like she's not sure what to make of the place.

"Dad, we're going to hang out in my room until the guys get here."

I beckon her toward the hallway. We have a little over two hours before the boys are set to arrive and I want to maximize the time with her. We haven't had time alone like this since before my punishment started.

"Sorry, I should have warned you," I say when we're both in my room with the door closed. "Dad's place is a *little* bit different from Mom's."

Hoshiko laughs. "The boys are going to love it here."

"Truly." It's so nice to be with her again. I've missed hanging out. "So, I have the best news—I was going to text but then decided to tell you in person. Mom said I can go to homecoming!"

Hoshiko jumps up and screams. "Yesssss! I knew it would work out!"

We start chattering about dresses and possible hairstyles. But when I bring up the possibility of driving together, Hoshiko hedges.

"Maybe. Let's talk about it later."

I frown, but I guess it's true that the last time we drove someplace together I got grounded for two months. Maybe it's better if Mom or Dad drives me.

"So, I want to hear more about a certain bespectacled gamer. What's the latest on you two?"

I flop back onto my bed. "Nothing new."

If I'm being honest, it's hard to admit to her all my feelings about Nathan. It's so embarrassing. I was so cocky with my foolproof plan to flirt with him without any consequences, and now *I'm* becoming the lovesick fool instead of Sophia. I peek at Hoshiko, wondering how much she suspects. We've been best friends long enough that she usually knows when I'm trying to hide something.

She raises an eyebrow but doesn't question me further. "I think we deserve a musical rewatch before the boys get here. Today feels like a *Hairspray* day."

"*Yes.*"

By the time we get to the final scene, Hoshiko and I are standing in the small space between the couch and the TV, doing the twist and belting out the words like we're onstage in NYC. Dad walks into the living room from the kitchen, but I ignore him. He's not making me miss the last notes in "You Can't Stop the Beat."

Hoshiko twirls next to me and I grab her hand as we fall backward onto the couch in a flurry of laughter. Applause comes from behind us . . . and there's more than just Dad clapping. We whip around to find all four boys clapping and laughing alongside Dad.

"Oh my God, when did you get here?" I ask.

"About halfway through the song," Dad says with a chuckle. "You two were so caught up you didn't hear the knocking. You're just the same as when you were little."

I cover my face with my hands, thinking of elementary school and all the evenings I'd spend singing, dancing, and dressing up in elaborate costumes. Clearly, Dad hasn't forgotten about that either.

"Are there home movies of that? I'd love to see them," Lucas says eagerly.

"That was plenty for me," John replies. "We could hear you from the parking lot."

The boys wander around, picking up Dad's action figures and pointing to some of the comics he has framed on the walls. Nathan exclaims about one of the retro gaming systems in the corner. I was wondering whether there would be any flirting or weirdness between us here, but he's acting like I'm just another friend. Which makes sense. There's no reason to put on a show since we have absolute assurance that neither Paul nor Sophia is going to show up. Still, it feels odd to be in the same room with him and not have his attention.

"And you have an arcade cabinet," Anthony says, giving it a reverent pat. "Based on the 1992 *X-Men* game?"

"You know it. Everyone's welcome to play a few games. No quarters required."

"Hold on, we need to focus," Nathan breaks in. "We're here for one thing and it's not show tunes or retro video games . . . as cool as those sound. It's Monty Python time."

"I'll show you around after. And pizza will be here soon." Dad eyes the group. "I have to go downstairs to the laundry room, but after that I'll be in the other room painting my Hordes army. But the walls are thin, so make sure you behave." He winks at Nathan and me before heading out the front door with a laundry basket. The others exchange a glance.

"What was that about?" Anthony asks.

I wince. "He thinks Nathan and I are together."

"And you haven't told him the truth?"

"It was too awkward. How do we explain without us coming across as totally pathetic?"

"I can promise you, there's no way to do that," Anthony says with a grin. "Although I could argue that Nathan's got exactly the right idea. He gets to flirt with multiple girls without getting in trouble."

I roll my eyes. "*Anyway.* Turns out Dad has Blu-rays for all the movies so we should be good."

"Before we start the movie, there was something I wanted to mention," Lucas interrupts. "Well . . . I guess not just me . . ."

He turns to Hoshiko, and I gasp when I see Hoshiko's cheeks flush pink.

She nods at me. "Lucas and I are going to homecoming together!"

"Ahh!" I swat at Hoshiko. "I can't *believe* you didn't tell me earlier! That whole time we were singing our hearts out and it never popped into your mind?!"

"I'm sorry, I know, I know, I'm a terrible best friend. But I was planning to tell you as soon as Lucas got here."

He takes a step toward me. "Don't be mad at her. It was my idea to wait until we were all together. I know it was killing her."

I want to be mad at Hoshiko. I *am* mad, at least a little. She's my best friend—how could she keep this from me? I should have gotten a text the second she said yes! But as soon as I look at them, the anger fades away. She's so excited she's practically shining, and that's nothing compared to the way Lucas is looking at her right now. It's as if he's staring at an angel dropped to Earth. Or, you know, Idina Menzel.

Hoshiko tilts her head at me, and I reach out and pull her into a hug. "I'm too happy to sulk!"

"Eeeee!" She squeezes me. "I can't wait! We're going to have so much fun!"

"Did you get a date too?" John asks me. "Won't that mess up all this weirdness you've got going on?" He gestures between Nathan and me.

"No date, just permission from my parents."

"She's my date," Hoshiko says, and leans her head on my shoulder.

Lucas frowns at Nathan. "She wouldn't have to be your date if someone would just step up—"

"And here we are!" Nathan practically yells, and waves the Blu-ray box above his head. "No more talking. It's time to get serious."

The others don't need to be told twice. Lucas claims the overstuffed recliner and beckons Hoshiko to squeeze in next to him, which she happily does. She's practically on top of him. She's going to need to do some serious talking the next time we're alone. I need *all* the details about Lucas. John and Anthony both plop onto the black faux leather couch, leaving only the center cushion open.

"Go on." Nathan gestures to the seat.

"No, I don't want to make you sit on the floor. You love this movie."

"I've seen it a billion times. And your dad will think I'm rude if I make his daughter sit on the floor."

"I really don't mind."

"Riley—"

"*Here,* both of you sit on the stupid couch and I'll sit on the ground if that means you'll shut up." John waves at the screen, where a knight pretends to gallop through a field while another guy claps coconut shells together. "We're going to miss the European swallow part."

Anthony snickers and Nathan and I exchange an awkward glance before silently sitting. Dad's place is small, which means he has an apartment-sized couch, and our legs are pressed against each other from hip to knee. I try to cross my legs to give us a little space and keep my eyes on the screen. Lucas looks at us before whispering something to Hoshiko.

Luckily the movie—while totally bizarre—is funny and keeps my attention. It helps that all the boys know it by heart. After a bit, a knock on the front door announces that the pizza has arrived.

"I fart in your general direction!" Dad cries as he comes out of the other room.

"Your mother was a hamster and your father smelt of elderberries!" John quotes back automatically, and pauses the movie.

"And you guys make fun of us for knowing the words to *Hairspray*," Hoshiko says.

Dad deposits the pizza boxes on the coffee table in front of us. I jump up and away from Nathan, but based on Dad's knowing smirk, he saw exactly how close we were sitting a moment ago.

"We didn't make fun of you," Anthony argues. "If I'm not mistaken, we were clapping."

"That was pity clapping," I reply, and grab a slice of mushroom and sausage.

"Nobody pity claps us!" Hoshiko says.

"Exactly!" I jab my pizza at the guys like a sword.

Everyone takes their slices and a Mountain Dew (Dad's

drink of choice) and settles back to watch the rest of the movie. I think about sitting on the edge of the couch so I'm not pressed against Nathan, but he beckons me back. Everyone chuckles over something about a witch, but it's hard to pay attention when shivers go through me every time Nathan shifts and another part of his body touches mine. I turn a bit so I can see him more easily.

"I've been wondering something. If I'm able to bring back the musical, will you make an exception to your after-school boycott and come watch it? It would be a real coup for me if I could get the notoriously anti-school Nathan Wheeler to attend."

He tilts his head as if debating and then comes closer. So close that his mouth is only inches from mine.

"I could be persuaded," he whispers, "under the right conditions. Maybe I'll even bring a bouquet of flowers to make Paul jealous."

"Make it sunflowers, then. They're my favorite."

"That sounds like you."

"In case you weren't aware," Lucas says loud enough that Nathan and I both jump. "Sophia isn't here right now. And neither is Paul. So, you really don't need to keep the fake flirting up for us."

"Shhh!" I look around to make sure Dad isn't lurking in the doorway. "We weren't fake flirting."

He and Anthony exchange a knowing look. "Right, sorry. Regular flirting it is."

My cheeks flame and I take a huge bite of pizza.

Chapter Twenty

For the last ten minutes at lunch on Monday, the boys have been debating Marvel versus DC superheroes, and I never thought a debate I didn't care about could be so hilarious.

When the bell rings, Hoshiko and I wave goodbye since we don't have our next class together and I head down the south hall. A hand slides into my own and squeezes. I squeeze back before I think about it and look into Nathan's green eyes. His hand used to feel strange in mine, but now it feels weird when he's not holding it. Still, I'm not sure why he's walking next to me. Nathan and I don't walk to class together after lunch.

"What's up?" I look over my shoulder to search for Paul. "Did you see him someplace?"

Nathan shakes his head. "Nope."

I blink in confusion. If Paul isn't around, then what's Nathan doing? I slow at my locker. I need my notebook for English later today, but I also need a moment to settle myself. Nathan isn't helping that, though. He lets go of my hand but leans against the locker next to mine, looking so calm and gorgeous that I want to throw myself at him and kiss him until he forgets Sophia's name.

"Don't you need to get to class?" I ask, my voice wavering.

"We still have a few minutes. I wanted to talk to you about something I've been thinking about."

"Okay."

"So, all this fake flirting we do around Sophia and Paul . . . do you ever feel like it's hard to keep track of what we're supposed to be doing and when? I'm getting jumpy tracking Paul in my peripheral vision all the time. He probably thinks *I* have a crush on him the way I watch for him."

My hand freezes as I pull out the notebook. I can predict his next words before he says them. He's going to suggest we call it off. I've been wondering when this might happen.

Nathan shifts a little closer. "Maybe we should . . . I mean . . . What if we stopped turning it on and off? What if we just faked it all the time?"

The notebook clatters to the linoleum tile and we both reach for it at the same time. I couldn't have heard him right. My gaze locks on his as we slowly stand in unison.

"You want to . . . what?"

He hands the notebook to me, a small smile tipping up his lips now. "It's like method acting, right? We fall so deep into the roles we're playing that it doesn't feel like we're faking it anymore. And then we don't need to worry about being caught."

My mouth grows dry. *Fall so deep* . . . Oof, I'm already

falling and I don't know when I'm going to hit bottom. "Are you serious?"

"It just makes sense. Otherwise, it's only a matter of time until we let our guard down and Paul or Sophia figures out this is all a ploy. As it is, our whole table is one joke away from blowing our cover. What if Paul finds out you actually *did* make this up? Or Sophia realizes we're only trying to make her jealous? Neither of us would ever live it down. We need to do whatever we can to sell this."

My thoughts swirl like a tornado. It's true that there would be no recovering if either of them found out. But how likely is that to really happen? Even if Sophia or Paul saw us when we weren't actively flirting, would we really look that suspicious?

At the same time, who am I to argue if this means more time with Nathan? More heated looks, more toe-curling whispers and fingers running through my hair . . . Maybe I don't care what his reasoning is. Maybe I shouldn't fight him or quit my job at the store.

Or maybe I need to fight with everything I have before I get so lost in this deception that I can't find my way out. I can't decide if this is the best idea in the world or if it's only going to lead to my demise.

"What about Sophia?" I ask to buy time. "Won't we put her off if she sees us together too much?"

"I don't think so. If she starts to hint at that, then we can pull back. But I think she likes the competition. She likes to win."

My body seizes at the idea.

"What?" he asks.

"Nothing. It's just . . . I mean, I know this is the point, but doesn't it bother you at all? That she'd think we were together and then purposely try to break us apart? She'd be trying to get you to cheat on me with her."

His eyes widen. "*Cheat* on you?"

My cheeks heat and I wave the words away. "You know what I mean. From her view, that's what you'd be doing."

"And that bothers you?"

"It makes me question whether she's good enough for you." The words come out before I can shove them back down my throat.

"When did you start caring about that? I thought this was all an elaborate ruse to save face for Paul."

"It is. Of course. I just hate wasting my efforts for some-one who isn't worth it."

"Is it really that much effort to pretend you like me?" he whispers. He runs his fingers through my hair. He must know the way his touch burns through my skin despite my steady breathing. His gaze is so soft that it's almost impos-sible to believe he's acting.

The question rises in my mind: Is it possible that he *isn't* faking anymore either?

I narrow my eyes at him, trying to discern his emotions through his expression, but he gives nothing away. And I won't be the one to ask. If he's going to claim this is all fake, then I'll flirt right back. I'll meet him toe to toe every time. And if it finally gets to be too much and he wants to know what the truth is, then he'll have to be the one to break and ask me. No way am I putting myself out there only to find that he really *is* this good of an actor.

"Hey, Mr. Wheeler! How about you take your hands off Ms. Morris and you both get to class before I write you up?"

Nathan jumps back like Mr. Stevens shocked him with a Taser. "Yes, sir. On my way." He jogs backward a few steps and looks over his shoulder to double-check that our history teacher is still striding away. "You're riding to the store with me, right? I'll see you then!"

He jogs farther away and I wave to him as if nothing is wrong, even though I'm about to collapse into my locker.

I spend the rest of the day in a fog, replaying those few minutes with Nathan and trying to figure out what's going on with him. It's only at rehearsal after school that I can finally focus. People have memorized their lyrics and small bits of choreography and it's starting to look like an actual performance. But the Three Little Pigs still aren't projecting, Papa Ogre is giving me a hard time about the Shrek mask he needs to wear, and the costumes are a disaster. I can't believe how fast time is moving. Homecoming is this Saturday and the big meeting is the Wednesday after. I've got to pull this together.

I'm almost to the school exit, busy running through my mental to-do list, when a voice pulls me from my thoughts. "Riley? Hey, wait up!"

Ugh.

It's Paul again, looking every inch the leading man with his perfectly cut hair and bright white smile. I know for a fact his hair didn't look like that after he pulled off the Shrek mask in the auditorium minutes ago, which means he must have ducked into a bathroom before finding me. For some reason the vanity annoys me.

"I don't have a lot of time. Nathan is picking me up today." I give him a pointed look.

"That was a great rehearsal," he replies with zero acknowledgment of what I just said.

Sighing, I push open the door that leads out into the parking lot. It's a cool October day, but the sun is bright and I have to shield my eyes with my hand.

Even still, my gaze immediately latches on to Nathan in the distance. I figured he'd be waiting in his car for me, but he's leaning against the driver's side door. Why do guys have to look so good when they're leaning against things? It's just a form of laziness, all this leaning. It shouldn't make my heart speed up, but here we are. He pushes away from the car and strides toward me.

"I have to say, I don't get the two of you." Paul's still next to me for some godforsaken reason. "You have nothing in common."

I glare at him. "Well, you and I had lots in common and we know how that worked out."

"Riley—"

"Okay?" Nathan asks me, his voice tinged with worry as he comes to my side.

I reach for his hand, and he easily gives it to me. "I'm better now," I say mostly to myself. And I mean it. I'm more relaxed just having him close.

Paul surveys us. "So, will I see you at homecoming?"

Nathan and I glance at each other. He might have said we

should start faking all the time, but I know he didn't mean *all* the time. Not when it comes to the school dances he loathes.

"I don't think—" I start.

Nathan's hand tightens around mine, and he pulls me closer so that our arms are touching from shoulder to wrist. "Of course we'll be there. I'm already looking forward to seeing what Riley wears." He gestures down at my oversized strawberry sweater. "I'm sure it'll pull all eyes to her. Though that happens no matter what she's wearing."

I look up at Nathan in total shock. *What?*

He must see my confusion because he kisses my temple as if to remind me of what we're doing.

"Okay, uh . . . cool." Paul sounds hesitant, like he can feel some tension or weirdness between Nathan and me and isn't sure what to make of it. "I'll look for you. If you need me, I'll be the one in the red BMW. My uncle's letting me borrow it for the dance." He winks and walks out to the parking lot.

"You shouldn't have said that," I tell Nathan once we're safely in his car and driving away from school. "What am I going to say when he realizes you didn't come with me? It's going to be even worse."

He snorts. "If Paul saw you at homecoming without me at your side, you wouldn't need to worry about explaining anything. He'd be too busy falling over himself begging you to take him back."

I stare at him in horror. "What are you talking about? That's ridiculous."

"Uh, *you're* ridiculous. Have you seriously not noticed the way he watches you? Or the waves of jealousy wafting off him whenever I come up beside you?"

"Nathan, *he* dumped *me*. He's dating Lainey. He doesn't want to date me again; he only wants to make sure I know what I'm missing."

He continues driving straight down Chestnut Street when he should have made a right, then turns abruptly into a narrow alley and accelerates. I think Nathan could have been a NASCAR driver in another life. "He's totally hung up on you. When a guy really dumps someone, he doesn't keep coming around like this. He's not over you."

I roll my eyes in exasperation, but I can't push the idea away. I replay my recent interactions with Paul. He's been talking to me a lot more after rehearsals and he did ask about driving me to the store. But he's still dating Lainey as far as I can tell. Even if Nathan is on to something, I couldn't care less. The whole idea of Paul wanting me back is gross.

"You're quiet over there. Are you debating the possibility of getting back together?" Nathan asks. Maybe I'm imagining it, but he sounds annoyed.

"He's too full of himself to ask me out again. It would be a blow to his ego. And you're distracting from the real subject—how I'm going to save face when you don't show up at the dance with me."

He turns down another back alley—one I never knew existed. I'm about to ask him where he's driving us when we pull out onto the road in front of the store. So *this* is how he gets here before Dad and me. He's found some secret back way through town.

"I don't know why you keep saying that—I wasn't lying to Paul," he replies. "I'll be there with you."

"But you hate school functions. You swore you wouldn't go."

He gives a small shrug. "What can I say? I'm getting addicted to shutting down Paul when he makes assumptions. I'm starting to understand what compelled you to blurt out my name in the first place."

I sit back in the seat and stare straight ahead. We're going together? My body feels tingly at the idea, and I try to remind myself that we're not *really* going together. He didn't ask me of his own volition, and he's not taking me as his date. It's just more pretending.

"Is that okay?" he asks when I don't respond. His eyebrows furrow in concern. "I just assumed you'd want to go together, but if not . . ."

"Yeah, no, it's definitely okay. Thank you for agreeing to it." I smile. "It'll be fun."

"I'm a horrible dancer."

"That's okay. I'll teach you a couple moves."

My emotions are a soft-serve swirl of excitement and trepidation. An entire evening with Nathan at my side, with his hands on me as we dance—it sounds like heaven. But I know pain is lurking in the wings, waiting to pounce on me. I never thought of myself as a masochist, and yet I can't seem to stop myself from sprinting right toward the pain.

Chapter Twenty-One

Nathan's true to his word all week and by the time our Friday D&D game arrives, I'm barely holding it together. I don't know how he's able to fake it so thoroughly. He acts like the perfect boyfriend from the moment I see him in the hall each morning to the last minute at the store in the evening. My whole body tingles from the memories. Our hands clasped tightly as we walked between classes, our legs pressed together at the lunch table as we ate walking tacos, his lips pressed into my hair and against my temple. Oh, his *lips*. I haven't thought of much else all week. The only way I can handle it is to up the ante every time he does. If he takes my hand, I squeeze it and lean into him. If he hugs me, I take the opportunity to whisper teasing insults in his ear. How far can I go before he finally pulls back in shock? But nothing I do gets that reaction.

Well, I haven't kissed him yet. I imagine that would do the trick.

We keep dancing around it, getting closer but never going all the way, and it's driving me out of my mind. I keep wondering, *Will this be the time? No. Maybe* this *time?* How is he not pulling his hair out with agony? But he's so chill. He really must have no interest in me.

"You ready for the game?"

I jump at his voice and almost drop the board games I'm holding. Dad asked me to reorganize the shelves before our D&D game starts, and I've been using the time to be away from Nathan and calm my thoughts. I couldn't fail harder if I'd rolled a one on a d20.

Nathan takes the games from my hands and stacks them on the shelf before turning back to me. "You okay? You've seemed a little off today."

Probably because I can't stop imagining kissing you until we both collapse from exhaustion and knock all the games off these shelves.

"Yeah, sorry. Just thinking about the musical."

"Of course. What else could you possibly be thinking about?"

I don't meet his eye. For once, the musical is the last thing on my mind. "You're one to talk, Mr. D&D."

"Oh, please, I have a ton of things on my mind. D&D, Magic, Warhammer." He ticks them off on his fingers. "I may even have a few Monty Python quotes rolling around in there."

I try to smile and walk to the back room. Anthony and John are at our usual table, but I'm surprised that Lucas is missing. I glance around the room, but there's no sign of him. And no Hoshiko either. I look at my phone in case she's texted to say she's running late, but there's nothing. Granted, she's always running here from dance, but she's usually good at telling me if something comes up. And Lucas is never late. I bite my lip—maybe they're together? I send a quick text to check.

Nathan stands behind me, but a glance over my shoulder at him tells me he's also noticed their absence. Just then, Sophia walks into the back room, looking like an ethereal fairy with her waves of red hair and a crown of fake flowers. The activity in the room slows as everyone stops to look at her. I'm sure she loves it.

I sense Nathan step closer behind me. He plays with my hair, smoothing it away from my face and down my back. It's so calming that I have to school myself so I don't purr like a cat.

"Are you leaving your hair down tomorrow?" he whispers.

I smile smugly. He keeps trying to find out what I'm wearing to homecoming, but Mom and I just found a dress two days ago and I'm keeping it a surprise. At least I can keep him in suspense about this.

"Possibly," I whisper back. "Do you like it down?"

"Yes." He gathers it up into a low ponytail and releases it.

"Interesting. I might put it up just to mess with you, then."

"That's cool." His hands fall on my shoulders and then slide down the length of my arms. He leans forward so his chest presses against my back. "I like when you mess with me. I like everything you do with me." His lips brush the back of my head and shivers run up my spine.

But instead of swooning at his words, I snap. It's too

much. I can barely hold it together when he touches me, but his words? It's impossible to hear them, knowing he's whispering in my ear because Sophia just walked in. I can't take it anymore.

I swirl around, jutting out my chin. I know everyone is watching but I don't care.

"You shouldn't say things like that." I pinch his arm.

"Ow!" His jaw drops open in shock. "You pinched me."

"You deserved it."

He blinks, clearly confused. Hesitantly, he beckons me farther away from the table, where I'm sure everyone is trying to eavesdrop with great delight.

"Hey, I'm really sorry. I didn't realize I was crossing a line. I just . . ." His shoulders hunch and his expression is so full of concern and remorse that I can't hold on to my anger. I look down at my feet.

"Tell me what to do," he continues. "Or not do. Was it the hair? Or the kiss . . ."

I shake my head, abruptly feeling like I might cry. "I don't know. It's . . . weird when you say nice things like that to me. It's too much."

He straightens. "You don't want me to say nice things?"

"I'm used to jokes. Or teasing. Just stick to those instead of lying."

"I wasn't lying. I love when you mess with me."

He thinks he's helping, but he's really not. He's only making this *so* much harder.

I look behind me. The entire table is staring at us, even John. Sophia's eyes are narrowed like she's appraising us.

I groan.

Nathan doesn't seem to care what everyone else is seeing. He closes the small distance between us. "Do you want me to pull back?" he asks in a whisper. "Just tell me the rules and I'll follow them."

My stomach flips. The rules . . .

Don't look at me like you want to kiss me unless you actually do.

I take a breath. "I'm fine. Just . . . yeah, we should pull back. I don't have the energy to keep this up tonight."

Nathan's face flashes with hurt and I look away. Lucas bustles into the room at that moment, Hoshiko a few steps behind him. Nathan and I turn to each other in surprise, our awkwardness forgotten momentarily by this new revelation. Since when did they start arriving to the game together? And where were they before this?

There's something more happening with Lucas that she's not telling me, but I'm still desperately happy to see Hoshiko. Nathan and I return to the table and she takes me in. Her face flashes with worry, but I shake my head. I can catch her up later.

"Okay, sorry I'm late," Lucas says. "Tonight is a big night for the campaign so we need to focus. No messing around if we want to finish this part of the quest tonight." He pulls his books and dice from his bag and sits down, looking around the table with a serious expression. For once, I'm relieved to focus solely on the game and ignore Nathan and Sophia. "At our last session you made your way to the edge of the swamp you believe the hydra to be located in. You can continue to explore around the edges or you can venture deeper in."

"No more exploring. It's time we kill this thing," Nathan says, and mimes holding up the magical sword we retrieved for him two sessions back.

"And get our treasure!" Anthony cries.

Hoshiko and I exchange an amused glance and nod along with the others. I wasn't sure she'd make it more than a few sessions, but between hanging out with me and her new favorite DM, she's really gotten into it.

Sophia's rogue leads the way through some random encounters, and soon we're all in a desperate fight to stay alive against the hydra. Round after round we battle against it, each taking damage as we cut off one of its heads only to have two grow back when it escapes the fire damage. Everyone else is on the edge of their seats, speaking louder and faster than usual, cheering when one of us manages to cut off a head and groaning when someone's hit points drop. I try to match the enthusiasm of the others, but I'm struggling. My thoughts are still swirling around what happened with Nathan so that it's impossible to sink into my character and the story line. It's so bad that I find myself peeking over my shoulder, half hoping Dad will be in trouble with a customer and I'll have to leave to help him.

John finishes his turn by casting bolts of fire at the monster. "I don't know why we wasted time searching for that sword, Sol, when I'm the one who's about to kill this thing."

"No way, the kill is mine. I can't miss with Elphaba to inspire me like always." He smiles at me. "I'm unstoppable with you at my side."

My heart stutters and I look down at my dice. My perfect dice that my perfect fake boyfriend bought for me. I know we're both playing characters—right now and in real life—and I know this is just a game. But I don't think I can play much longer.

"You're next, Elphaba. What'll it be?" Lucas asks.

"I'll heal Anthony."

"Okay."

"And . . . that's all."

Lucas blinks in surprise. Sophia gives me her full attention and Nathan leans close. "You forgot to use your inspire ability to buff me."

"I'm going to save it."

"Save it?" Nathan looks at me as if I just told him I plan to punch him in the face later tonight.

"I can only use it a few times per day, and the party might need it later."

"I know, but . . ."

I mess with the dice rather than look at him. Without my help, Sol is no match for the hydra. The rest of the party jumps in to help, but ultimately John is the one to take him down. The group erupts into shouts and high fives when we realize we actually won. Anthony jumps up and pulls us into hugs before running through the room and hugging other random customers. Even Hoshiko does a victory dance.

After a moment, Lucas leans into the table, his face suddenly menacing. "Well done. But it looks like Elphaba knew something the rest of you didn't when she decided to save her ability. Perhaps she can predict the future in addition to singing a mean song because . . ." He pauses and slowly stares around the table, making sure to meet each of our confused gazes before moving on. "You thought the hydra was your final foe, but you were mistaken. What you failed to realize when you stole Sol's magical sword was that you disturbed the eternal resting place of the ancient king you were stealing from—and he is *very* displeased. He has returned to this plane as a wraith, and he is waiting at the edge of the swamp to retrieve what is rightfully his. And destroy the ones who stole it." Lucas leans back and crosses his arms over his chest, looking extremely pleased with himself.

Nathan gasps and John leaps out of his chair. Anthony and Sophia both groan and drop their heads to the table. I'm not sure how hard it is to kill a wraith, but I'm guessing it's not easy.

"This is impossible. We can't take on a wraith now—our hit points are already decimated!" John complains. "You want to make sure the entire party dies."

"It's sadistic, man," Nathan says. His body is turned away from me, and I can't help feeling that he's purposefully ignoring me now. Not that I can blame him.

"It's not sadistic." Lucas lifts his chin defiantly. "Well, okay, maybe a bit. It's one of the benefits of DMing. But it's *not* impossible. There's six of you now and if you all work together, there's a chance the party can make it through alive."

"The same chance that one of us will win the next Mega Millions jackpot, buy a yacht, and take the group on a year-long trip around the world," Anthony mutters.

"Is that a possibility?" Hoshiko asks. "Because we should be working harder toward that."

The group is still buzzing with the surprise campaign twist when Dad comes around a few minutes later to remind us that the store will be closing soon. "You all need to get your sleep tonight so you'll be ready for the dance tomorrow," he says with a smile. "Everyone excited?"

Lucas grins. "Can't wait."

"We'll be short-staffed," Dad replies, nodding at me and Nathan, "but the customers will have to wait. There's no way I'm missing the chance to see two of my favorite people going to their first homecoming together." He beams at us.

Everyone whips around to look our way. I force myself to give him a weak smile. "Thanks, Dad. I'll come up front to help close in a second."

"Sure, take your time." He squeezes Nathan's shoulder and walks away.

Sophia leans back, eyes flaring, and I flinch. "I didn't know you two were going to homecoming together," she says.

"Yeah . . ." Nathan turns to me.

He's barely made eye contact with me since I refused to use my ability to help him, but suddenly his gaze is intense and unreadable. Does he want me to give Sophia some excuse about why we're going together? It's dangerous for him to let me explain rather than jumping in himself. All I want to do is snarl at her like an injured animal and growl *mine*.

But he's not mine and I'm so tired of pretending otherwise. It's officially time to step aside.

"We're just going as friends," I say, and gesture around the table. "A group of us are all going together, and I couldn't get a date. Nathan was nice enough to come with me so I wouldn't be alone. Nothing more going on than that—Dad just has a vivid imagination."

Nathan's eyes widen in shock. Actually, everyone at the table is looking at me like I just pronounced I'm boycotting the Tony Awards this year.

I stand. "I should go help Dad." I nod at Sophia and stride away.

There. It's done. And I only feel a little like crying.

I grab the carpet sweeper in the front closet and start running it over the floor indiscriminately.

"Well, *that* was interesting," Lucas says a few minutes later. The rest of the group, not including Nathan and Sophia, crowds around me at the front of the store.

"If they actually start dating, Sophia is going to chew him up and spit him out," Anthony says to no one in particular.

I shrug. "It was time. We started this whole thing so he could date Sophia and she's clearly interested in him now. I didn't want to torpedo that."

They exchange glances.

"I would have liked it a lot more if you two got together for real," Anthony says. John nods. Hoshiko wraps an arm around my waist and squeezes me.

"Sorry, Riley," Lucas says quietly. His face is so full of sympathy that I can't stand it. I know my cheeks are red and my throat feels so thick and dry that I can barely speak.

"For what?" I push the sweeper harder. "This was the plan from the beginning. I flirt long enough for Sophia to get jealous and then he gets the girl. If anything, your reaction just shows what an amazing actress I am."

Lucas looks skeptical. "Yeah, but . . ."

"No buts. It's all good."

Hoshiko looks at her phone and sighs. "I'm sorry, Dad's here to pick me up." She pulls me into a hug. "We'll talk when I come over tomorrow to get ready, okay? Love you."

"Love you." I squeeze her tighter before letting her go. The others follow her out. I turn off my brain and mindlessly sweep.

Sophia strides out of the back room next, her hips swaying and her face beaming. She twirls her fingers at me in a little wave. "Bye, Riley!"

I blink at her as she leaves the store and my whole body grows heavier. There's only one reason she'd be that happy.

Now it's done.

A moment later, a shadow falls by my right side and there's only one person it could be. "Hey," I say without looking up.

"Everyone left so fast," Nathan says. "Usually they hang around until your dad shoves them out the door and locks it behind them."

I shrug.

"So, what happened back there? Why did you tell her we're going as friends?"

"Because we are."

"I know. Of course I know that." He blows out a breath and runs a hand through his hair. "But she didn't. That was the whole point."

I drop the handle of the sweeper and turn to him, hands on my hips. "*No*, the whole point was for you to date her. Right? And I saw a perfect opportunity for that to happen. Let me guess, she asked you out after I left?"

He takes a step back. "How good is your hearing?"

"I didn't need to hear. I knew."

He puts a hand on the back of his neck. "She asked me to go to her school's homecoming. It's next weekend."

I wasn't expecting that part. It's irrational, but it hurts more than if they were going on a regular date. I fight to control my expression. "And you said yes?"

He hesitates. His gaze sweeps over my face before dropping to my mouth and then the ground.

"I did."

"Good. I'm happy for you." My voice is so calm. I might be tired, but I can still pull off this last conversation. "So, we did it. It's happening. This thing we agreed to ended up being really successful, huh?" I look around, realizing where we're standing. "And it all started here, in this aisle. I guess this is a fitting place to call it off."

"Call what off?"

I frown. "Everything. The flirting, the pretending, the dance."

Nathan shakes his head. "But what about Paul? What about tomorrow?"

"I can handle Paul. I never should have let him get to me the way he did, but I don't care about his opinion anymore."

I assume Nathan's going to look relieved, but instead his expression hardens. "I'm not going to abandon you."

"It's fine," I say, but my throat is tight and I have to turn away before he can read my expression. Really, I'm only upset with myself. I have no one else to blame for getting into this ridiculous situation. I'm the one who convinced him to start this.

"No." His voice is fierce now. Agitated. "The dance is

tomorrow—I'm not backing out on you the night before. Your father would never let me step foot in this store again if I did."

"Oh . . . fair point." I chuckle humorlessly. I wish he had a different reason, but he's not wrong about Dad. He'd be livid if he found out I was suddenly dateless.

Nathan puts a hand on my arm. "I'll be there tomorrow at five to pick you up, okay? But we'll drop all the other stuff and just be our regular selves. Friends. Assuming you still think of me as a friend?"

"You're my annoying coworker sometimes, but yeah. We're friends."

"Good. And you still won't tell me what you're wearing tomorrow?"

That makes me smile for real. "No, that's staying a surprise."

"Fine." He looks at me another second and then turns away. He only makes it a few steps before he comes back. "You might not care about Paul anymore, but that guy still annoys the crap out of me. I may have to slip back into my boyfriend role one more time if he starts bothering you tomorrow."

I laugh lightly. "I won't argue with that."

In fact, I wouldn't be opposed to slipping Paul twenty bucks to come around just so Nathan will brush one more kiss against my temple. But I know that's not what either of us needs. Nathan has been dreaming about Sophia for months and now—because of my plan—he finally has her.

Chapter Twenty-Two

"**D**one! You look beautiful."

Hoshiko steps back and looks me up and down. Homecoming is tonight and my parents agreed that she and I could spend the whole day together getting ready. We did each other's nails and hair, and we've spent the last hour up in my room, dancing to Taylor Swift while we did our makeup and finished getting dressed.

"Thanks, but you're going to put the rest of us to shame," I tell her.

Hoshiko grins and does a graceful spin across the room. "I hope so."

There's no need to hope—she chose a blue sequin dress that's way more formfitting than I thought her mom would allow. It accentuates every detail of her dancer's body and Lucas is going to pass out when he sees her. As he should.

I brush my palms down my dress and swallow my nerves. I'm starting to wish I had warned Nathan about what I'm wearing instead of keeping it a secret. He must know I would choose something dramatic, but this dress is over the top even for me. There were few options left when Mom and I went shopping a few days ago, but then I saw this one and couldn't pass it up . . . although other people obviously could since it was on a deep discount.

It's a short strapless dress completely covered in dyed pink, blue, and purple ostrich feathers, with a wide neon pink belt cinched at the waist. I paired it with Mom's bright green heels, because why not, and after *much* debate, I kept my hair down in soft waves. I was tempted to put it in a high bun just to spite Nathan, which Hoshiko was in favor of, but . . . well, I want him to bitterly regret that we're going as friends. It's petty and pitiful, but it's all I have right now.

"I still can't believe he agreed to go with Sophia," Hoshiko mutters into the mirror as she messes with her earrings.

"I don't know why you and Lucas are so shocked about it. Of course he was going to say yes."

"You haven't had to sit across the table and watch Nathan for weeks like we have. You don't know what he looks like when he's looking at you. *No one* is that good of an actor."

I huff in pretend annoyance. "Not even me?"

She gives me a half-smile. "I love you, but let's not pretend. When it comes to Nathan, you're kind of a lousy actress."

"Ouch! Way to cut out my heart." I grasp my chest dramatically.

"I know this isn't how you were hoping homecoming would go, but we're still going to have an amazing time. We're wearing beautiful dresses and we get to spend the night dancing together. Tonight is made for us."

"True. And then we can come back here and analyze every detail. How could it be a bad night?"

"Exactly!"

"The boys are here!" Mom calls from downstairs. Her voice is so excited that she almost sounds like a teenager herself.

Hoshiko and I grin at each other and head for the stairs. For a second, as we descend, it's like the living room is filled with paparazzi. Way more people than I imagined fill the space and they all have their phones up as they ooh and aah. I spot Hoshiko's mother, father, and little sister, along with Lucas's parents and grandparents. Dad stands next to Mom. This is the first time I've seen them together since they grounded me. Luckily, they're both smiling this time.

Lucas takes a step toward Hoshiko and his face is exactly how I imagined it would be—slack-jawed and overwhelmed. I'm so caught up watching them that I don't notice Nathan until I'm on the bottom step and he's right in front of me.

"Riley."

One look at him and I'm light-headed. He's . . . devastatingly handsome. More than I thought possible. He's always been cute with his floppy hair and black-rimmed glasses, but now it's like he's a totally different person. I figured he'd wear some khaki pants and a tie he borrowed from his dad, but he's in a *suit*. A beautiful dark gray suit that makes him look like he's going to a movie premiere instead of a high school dance in the middle of Ohio. And his expression . . . if I didn't know better, I'd say he was as slack-jawed as Lucas. Maybe even more? As if he can hardly believe it's me.

"Hey." My voice comes out as a whisper. "I guess this

whole time I should have been asking what *you* were wearing—this suit is amazing. I didn't even know you owned a button-up shirt."

He looks down self-consciously. "My mom took me out to get everything. I don't dress up much."

"You don't say."

He grins ruefully. "You look . . . Wow. That dress."

"Yeah." I rub my hands over the feathers, feeling silly. What was I thinking wearing a dress like this? People are going to make bird jokes all night.

"Do you mind?" He hesitates and reaches out to touch a feather. "Oh, they're so soft!" He laughs. "I thought it might be itchy or poky or something."

"It's pretty unusual, I know. You shouldn't have expected anything less from me." I shrug.

"The dress is perfect. You look perfect."

Our eyes meet and I feel it, that spark that makes me wonder if Hoshiko is right. Does he really think I look perfect? Do friends say things like that to other friends? Then I realize that people are still taking pictures and videos of us, and I step back. "Where's your mom? I need to compliment her style."

He rubs the back of his neck awkwardly. "They couldn't come. You know . . . work and stuff. I think she felt pretty guilty, which is why she spent so much money on these clothes."

I glance around the room. Nathan is the only one with no family here. No one to fuss over him or make him pose for photos or talk about how they can't believe how grown up he looks now. My parents can be overprotective and frustrating, but they're always here, no matter what. I took it for granted—the fact that both Mom and Dad came to every performance and event. But standing here, it's clear that not everyone has that.

I slip my hand into Nathan's without thinking and squeeze. "Give her my compliments—it's really cool that she did that. Now, let's get these photos finished so we can go eat."

We meet up with Anthony and his date, Kenzie, at one of the only nonchain restaurants in town. Nathan's parents must have lectured him about manners because he pulls out my chair for me. I pause when I see all the place settings.

"I'm surprised they sat us at such a big table." We're at a table big enough for eight, but there are only six of us and I know for sure that other larger groups are still waiting for seating.

Lucas, Anthony, and Nathan exchange an excited look. Which makes Hoshiko and I exchange a scared one. What are they planning?

That becomes only too apparent about twenty minutes into dinner. We've just gotten our bread and side salads when a commotion sounds behind us. I turn and gasp. John is striding toward us, looking like he just walked out of a Lord of the Rings movie. He has on a navy blue tunic and black pants, with a heavy black cloak billowing behind him. He's hung multiple glass bottles and a leather satchel on a leather belt. And he's not alone. Next to him is a tall Black boy dressed as a knight, complete with armor that clanks and a superlong sword in a scabbard.

"Yes, you made it!" Anthony cries. The entire restaurant has paused midbite to stare.

I yelp and start clapping. "Oh my God!"

John rolls his shoulders back. You'd think he'd be self-conscious being dressed as a wizard in the middle of a fancy(ish) restaurant, but he looks more confident than I've ever seen him. The boys sit down in the remaining seats, though they have to mess with their cloaks and swords to fit comfortably.

"Hey." The other boy waves to the table. He looks a bit more nervous. "I'm Jordan. The boyfriend."

My grin gets even wider. I don't care what else happens, I love tonight. "Hi! I'm Riley."

Hoshiko introduces herself, and it turns out the guys convinced John and Jordan to come to dinner before LARP-ing since they flatly refused to skip it for the dance.

"Are you sure we can't convince you to come?" Hoshiko asks. "I really need to see a picture of you both in those costumes doing a classic homecoming pose."

Jordan pushes his sleeves up and butters a roll. "I said the same thing, but John is *very* serious about LARPing." He gives John the kind of loving but exasperated look that couples give when they've been together a long time.

John returns it. He was born to wear this costume because his personality is raised to the power of ten in it. "It's impossible to dance in these robes anyway. I'd much rather kill some monsters."

"Where did you buy those?" I ask. My mind is already returning to the possible musical. We probably won't have the budget to buy fancy costumes, and I doubt we need anything like what they're wearing, but maybe the costume company has something we could afford for the leads.

"Oh, we're too broke to buy this stuff. It's crazy expensive, and my mom insists it's a waste of money. Luckily, there are a ton of tutorials out there."

I drop my knife and it clatters on the plate. "You *made* those costumes?"

Jordan grins and does a tiny bow. "Hours and hours of work. Our friend Marjorie is a whiz with a sewing machine, so that helps."

Nathan chuckles and I turn with narrowed eyes. "What?"

"I should have told John to ask *you* to join the LARPing group instead of me. One look at the costumes and you would've been a goner."

"I do love a good costume." I sigh lustfully at the faux fur lining of John's cloak.

Nathan leans toward me and I'm reminded that, as cool as a silver chest plate is, nothing looks as good as he does in a suit. I have a sudden desire to grab his tie and pull him even closer.

"I can always drive us back to the Holiday House after the dance," he whispers. "Maybe we can sneak a few costumes off the mannequins before we get caught."

"It's a date."

He winks and tingles run down my legs. It's really hard to only be friends when he looks like that.

My nerves ramp up when Nathan pulls into the high school parking lot after dinner. All around, couples are walking toward the front doors, holding hands and laughing. To our left, Paul gets out of his uncle's BMW and takes Lainey's hand. He's got on a baby-blue suit—he always did have my dramatic flair—and she's wearing a long silver dress that might as well have been poured over her. Paul spots me and nods. Lainey's eyes widen when she notices what I'm wearing.

"Hey, Riley. Nathan." Paul gives me a once-over. "Quite the dress."

Great, the dress discourse is starting already. I'm not going to let him get to me, though. I do a little shimmy so all the feathers flutter. "Perfect for dancing."

Nathan glowers at Paul and takes my hand. "See you inside," he says gruffly. We stride toward the entrance, Nathan muttering to himself.

"What?"

"I just hate that guy."

His loyalty warms me. "Thanks."

Nathan looks down at our clasped hands and takes a breath. "I'm sorry, I shouldn't be doing that. I know you told me to cut all that out tonight." He releases my hand, and the air is cold on my palm.

"It's fine. I didn't even notice." I give him a small smile. "I guess we've gotten into some habits, huh?"

"Yeah. But I don't want to upset you again."

"I've already pushed last night from my mind."

"Well, I haven't. Didn't I cross a line because I said something nice to you earlier? I was a bit worried you'd slap me after I complimented your dress." The glimmer in his eye is half teasing, half wary.

"That was strike one."

He chuckles. "Seriously, though, Riley."

"Stop worrying. I was . . . tired. Let's just forget everything and have fun. No rules tonight."

He takes me in, as if weighing my truthfulness. "Okay. No rules."

Chapter Twenty-Three

We walk into the school and find our friends huddled around a table at the edge of the gym. The homecoming theme is "Winter Solstice," which is a little weird because it's only October, but at least the gym looks pretty. The space is dim except for the Christmas lights that have been strung across the ceiling. Someone's made a ton of paper snowflakes that hang above our heads, and there's a photo booth covered in white balloons and paper snowflakes as well.

"I feel like I need a winter coat," Lucas says.

"More like a calendar," Nathan replies with an eye roll.

Okay, so he isn't won over by school functions yet.

"Forget about the decor. What are we waiting for—let's go dance!" Hoshiko pulls Lucas toward the center of the gym where people are starting to congregate.

I look at Nathan. "Ready to start having fun?"

"Does that mean we're going for a drive now? We can pick up more Pop-Tarts."

I take his hand and drag him toward the floor. Anthony and Kenzie follow us and we form a small and slightly awkward circle, shimmying and shaking to the music.

"And next up is a special request from Principal Holloway," the DJ announces. I recognize his voice as the middle-aged man who runs the local easy-listening radio station in town. Not exactly the coolest choice for a DJ, but we're limited around here.

I swivel to Nathan as Michael Jackson's "Beat It" pumps through the speakers. Around us, most kids groan and walk over to the refreshment table, while a few clap and start dancing.

Nathan lights up. "Eat it!" he belts out with Lucas, who clearly also knows the Weird Al version.

"You're singing the wrong version!" I shout over the music.

"Nah. This version is okay, but it's not as good as the original."

"You've got that reversed."

"You're reversed," he calls, and twirls me in a circle.

We're all dancing in a frenzy now, jumping and yelling whatever words we can remember. Michael Jackson fades into Beyoncé and I'm too busy laughing and dancing to pay attention to the time or what's happening with the other students. Hoshiko is pulling out some salsa moves, Anthony is next to her doing a horrible version of the running man, and I have to bend over I'm laughing so hard. The cramp in my side is totally worth it.

Eventually the music stops so that Principal Holloway can make an announcement and we all sit down at one of the tables. They're covered in blue plastic tablecloths with snowflake-shaped confetti sprinkled on top. Clearly the school's budget issues extend beyond the musical, but the dim lighting makes it all a bit magical.

"Do you want me to get you some water?" Nathan asks.

"Yeah, thanks."

Lucas leaves at the same time, and I assume he's going to get drinks as well, but he heads in the opposite direction.

I turn to Hoshiko. "Are you having a good time with Lucas? You two look cute together."

Her eyes shine as brightly as stage lights on the opening night of a new show. She glances around, checking to make sure he isn't back yet, and leans in. "Riley, I like him. Like, *really* like him."

My heart fills at her words. There's nothing more wonderful than seeing your best friend happy. "Well, clearly the feeling is mutual. He couldn't take his eyes off you back there."

"Do you think? I—" She breaks off and sits up straight.

I look around in confusion. "What's wrong?"

"This song . . ."

Lucas jogs across the floor toward us, his hand outstretched. He stops in front of Hoshiko. "Shall we?"

She squeals—literally squeals—and flies out of her chair. "Are you sure?"

"One hundred percent sure."

They run back onto the gym floor, and I look at Anthony, but he shrugs in confusion. I have no idea what's going on.

"Am I hallucinating right now?" Nathan asks me as he

comes back to my side. He hands me a bottle of water without pulling his eyes from the dance floor.

And then I see what he's staring at.

"Are you seeing Lucas and Hoshiko doing a choreographed dance number to 'Uptown Funk'?"

"Yep."

I start laughing. "Then your vision and sense of reality are intact."

I can't stop staring. They're doing grapevines, kicks, jazz hands, the whole thing. Lucas is clearly not a dancer—he can barely keep up with Hoshiko's easy grace—but he's so enthusiastic it doesn't matter.

"Whoa, this boy must really be in love to make a fool of himself in front of the whole school," Anthony says from my other side.

I bring a hand to my mouth. He's right. I don't think anyone would do that unless they were desperate to impress the person they're dancing with.

Nathan's shoulder brushes mine and I lean into him. "Wow . . . ," I whisper.

"Yeah . . . he's a *horrible* dancer."

I look over at Nathan and we both crack up. He really is. But he's also adorable and suddenly I'm intensely grateful I took Mom's car, worked at the game store, got pulled into D&D, and pulled Hoshiko in with me. Because if that led to her finding someone who looks at her with such adoration while doing a very wonky Charleston step, it was worth every moment.

Nathan is still laughing and puts a hand on my arm to

steady himself. Heat flares through me at his touch. It was worth it for multiple reasons.

The song fades into a slow one. I expect Hoshiko and Lucas to come back to us so we can hear every detail of how this happened, but Lucas wraps his arms around her waist and they start slow dancing, oblivious to the rest of the world.

Nathan and I glance at each other and then look away. I cross my arms in front of my chest. Dancing with the rest of the group is one thing, but slow dancing feels really intimate.

He bumps his shoulder with mine. "Want to?"

I expected him to be resistant to all forms of dance, but he's smiling warmly. He holds out his hand.

"Um . . . okay."

I swallow and follow him out onto the floor. After a moment of awkwardness, I put my hands on his shoulders and his go to my hips. I take a shallow breath.

"So, you had no idea that was going to happen?" he asks.

"Zero idea. I'm miffed they kept it a secret."

Nathan freezes mid-sway. "Wait, that's where he's been!" He looks down at me, his face shockingly close. "All those times he blew me off or was late to the game store. He must have been practicing that dance with Hoshiko! Though, after seeing that, he probably should have blown me off more often."

Our eyes meet and we crack up again.

"He must *really* like her to give up all that game time," I say.

"Definitely." We sway back and forth for a few moments. His voice is softer when he speaks again. "Guys don't tend to skip their favorite things unless they really like a girl."

"I don't know about that. You gave up a night at the store to be here."

"I did give that up, didn't I? Though I'm not sure the store would be much fun anymore without you there."

"That's a switch. I bet at the beginning you were counting down the weeks until I was gone."

"I was counting the days." His grin is wicked. "Actually, at one point I was counting the seconds."

I laugh and his hands tighten around me until we're pressed together.

"Let me guess, that was the day I pulled you into the mess with Paul?"

He looks away from me and across the dance floor. "No. That was a good day." He runs his hands up my back and through my curls. "You left your hair down." His eyes soften and he tilts his head down. "Did you mean what you said about forgetting the rules tonight?"

Is he . . .

Are we about to . . .

I pull my eyes from his and glance around the dance floor. Is Paul here? Is that why Nathan's acting this way—for Paul's benefit?

Because I *really* want to kiss Nathan right now, but I don't want it to be fake. I don't want anything about us to be fake anymore.

I scan the crowd as we sway in a slow circle, but I don't see Paul anywhere. My chest expands with relief and anticipation.

I look back to him. "I meant it."

He leans closer, achingly slow as if waiting for a hint of

hesitation from me, so I rise up until my lips reach his. He pulls me even tighter to him and I wrap my arms around his neck. Fireworks flame behind my eyes and through my brain. No kiss I've had has felt like this. Like I'm floating and free-falling and totally weightless all at once. Like I could do this for a millennium and it still wouldn't be enough.

Eventually we pull away and I open my eyes to meet his gaze. He had to have felt that, too, right?

But something behind him pulls my attention. We'd kept turning in a slow circle as we kissed, and now I'm facing in the opposite direction than I had been before. And standing at the end of the dance floor, staring at me, is Paul. He must have been there the whole time, watching us. Did Nathan see him before? Is that why he kissed me—because Paul was watching us?

"Paul!" I exclaim, and pull away. I suddenly feel ill. "Paul's here. Did you see him?"

Nathan recoils. "What? I mean, yeah."

I take another step away and bump into the couple next to us.

"I didn't realize . . . that he was close to us." I shake my head. "I need to run to the restroom."

"Riley, wait." Nathan reaches for me. "Are you okay? Was that too much?"

I shake my head. "I'll be right back."

I push away from him and through the crowd and toward the tables that ring the dance floor. Nathan must have re-verted back to his fake "boyfriend mode" when he saw Paul lurking around the edge of the dance floor. My eyes fill with tears, and I try to blink them away. What was I thinking? That

Nathan really liked me? If that were true, then he wouldn't be going to homecoming with Sophia next weekend. I'd gotten so caught up in the moment that I hadn't realized what must be happening.

I want to be mad at Nathan, but that isn't fair. He's been playing his part . . . and doing a *way* better job acting than I ever have. I suck in a muffled sob and suddenly find myself in front of Paul. He must have followed me off the dance floor and to the edge of the gym.

"Are you okay?" he asks.

"What does it matter to you?" I snap. "Why are you following me?"

He takes a step back. "I saw you and Nathan, um, well . . . and you seemed upset after so I thought I should check on you."

My hands clench into fists. So, it wasn't in my head—he really was watching.

"Paul, I'm not yours to check on anymore. Go dance with Lainey and leave me alone."

He shrugs, looking sheepish. "Lainey broke up with me twenty minutes ago."

"Maybe because you can't stop bothering me."

"Yeah, maybe . . ."

I cover my face with my hands. I absolutely *cannot* have this conversation right now. I step away, but Paul puts a hand on my arm to stop me.

"Wait, listen, I miss you, Riley. Breaking up with you was the stupidest thing I've ever done." His eyes skim down my body. "You look so good in that dress."

I mouth curse words into my hands as horror and

understanding dawn on me. On top of everything else, Nathan was right about Paul this whole time.

Paul pulls my hands from my face. "Remember all the fun times we had onstage and goofing around in the wings? And when we went kayaking and spent the afternoon singing and annoying everyone else on the river? We were so good together, Riley. You have to miss me, too, at least a little bit?"

I squeeze my eyes shut. I'm not remotely interested in getting back together with him. But wouldn't life be easier if I was? I could forget Nathan. I could stop working at the store with no regrets. Everything would be so much easier.

Paul seems to take my lack of response for affirmation and pulls me in for a kiss.

Absolutely not. I twist sharply and he kisses my cheek instead.

"Stop! Let me go, Paul. I can't do this. We're over."

I jerk away and jog for the restroom like it's the eye of a hurricane. But not before I spot Nathan, huddled with Anthony and Kenzie, watching us from the corner of the room.

Chapter Twenty-Four

I'm still in the restroom ten minutes later when Hoshiko comes barreling in.

"Riley?" she calls.

I open the door to my stall. Her eyes widen when she sees me.

"What's going on? I just ran into Paul and he told me that you two might be getting back together? I thought you hated him! I tried to talk to Nathan, but he's being extra surly tonight. He really must not like dances."

"He didn't say anything?"

"Nathan? I could barely get two words out of him. Did you two fight?"

"No. I don't know." There are two other girls in here with us, but they're seniors and don't seem to be paying attention. I pull Hoshiko to the far mirror. "He kissed me," I whisper urgently.

"Paul or Nathan?"

I growl. "Paul tried to kiss me, but I ducked out of the way."

"So, you aren't getting back together?"

"*No*. He's the worst. I don't want to talk about him. *Nathan* kissed me."

"And you didn't duck that one?" she asks with wide eyes.

"I did not." I suck in a breath. "But it wasn't real. He was just faking it because Paul was watching us."

"Are you sure? Lucas and I swear there's something going on between you two."

It hits me that Hoshiko and Lucas are close enough now that they're going off on secret dance dates and having conversations about the rest of us. "Do you think Lucas knows anything?"

She shakes her head. "He's tried getting it out of Nathan, but he won't talk. They don't really have that kind of friendship."

"What is going on with you and Lucas, anyway? That dance! How long have you two been practicing?"

"He started coming to the studio two weeks ago." She shakes her head and grins with a faraway look in her eyes, like she's still imagining it. "I was so surprised when he asked to take a class with me. I thought he might be full of it, but I think he actually likes the classes. I've had such a fun time dancing with him and he's already talking about prom and—" Her mouth clamps shut and she whacks my arm. "Hey, stop trying to distract me! I'm here to check on you, not talk about myself!"

"But you're so much more interesting than me."

"Absolutely, but we'll have all night for that."

I grin and a jolt of joy goes through me at the reminder that no matter what's happening right now, Hoshiko is coming back to my house after to spend the night. Boys come and go, but best friends are irreplaceable.

A group of girls from our *Shrek* showcase come into the bathroom just then and shriek with excitement when they see us. We spend a few minutes complimenting dresses and hairstyles and discussing the upcoming performance. The girls move to the stalls and Hoshiko tugs my hand toward the door. She must know there's no way I want to discuss Nathan when there's a possibility of people overhearing us.

"Enough of the bathroom," she says. "You can't stay here all night."

"Sure I can." I lean forward and lower my voice. "I'm getting all the intel. It sounds like Emily Harris is having a rager at her house after this—her parents are going to be there and even bought the alcohol! And Sara has decided to go all the way with Eli. Good for them."

She groans. "Not cool. Let's go." She pulls me toward the door, then stops and inspects me. She uses a thumb to rub under both my eyes and adjusts one of the tendrils of hair that frame my face.

"Perfect. You might as well make all these boys lust after you."

"All the boys except Lucas," I tease.

She winks and we walk back into the gymnasium, which has lost the winter wonderland magic I felt earlier tonight. It's back to being a basketball court that hasn't been renovated in twenty years. A J.Lo dance anthem is playing and the vast majority of the students are jumping around together in the center of the floor. There are a few stragglers—a group of girls at one of the tables, a couple making out in the corner. I scan for Paul, but luckily he isn't waiting around for me. I hope he went home already or is back with Lainey. I don't have the bandwidth to deal with him.

I follow Hoshiko to the other side of the floor where Lucas and Nathan are sitting on folding chairs with Anthony. Anthony's face is flushed and he's breathing heavily.

"There you both are!" he exclaims when he sees us. "Come out with Kenzie and me."

Lucas stands so quickly that the backs of his legs hit the metal chair and it shoots backward. He looks between Hoshiko and me. "Do you want to?"

Hoshiko bites her lip. "I don't know . . ." I can practically feel her spirit splitting in two directions. Dancing is one of her favorite things in the world, but she won't leave me when she knows I'm upset.

I nudge her toward Lucas. "Go!"

"Come with me." She nods toward Nathan, who's sitting like a statue. "You should both come dance."

"I'm good," Nathan mumbles.

"Go ahead. I'll be there in a second."

She frowns but follows Lucas and Anthony out to the dance floor. After an awkward second, I pull Lucas's chair over and sit down next to Nathan.

"What happened back there?" Nathan asks. "Did I see Paul try to kiss you?"

"Yeah."

His expression darkens. "I knew I hated him for a reason. Unless . . . Are you two . . . ?"

"No. It just took him a minute to figure that out."

"I'm happy to break the news if he's still confused." He glares around the cafeteria.

"The Paul situation is officially done. And I have to give you credit—you played your part better than I ever imagined you could. You didn't just convince him we were together, you made him so jealous he actually came back to me begging."

I still can't believe that happened. I should be basking in the joy of watching my ex grovel before me. I should be jumping up and down with excitement next to Nathan on the dance floor. I won.

But sitting next to Nathan right now, trying not to notice how incredibly gorgeous he looks in his slightly wrinkled suit with his glasses askew, it doesn't feel like I've won anything. All tonight has done is show me what an absolute mess I've made of everything. My heart is going to collapse if I have to spend one more moment with Nathan while he pretends he likes me and I pretend I don't love him.

Because I do. I haven't let myself admit it or even think it until now, but I can't deny the emotions anymore. I love the way he accepts me for who I am, how loyal he is to his friends and the store and my dad, and that he came with me tonight despite his disdain for school functions because he wanted to make sure I was taken care of and happy. He's one of the best people I've ever known. I want him to think the same of me. I want him to choose me over everyone and everything else because there's nowhere he'd rather be. But he's still interested in Sophia, and I need to make my peace with that.

"Riley?"

I've been staring at him and shake myself. "We need to call it off now for real," I say. "No more boyfriend mode. You don't need to act that way anymore for Paul's benefit."

Nathan toes the ground. "Okay."

I take a deep breath to prepare myself for this next part. I feel sick, but I know it's ultimately for the best. Tonight has made my decision for me.

"Also, I've been wanting to tell you that my parents are releasing me from the store. No more probation. So I won't be stealing your hours anymore." I try for a small smile, like this is good news, but Nathan scowls.

"What? Are you serious? You're going to stop working?"

"Yeah. I think it's best if I step back from the store and the game."

"No, we need you for the game, especially after Lucas pulled that BS with the wraith in the last session! We won't survive without your character. And we need your help at the store too."

"It's just too much, Nathan. I won't be able to balance everything with my choir and musical commitments."

"How long have you known you were quitting?"

I cringe and look at the ground. "I hadn't exactly decided about it, but . . . Mom told me a week ago they were lifting the punishment."

"A *week*? You've got to be kidding me. That means . . . you knew you were quitting when we watched Monty Python together? You knew during every shift we worked since then and you never told me? You never told any of us?" He's sitting up straight now, his voice louder and eyes wide. I crumple more into my chair. I can't take the way he's glaring at me. Yet another example of me messing everything up.

"I'm sorry. I should have said something sooner. I just . . . I wasn't sure what I wanted to do."

He sits back. "But now—tonight—you're suddenly sure you want to quit."

I twist the bracelet I'm wearing and nod slowly. We're both silent, and distantly it occurs to me how strange we must look. All around us, people are laughing and dancing. "Y.M.C.A." plays so loudly I can barely hear Nathan over the chorus and resulting singing. And all I want to do is go home with Hoshiko and curl up in blankets.

"The timing makes sense," I say to fill the silence between us. "It will be too strange to play in the game with Sophia now. And I'm still really hopeful about bringing back this musical and when I do, the work is going to be all-consuming. There's nothing more important to me than making this musical happen."

"Nothing?"

"It's what I love," I whisper.

My heart splintered the moment I saw Paul watching us on the dance floor, and this conversation is cracking it open further. I can't stay here any longer with Nathan. His gaze might as well be pouring hot oil on a fresh burn. It's possible he hates me in this moment. He certainly doesn't like me.

Hoshiko and Lucas wave for us to come out onto the floor. I'm grateful for an excuse to escape. I point in their direction. "Looks like we're being summoned."

He glances over and grimaces. "You go without me. I'm not up for more dancing."

I stand, desperate to get away from this conversation but hating the idea of being away from him. He holds up a hand to stop me.

"Actually . . ." Nathan's voice cuts through the music and through my chest. "Hoshiko drove tonight, too, right? So she can give you a ride back to your house?" He runs a hand through his hair. "I think I might go home. Turns out I was right about school dances." He glares at the scene around him.

My heart plummets in my chest. "She can drive me," I say faintly.

"Cool." He raises a hand in goodbye, his posture stiff and expression pained. "It was good faking it with you. You really are a great actress, Riley."

Chapter Twenty-Five

Hoshiko and I stay at the dance for another hour because I don't want to pull her from Lucas and Hoshiko argues that staying might make me feel better. She's wrong, but at least her exuberant joy distracts from how horribly this night has imploded. I slump into my seat as soon as we get in her car. She looks at me with sympathy. "I'm sorry about you and Nathan."

I groan. "You guys predicted it would end badly from the beginning."

"If he's going to homecoming with Sophia next week rather than begging on hands and knees for you to date him, he doesn't deserve you. In fact, he's officially dead to me."

I chuckle. Nothing beats BFF loyalty. "I know this is probably impossible, but I'm going to try not to think about it until after the meeting is over Wednesday. Although I'm not feeling great about that either anymore. I hope the performance goes well, but even if it does, it's only part of the battle. What if the budget I'm proposing is too high? Or they're wanting more sponsorship from the community?"

"I know your brain is reminding you of every possible bad outcome in life right now, but let's try to be optimistic. You've done a phenomenal job pulling the showcase together and we're going to kill that. I already have my dance instructor on board to help with choreography when they agree to bring back the musical. And I bet you could get both of your parents to volunteer or donate as well if the administrators are looking for that—that is, if you actually told your parents what you've been doing lately." She raises an eyebrow.

I rub my hands over my eyes, no longer worried about my makeup. "Maybe. Assuming my parents don't flip when I drop this in their lap."

Mom practically runs out of the kitchen when we get to my house. "Girls! How was it?" Her eyes skim over me. "Big night?"

Code for: *You're a mess.* I guess I'm wearing my emotions on my face along with my smeared mascara.

"We did a ton of dancing." I try for a smile.

"Good! Well, come see what I've been up to." She beckons us into the kitchen. "I might have gone a little overboard."

Our pristine kitchen island is covered with snacks. There's a big bowl of cheddar and caramel popcorn, Twizzlers, cookies, drinks . . . and an entire charcuterie board because my mom can't help being extra.

"Wow!" Hoshiko grabs a handful of popcorn. "This is awesome."

"Thanks, Mom! This must have taken a long time."

She shrugs, but I can see she's pleased with herself. "I know you only get a few experiences like this in life, so I thought I'd make the sleepover a little more fun." She leans against the counter and gives me a knowing look. "I didn't realize Nathan was so cute. And say what you want, but it certainly looked to your father and I like you two were dating. You need to bring him around again so I can put him through the wringer." She winks.

I grab a chunk of cheese from the board and shove it in my mouth rather than respond. There's no way to reply that won't lead to more Nathan-related questions and the possibility of tears. And, bonus, if I fill up on cheese, maybe that'll dull the throbbing pain that comes every time his name is mentioned. It's worth a shot, at least.

Hoshiko takes my elbow and moves me to the stairs. "This looks so great, Mrs. Morris, but I think we need to change out of our dresses so we can really eat."

Mom nods and waves us away. "I want to hear all about Nathan later!" she calls behind me.

I muffle a groan and Hoshiko pulls me faster.

We stay up until two a.m., munching our way through Mom's snack buffet and dissecting every detail of Hoshiko's night with Lucas, when she knew she liked him, and the dance classes they took together. She brings up Nathan and Paul a few times, but I quickly pivot the conversation back to Lucas and she doesn't argue. I'm not ready to do a deep dive into my feelings about Nathan or how I'm going to act around him now.

We sleep in late and then spend the early afternoon making final touches to the musical proposal. A wave of nausea rolls through me whenever I think about the meeting Wednesday after school. Everything is riding on this meeting. It was almost impossible to find a time when Miss Sahni, Principal Holloway, a school board member, and a parent from the Music Boosters could all meet, so if I screw up, then it's all over. I hope I've done enough.

"It's going to be awesome," Hoshiko says. "They won't be able to say no!"

I smile weakly. "Let's hope so."

I flip through my papers again. At least I can say I've done as much as I can to prepare.

After Hoshiko leaves, Mom follows me back upstairs. "How are you doing?"

"Good." I sit on my bed and pull a pillow into my lap.

"Yeah? You seemed pretty down after homecoming. Did everything go all right?"

"It was fun. Mostly."

She wanders absently around the room, looking at pictures and posters she's seen a billion times. She's trying to be casual, but I'm not buying it. "Did something happen with Nathan?" she asks. "High school relationships can be really hard."

"He's not my boyfriend, Mom. I know Dad keeps talking

about it, but he's blowing things out of proportion. Nathan and I are just friends."

"Mm-hmm." She's clearly not convinced.

She wanders farther into the room and stops at my desk, where we've left the green stage makeup and the four hefty folders I put together with budget details about the proposed musical. Argh, I'd meant to store everything away before she saw them, but my head is all over the place and I totally forgot.

She studies the makeup. She knows enough about theater to recognize what it is. "Were you and Hoshiko working on something for school?"

"Um . . ." For a moment I think about making up a story, but if our showcase is successful this week, I'll have to come clean about the musical anyway.

"Actually, that's a project I've been working on . . . for the spring musical." I hand her a folder and tell her about the info I pulled together for the administration before launching into the performance. Her head jerks up when I get to the after-school rehearsals.

"You've been working on this musical? And you said those were choir rehearsals. You were lying about that?"

My breathing grows shallow, but I don't deny it. "I'm really sorry I didn't tell you everything. Miss Sahni *did* give us permission to use the space and we were rehearsing songs, but they weren't for choir. I knew you and Dad wouldn't agree to me getting involved in anything after school when I was still grounded, but I just . . . I couldn't give up on the musical, Mom. I had to see it through." I'm weirdly weepy and defiant at the same time. I knot my hands in front of me. "I've been directing the showcase numbers and I think with them we have a chance of convincing the administration to change their minds. Please try to understand."

The last words come out as a plea. I expect Mom's eyebrows to furrow together like they do when a contractor tells her they need to reschedule, but her expression stays impassive. She flips through the information in the folder and looks back up at me.

"How many students are in this showcase?"

"Twenty-five."

"And you're directing them? And you put together all of this information on budgets and musical licensing?" she asks quietly.

I nod and bite my lip. Is she bottling up her anger so she can explode after thoroughly questioning me? She never yells, but there's a first time for everything.

Instead, she sighs. "I hate that you lied to me. But . . . maybe I can almost understand why you felt the need to. If I'm being honest, I'm impressed that you found a way to work at the store, keep up with school, and run these rehearsals. It shows you've found a way to create some balance in your life."

"Really?"

She chuckles and shakes her head. "Yeah. If you're successfully juggling that many things, then you're definitely becoming more responsible. So, you're not in trouble again, at least not with me. *But* no more lying, okay?"

"Okay," I say immediately. I rock back on my heels. "Um, in that case . . ."

"*Riley.*" Her voice is sharper this time.

I hold out a hand. "Don't freak out. But Miss Sahni was so impressed with the showcase that she's offered me a position running rehearsals for the junior high show choir and assisting with other tasks." I can't help smiling at this. "It hasn't started yet, but it sounds super fun."

"Wow," Mom says. She puts down the folder and pulls me into a hug. "Congratulations, that's wonderful. So you want to accept the position?"

I nod, my cheek rubbing against her shoulder.

"Okay. Can I assume your father knows nothing about any of this?"

I nod again, scared of what she's about to say.

She pulls away and studies me. "Then that's the next thing you need to do. Particularly if you're planning to quit working at the store, which I have to assume you are."

I stare at the floor. "Yeah, I'm planning to quit," I whisper. Thoughts of Nathan and our terrible conversation at homecoming last night return. Telling Dad might be even worse, if that's possible.

"Then I'll drive you over now so you can tell him. And no, a text won't do it. He needs to hear it from you."

It's a somber ride to Dad's apartment. Dread pools in my stomach at the thought of talking to him about all this. Just last Sunday I was there with my friends, hanging out and watching Monty Python, and he seemed so happy to have all of us there. I hate having to ruin all the goodwill we've built up over the last weeks.

Dad's expression morphs from surprise to fear when he finds Mom and me at his door. "What happened?"

"Riley has some things to share with you," Mom says

gently. She gives him a sad smile, the closest I've seen to kindness between them, and takes a step back. "I wanted to give you some time to talk. Maybe you can give her a ride back to the house when you're done." She gives me a meaningful look and heads back to the car.

Dad beckons me inside, clearly still on edge. "This is all sounding very dire, so let me have it."

We sit down in the living room and I repeat the conversation I had with Mom about bringing back the musical and directing the showcase. If anything, Dad is even less concerned about it than Mom.

"I see why your mom wanted you to come clean about the real reason for the rehearsals, but I don't really care. Driving without a license is one thing, but staying after school to sing? Your mom and I should be grateful to have that be our biggest problem." He laughs. "I appreciate you telling us, though. Do you want a drink? I've got the latest flavor of Mountain Dew in the fridge."

For some reason, a comment from Nathan weeks ago pops into my head.

"Aren't you supposed to be watching your sugar intake?"

He jolts in surprise. "The doctor suggested it. How did you hear that?"

"Nathan told me."

He smiles knowingly and it puts me more on edge. "Of course, I should have known you two would be talking about everything now. But don't worry about it." He waves his hand dismissively. "Actually, tell me about homecoming. How are things going with Nathan?"

"Why did you tell Nathan about your health issues and

not me?" I ask instead of answering. My body is trembling slightly and I slide my hands under my thighs to keep them still. "And I don't understand why you talked to everyone else at the store about my recitals and performances, but you never talked to me."

He sits up straighter, his laid-back attitude gone with my tone. "We already talked about this. I wanted to tell my friends what a talented daughter I have."

"But you didn't want to tell me?"

I'm shocked that tears prick in the corners of my eyes. I don't know where all this emotion is coming from, but suddenly I'm bursting with frustration and sadness about how little we've really spoken over the years. All the missed opportunities to share stories or to hear his thoughts on what was happening in my life. Even now he's not telling me everything. And, sure, I haven't been good about telling him things either, but it's hard to be motivated when it's a one-way street. Particularly when I'm not sure how much he's even interested in my life outside of the store.

"I told you how much I loved your performances," he says, his face intense and serious.

"No, you didn't." I wipe a tear away and cross my arms. "Maybe you like my singing at the store, but you never talked to me about my performances or . . . or my *life*. I assumed it was because you didn't care, but then I heard that you were going around talking to everyone else about it and I just don't get it, Dad! Is it that you don't like talking to me? Or spending time together? I'm sure you would have rather spent your weekends with your friends at the store than with me being bored."

"Riley, *no*." He puts out his hands as if to touch my knee or maybe pull me into a hug, but I stand and step away. "No, that was never it. I always love spending time with you. I love you. I'm just, I don't know, I guess I'm bad at talking about things."

"Well, I must get it from you, then, because I'm quitting the store." I wrap my arms around myself. "That's why Mom brought me here—so I could tell you that. My choir teacher asked me to help with rehearsals in the evenings, and hopefully, I'll also be working on the musical this spring so I won't have time to work anymore."

He leans back like I slapped him, and the misery grows wider inside me.

"You're quitting?" His voice is quiet.

"I won't have time to do everything," I whisper.

"But . . . I thought you liked it. You seemed so happy, and you have your friends there. . . ." He's speaking slowly, like he's trying to put together a puzzle without all the pieces. "We were having such a great time. I wanted to keep building a stronger relationship with you."

More tears come, but I swipe at my eyes and swallow hard. "Why didn't you try sooner, then? And why do I have to work at the store for us to have a relationship? We could have always had one, but you never seemed that interested."

He stands now. "That's not true."

"You didn't even want to drive me from school to the store. You got Nathan to do it instead."

He looks incredulous. "Are you serious? I did that as a favor to you. I figured you'd want the extra time with him. I've always wanted to spend more time with you—to know you better. But you and your mother built a little fort and kept me on the other side of the moat." He takes a deep breath. "I'm glad you're so close to your mom, but it's been hard to find ways to connect."

Guilt cuts through me, followed immediately by defiance. Am I not allowed to be close to Mom?

"If the only way you can connect with me is to guilt-trip me into staying at your store so we have something in common, then you aren't trying very hard."

Dad flinches and turns away. As soon as the words are out of my mouth, I feel sick—I didn't come here to hurt him. But I can't bring myself to take them back either. They've been waiting to come out for a long time.

We stand in silence and then he clears his throat. "Message received. You're turning in your notice."

I stare at the ground. A moment later, keys rattle.

"I'll drive you back now. Sounds like you have a busy week ahead of you."

Chapter Twenty-Six

I can't help searching for Nathan as I walk through the halls Monday morning. A tiny part of me hoped to see him standing out front, waiting for me. And when I get to my locker, I hold my breath in case he's somehow figured out the combination and filled it with paper hearts that'll flutter to the ground when I open the door. Or stuck in a note about how he's desperately in love with me.

Of course, there's nothing like that. Nathan has never struck me as a particularly romantic guy. And if he was, he wouldn't be using his skills on me, particularly after how we left things Saturday.

The meeting with administration is only two days away now. I will myself to focus on that—and that alone—as I shuffle from class to class. When lunch period comes, I spend the time in the choir room with Miss Sahni rather than face Nathan at our usual table. I'm a coward, I know, but tell myself I'll deal with everything after the *Shrek* performance. I just need to make it through the showcase Wednesday.

"Are you sure I can't convince you?" Hoshiko asks me after the *Shrek* rehearsal the next afternoon. It's our last day of rehearsal and I'm keeping everyone longer than usual. The songs have come together, but people are still missing cues. We need this to be perfect.

"It's not a good idea," I say in a voice that I hope gives some finality to the decision.

"You can't skip D&D tonight," she argues. I guess my tone wasn't enough. "We're taking on the wraith king tonight. The boys spent all lunch talking about it. Which you would know if you'd eaten with us." She gives me a sharp look.

I wince. "Miss Sahni needed to talk to me about the upcoming show choir performance. They're struggling with their harmonies."

"Riley, you can lie to Nathan all you want, but don't lie to me. I know you're avoiding everyone because of homecoming."

"I'm not avoiding you."

"Well, obviously." She leans her head on my shoulder. "You couldn't if you tried. I'd track you down."

I chuckle lightly, but my chest aches. A little part of me thought Nathan might do the same. That he'd miss me enough to come find me.

Hoshiko lifts her head and studies me. "I'm pretty sure he thinks you hate him, by the way."

"Nathan or Paul?"

Thankfully, Paul has kept a wide berth since the dance and I've done the same. If there's one good thing that came out of homecoming, it was that Paul wants nothing more to do with me.

"Stop trying to change the subject. You know who I'm talking about. If you'd just talk to Nathan—"

"It's too much. Too soon. He'll take one look at me and know exactly how I feel about him."

"And would that be such a bad thing? Maybe it'll finally wake him up to what he's missing."

"If he can't realize that on his own, I'm not going to help him. He can keep Sophia."

We both scowl at her name. "Just come and sit next to me and Lucas tonight at D&D. I'll keep you entertained and distracted. The guys miss you."

I slump. I miss them too. I know I can't go on like this forever—hiding away during lunch periods and avoiding everyone but Hoshiko. I need to be okay with Nathan and Sophia. But there's also the fact that I haven't spoken to Dad since I told him I was quitting. I'm not sure I can walk back into the store ever again now.

"Let's just get through tomorrow and then we'll see," I tell Hoshiko. She regards me sadly but doesn't argue.

I clap my hands twice and call to the group. "Can we run that again?"

I'm up early the next morning. Rather than go to D&D, I spent last evening texting Hoshiko for updates (Sophia didn't show, Nathan barely spoke all night, and they ended early after killing time in the swamp to avoid the wraith) and searching my closet for an outfit that tells Principal Holloway I'm serious but fun, ready to work but not a stick-in-the-mud. Unfortunately, I'm not sure I have that outfit. Mostly my clothes look like a paint factory exploded onto them. So I did the best I could—navy-blue pants and a pink button-down with tiny red hearts all over.

Hoshiko finds me before my first class. She looks me up and down and nods approvingly. "Love your outfit. But we have a few problems."

I freeze. "What?"

She sighs and pulls me toward World History. "Sara's mom wasn't able to get the costumes like she said she would, so it looks like the audience will need to use their imagination. And . . . I just heard Henry is home sick today."

Horror flies through me and I spin toward her. "You're telling me half the fairy-tale creatures don't have costumes? And we have no narrator." I look at the ceiling and groan. "He can't be sick! We *need* him!" Henry is one of the linchpins of our showcase. We start the first song with him narrating Shrek's young life—in a pretty convincing Scottish accent, I might add—and without him the show won't make as much sense. "Can we convince him to come in after school? He can stay far away from everyone so he doesn't spread anything."

She shakes her head, looking forlorn. "Strep throat."

I drop my head in my hands. All I needed was for this one day to go smoothly, and I can't even get that. What else is going to go wrong? Will Paul forget his Shrek mask? Will laryngitis suddenly burn through the school until no one has a voice?

"We were already teetering on the brink. I was so busy with rehearsals that I never found community sponsors, and without them the budget will be too high for Principal Holloway and the Music Boosters. We can't have anything else go wrong."

She steps in front of me and puts her hands on my shoulders, stopping my progress down the hall.

"It's all going to work out. Okay? We'll make a game plan at lunch. You *will* be with us for lunch, right?"

I hesitate and then nod. To be honest, I'd take about any excuse to get out of facing Nathan today, but she's right. We need time to brainstorm solutions. The bell rings.

"We'll make this work," she tells me again. Her face breaks into a small smile. "The show must go on."

I swallow a lump in my throat and head for class. First period comes and goes without me thinking of anything but the performance. I'm still a ball of nerves in geometry when the door opens and an office worker hands a note to our teacher.

Mr. Fleishman frowns and flicks his eyes up to me. "Riley? You have a call from your mother in the office."

A prickle of fear goes through me, pushing away my obsessive theater thoughts. Mom is calling? At nine in the morning? Central has a strict no cell phone policy during class, so I haven't been able to check for messages lately, but usually she'll just text and I can reply between classes or during lunch. If she can't wait, something must be seriously wrong.

Hoshiko glances over at me with wide eyes.

"I'll be right back," I whisper. I stumble out of my seat and out the door, knowing the whole class is staring. I zoom through the hallway, down the stairs, and through another hall, practically running by the end. My body was jangling with anxiety before this, and now I'm like a live wire. When I get into the office, the assistant hands me the phone without a word.

"Mom?"

"Riley. I'm so sorry to call you out of class but your dad . . ." She pauses and fear tightens around my chest. "He's in the hospital. I just got a call from Curtis at the store. They were both there early catching up on stocking and I guess your father started having chest pains and trouble breathing so they called an ambulance and—"

"Is Dad still alive?" I can barely get the words out—they scrape against the back of my throat painfully.

"Yes. Yes, he's alive."

I unclench slightly. All eyes in the office are on me. They aren't pretending to give me privacy or acting like they're working. I keep my own eyes glued on the Post-it notes on the desk.

"Was it a heart attack? Is he going to be all right?"

"I don't know. I only know what Curtis told me—that an ambulance came to pick him up and he's being admitted to the emergency room. I thought about not calling until I knew more—I know you have your performance after school today and I'm so sorry . . . but it didn't feel right not telling you. I'm heading to the hospital now. Do you want me to—"

"Come pick me up. I want to be there with you." I swallow tears. "And Dad."

"I'll be there as soon as I can."

I think I hand the phone to someone and sit down. When Mom comes into the office, I'm holding a cup of water and I don't know how it got in my hand. All I can think about is Dad. What if it was a heart attack? What if they didn't call 911 in time and he died on his way to the hospital? What if Mom tells me we weren't fast enough and now he's gone? Memories of the last time we were together revolve through my mind. His expression when I told him I was quitting . . . the sharpness of my words when I accused him of not trying hard enough to spend time with me . . . Why did I say those things? Why didn't I go to the store last night? I should have gone. I should never have quit in the first place—it was selfish of me. I'll never forgive myself if anything happens to him.

I grab Mom's hands as soon as she's close and search her face for signs of more horrible news.

She squeezes softly and shakes her head. "No more news yet, which is a good thing."

I exhale. There's still time to see him and make this right.

The car ride is silent, but my chest tightens further as we pull into the parking lot and walk into the emergency room. How can this parking lot look so normal? How can people drive past like nothing is happening? Don't they know my father is in here? Everyone should stop and take a moment to think of him.

Mom sits down next to me after talking to the person at the desk. "He's back for testing. She warned me it could be a while and we should get comfortable."

I know this isn't "good" news, but it feels like it. If they're running tests, it means he isn't dead or close to it or they'd be standing over his bed with those big paddles they rub together on hospital dramas.

She gives my shoulder a little squeeze. The waiting room is almost empty and quiet this early in the morning. This hospital is small and a little run-down, with fake pumpkins and fall foliage in the corners of the waiting room and an old TV playing a morning game show. It's the opposite of warm and welcoming.

Mom pulls out her phone and I follow suit. I haven't looked at it since before second period and now I see it's flooded with texts. Hoshiko has sent at least ten and a quick skim shows me her increasing worry. She usually uses a ton of emojis and exclamation points, but whenever she's upset, her texts get a lot more subdued.

People are saying your dad is in the hospital. Is that true? Are you okay? I'm so sorry

We're all freaking out. The guys are talking about skipping out on school

My heart twists to see her messages. I reply, telling her everything we know.

I expect her reply to be immediate, but of course she's in class and won't be able to check her messages until she's between classes. The thought brings me back to the reality of today. The showcase—the *meeting*—is happening this afternoon. We're scheduled to rehearse one last time directly after school and then I'll present my proposal to everyone, and we'll perform at four. I shake my head absently. There's no telling how long Dad will be here. It could be hours, maybe overnight or even longer, depending on what the doctors find.

I expect heartbreak to wash over me at the idea of missing the meeting. Instead, I can barely feel anything for it at all.

I'll text you again when we know more. I'm so sorry about missing today. Maybe tell Miss Sahni to cancel the meeting?

To my surprise, her reply comes within seconds.

No, we aren't canceling. You've done plenty, Riley. We'll take care of the rest.

I stare at my phone, my throat growing thick. I want to throw my arms around Hoshiko and pull her tight. There are so many big and little things for them to think about. Who is going to narrate? What if Mitchell forgets his lyrics and looks to me for the words? How will it work if only some people are in costume? I breathe through my nose and close my eyes. It's out of my hands now.

"Riley?" Mom whispers. She looks down at my phone and back up at my face. "What's going on? What are your friends saying?"

I shake my head and put my phone away. "Nothing. They're just worried."

"Okay." She purses her lips. "You know, it's all right if you need to leave for your performance this afternoon. Your dad will understand."

"*No.*" My voice is loud and echoes in the empty linoleum room. "No, I'm not leaving."

I glare at her, and she nods slowly and pats my leg. The school meeting will happen or it won't. The showcase will go well or it'll be a disaster. Either way, it's just a show. There will be others. Right now, the most important thing is seeing Dad.

I stare at the clock for the next hour. It's easier to turn off my thoughts if I watch the second hand steadily tick by. Another group comes into the waiting room, an older couple, and it jars me out of my trance. I open my phone and notice another text—a single one from Nathan. It came in just after Hoshiko's, but I'd missed it.

Just walked into American History and heard about Joel. I'm two seconds from skipping class and coming to find you at the hospital. Should I?

My stomach swoops. I imagine Nathan walking through those doors any second now. I imagine him wrapping his arms around me and squeezing me so hard the little shattered pieces in my chest press back together. I want it so much it's physical.

I wipe a few tears from my eyes. Why did I think I could shut him out after the dance and pretend like my life hadn't been permanently altered by him? It's only been a few days and I already miss him so much. I was a fool to let him leave homecoming like I did—I was so scared he wouldn't see me the way I see him that I couldn't get the words out. But I don't want to lose him. I want him here next to me, holding my hand and telling me that Dad is going to be okay. I want him texting me, and driving me down country roads, and gazing at me like he can't wait to kiss me again. I'm not sure if we're too far gone for that to ever happen, but sitting in a cold hospital waiting room has a way of taking all the blurry edges of life and tightening the focus until the important things pop into the foreground.

And what I see is Nathan.

I have to tell him how I feel. He deserves to know, even if it comes to nothing. Even if he tells me he'll never fall for me the way I've fallen for him.

My fingers twitch to text back and ask him to come. I would love to sag against him right now. But I text Nathan back something vague and polite instead. I desperately need to talk to him, but it will have to wait until I know about Dad.

Chapter Twenty-Seven

Mom gets me a cup of hot tea and we sit in the waiting room for two more hours. Eventually someone comes in to tell us that they're keeping Dad overnight for observation and moving him from the ER to a room on the fifth floor. Mom has to answer questions about medical history and the hours are interminable before we're finally able to see him. I try to steel myself on the elevator ride up, but I can't breathe when I walk into his room. He's sitting up in bed wearing a hospital gown with multiple machines attached to him. I'm not sure I've ever seen Dad without one of his gaming shirts on. But before I can completely lose it, he sees us and beckons us into the room.

"Riley! Shannon!"

He holds out his arms for a hug. I study him, looking for an edge of anger or resentment from our last conversation, but he only seems delighted to see us. I gingerly lean in.

"How are you feeling?" My voice cracks and his arms tighten around me.

"I've been better, but just seeing you makes me happier. If only I didn't have people coming in to prod me and ask me more questions every two minutes."

"Dad, you're in the *hospital*." I pull back to give him a reproving look. "Of course you're going to have people prodding you. Did they say what happened? Did you have a heart attack?"

"No, it wasn't a heart attack. Not exactly—just a heart attack *scare*. They said I'll need to start taking cholesterol medication and make more life changes, but I'll be fine."

Mom and I exchange worried glances.

"Is your doctor going to come around soon?" Mom asks.

"She came and left, but I'm sure the nurses will be back. Now, how do I change this channel? It's so boring here."

Mom huffs a sigh and lifts a huge remote that's attached to the bed. It has buttons for the TV and others to raise the bed to a seating position.

"Thank you." Dad's eyes linger for a moment on Mom's face and I get the impression that he's saying thank you for more than showing him the remote. I shift, wondering if I should excuse myself so they can talk, but Mom gets there before me.

"I'm going to run down to the cafeteria and pick up some snacks," she says. "I'm starving."

Dad and I sit silently and watch a *Seinfeld* episode for a few minutes. It's so surreal to be here watching TV, like my whole world didn't almost implode. I gather up my courage to speak.

"Dad . . . do you really think you're going to be okay?" My voice is shaky even though I try to sound strong.

He puts out his hand and I squeeze it. "Yeah, I'll be okay. I'm so sorry to put you through all of this."

I shrug.

"Thanks for being here. It really means a lot."

Unsaid words hang between us. We both know that a few months ago, I might not have been at his bedside in tears.

"Riley, I'm so sorry for anything I did these past years that hurt you. You were right, I should have made more of an effort to talk to you. I should have told you how luminous you are every time you're onstage, because you are. You're amazing."

I shake my head. "You don't have to do this. It doesn't matter. I'm just glad you're going to be okay."

"It does matter." Dad's voice is more serious than I've ever heard it. "It's true that I don't know how to talk about theater. I don't know the jargon. Plus, that was something you shared with your mom. But that doesn't mean I wasn't impressed or proud of you. You've always been the best thing in my life. I should have done a better job making sure you knew that." He lays his hand on my shoulder and tears prick my eyes.

"Can I tell you a secret?" he continues.

I nod.

"I'm glad you took your mom's car back in August."

I snort and the sound pulls me from my sadness. "You both seemed pretty furious at the time."

"Well, sure. You could have died, you could have killed Hoshiko, you broke a ton of laws. We let you off really easy."

"Way to be dramatic," I mutter.

"But having you at the store was . . . well, it has been the best thing to happen to me in a very long time. I've absolutely loved it."

The tears are back again, stronger than ever. I wipe at them and turn in my chair until my back is to the TV. "I'm sorry I said I was quitting. I'm sorry for all the things I said before, and for not trying harder to spend time with you, and for generally being a bad daughter. I'll cut out the other extracurriculars so I have the time."

"Because you feel guilty?"

"No," I say in a totally unconvincing voice. "But I don't want to do anything that gives you more stress or worry or anything. I was being selfish before."

"Riley." Dad turns off the TV and gives me a sad smile. "Nothing you did caused me to be here. The only causes are bad genes and a lifelong love of deep-fried foods. And you aren't being selfish. I was the selfish one—wanting to keep you at the store when you have other things you love doing. I only want you to be happy."

"But I love being at the store."

He squints in confusion. "Well . . . okay, I'm glad to hear that. But the important thing is that you don't need to come to the store for us to spend time together. There's lots of stuff we can do. We can go buy more pumpkins for the store—or holiday decorations! We could try cooking some of the healthy food I'll be eating soon. Maybe you could even take me to one of the musicals you love so much?"

"Yeah?"

"Absolutely. We're getting the best seats in the house as

soon as I'm out of a hospital gown. And in the meantime, you should spend your evenings doing whatever makes you happy. If that's not the store, then that's totally fine. But you're always welcome."

I look at Dad in his wrinkled gown and bedhead and my heart swells. I've spent years keeping my distance from him because of bitterness and some sort of misconstrued loyalty to Mom. I've missed so much time, and I was close to missing so much more. I was being ridiculous. I love him. He's my father.

I lean in and hug him harder than when I first came into the room. He makes a little *oof* sound and squeezes me back. For the first time in hours, I take a deep breath.

Chapter Twenty-Eight

Dad turns the TV back on and we sit together through the end of the *Seinfeld* episode and the start of a new one. It's the Puffy Shirt one, and it's good to hear Dad's chuckle. I keep waiting for Mom to come back, but she's clearly biding her time somewhere else in the hospital.

A nurse comes in to check on Dad, and the *Seinfeld* marathon turns into a talk show. I sneak a glance at Dad. He clears his throat.

"You know, you never did tell me how homecoming went. Did you and Nathan have a good time?"

I know Dad's making an effort, so I do the same, even though this isn't a feel-good topic. I tell him about John and Jordan coming to dinner in their LARPing costumes and about Hoshiko and Lucas's choreographed dance and he laughs at all the right places. If he notices that I haven't mentioned Nathan, he doesn't point it out. I think about leaving it since we're doing so well, but I need to be truthful with Dad if we're going to have a chance at a better relationship.

"Actually, I need to come clean about Nathan. I know we let you believe that we were dating, but that wasn't true. We were just . . . pretending . . . for reasons that I'd rather not go into unless you really need to know. But he doesn't actually like me."

"Sure he does," Dad says immediately.

"Dad." I roll my eyes. "It was an act."

"Riley, I've known the kid for years. I taught him D&D, and he's not good at acting. He might have said it wasn't serious, but he likes you."

Hope flutters in my chest while I try to mentally squash it into oblivion. Dad is smiling in that way parents smile when they think their kids are adorable, and I smile back. I'll take his patronizing smiles every day if it means he's here with me.

"I want to hear more about your musical you mentioned before. What's happening with that?"

I glance at the clock. By now school is done for the day and the group will be wrapping up their last rehearsal before the administration comes in for the meeting. I feel guilty, abandoning them after all the work we've put into the showcase, but hopefully they understand why I need to be here.

"I guess we'll see what happens," I say in a nonchalant tone I didn't realize I possessed. "There's a meeting with teachers and administrators today to present the plan and put on a performance, but obviously I can't be there. Hoshiko said she would take care of things and she can do anything she puts her mind to. So, maybe it'll all work out."

His bushy eyebrows rise high on his forehead. "Your meeting is today and you're sitting here with me watching *Seinfeld*?"

"Of course. I wasn't going to stay at school once I found out you were in the hospital."

"You don't need to be here now, though. Look at me—I'm fine!" He waves his arm and his IV flops around.

"Dad!" I yell, aggravated. "You are not fine! Curtis had to call nine-one-one this morning. You're talking to me *while lying in a hospital bed*. You're as far away from fine as I've ever seen you!"

"Oh please, I'm stable. They're only keeping me overnight so they can run a stress test in the morning. Right now my biggest worry is if they're going to stick me with the no sugar, no salt dinner menu tonight. What time was your meeting scheduled for?"

I glance at the clock again. "In about ten minutes."

Dad groans. "You have to go. You'll be late, but hopefully you can get there for part of it. Call your mom and tell her to come up and get you."

"It's too late, don't worry about it."

"No, if you've been working on this for weeks, then you need to be there today. Use me as a sob story if anyone is upset about you being late—they won't be able to say no."

I try to shrug him off, but when Mom returns a few minutes later with chicken wraps and Diet Cokes, Dad is adamant that she drive me back. Surprisingly, she agrees.

"There's nothing you can do at the hospital right now and the nurses' station said the doctor won't be back around until the morning, so there's no point waiting for more news." She hands me my wrap and grabs her keys from her purse. "Text Hoshiko and tell her we're on our way."

I want to fight more to stay at the hospital, but it's hard when both of my parents are on the same page and ushering me out of the room. And, now that I'm sure things between Dad and me are okay and that he's not about to keel over, I am anxious to see everyone.

I try calling Hoshiko from the car, but she doesn't pick up. Either they're about to start the showcase numbers or she's running around like a madwoman because everything is falling apart. I'm scared it's option two. I'm nauseous and wish I could teleport to the school, but it's a fifteen-minute drive. At least I can be there for moral support no matter what happens.

"I can get a ride back to the hospital or call you when I'm done," I tell Mom when she finally pulls into the parking lot.

"No, I'll come in with you," Mom says. "That way if any-one has questions about what happened this afternoon, I'll be there to address them." Mom's gaze is fierce and I blink in surprise. I wasn't imagining that she'd care this much, espe-cially given everything else that's happened today. She must read my expression because she continues. "I noticed you didn't once hesitate to stay at the hospital."

My eyes widen in horror at the alternative. "I wasn't going to blow off Dad. What if something had happened?"

"I'm so glad you have your priorities in order." Mom grabs her purse. "Now let's go convince those administrators!"

We hurry through the hallway toward the auditorium. My plan is to enter through the backstage side door to find out what's happening and how I can help, but then an amplified voice grabs my attention. It's coming through the main auditorium doors. And the accent is Scottish. But I thought Henry was sick? Did Hoshiko convince him to come anyway?

I crack open the doors, Mom at my heels. To my utter shock, Lucas is standing on the edge of the stage with a microphone, narrating the opening of *Shrek*. And he's really good.

My hand flies to my face. The auditorium is completely empty except for a small row of adults in the center middle. I can pick out Miss Sahni and Principal Holloway, plus two other people who must be the member of the school board and the Music Boosters president. Hoshiko and Terrance begin their section, singing as Mama and Papa Ogre, and they sound beautiful. Hoshiko pulls all focus to her. Her voice is strong and crystal clear, and her wig and green makeup look perfect.

I bite my lip, debating what to do. I don't want to distract anyone onstage by rushing to the front where I would usually stand as director. Instead, I creep down the side of the auditorium. If someone misses their mark or things start to break down, then I'll jump in. But none of that happens.

The performance isn't perfect, of course. We don't have professional lighting, so it's hard to see everyone depending on where they stand onstage, and it looks a little sparse without real sets, but it's still captivating. Paul, as the grown Shrek, even gets a loud chuckle from the principal when he pretends to use a toy skunk as deodorant. I squeeze my eyes shut in relief. Maybe this will actually work. . . .

The second song begins, and I hold my breath. This one was always the biggest risk. We've got sixteen people with singing roles. And since half of them won't have costumes, it's going to be significantly harder for the administrators to understand what the song is about. Except, when the cast comes out onstage, everyone *does* have costumes. Some are pretty simple—brown ears to suggest they're the Three Bears or elaborate wings for the Tooth Fairy. But they have something. I do an excited, nervous dance and Mom squeezes my shoulder. They figured it out somehow!

I tiptoe quietly through the auditorium, making my way toward an empty row of seats in the center. When the cast marches to the front of the stage for the end of the song, I raise my hands like I'm directing a choir. They catch sight of me one by one and everyone projects just a bit louder, their voices harmonizing and filling the auditorium. Tears fill my eyes until the cast members are blurry watercolor versions of themselves.

The song ends and applause echoes in the auditorium. Not a huge amount since there are only a handful of us in the audience, but Mom claps loud enough for a dozen people. I jog to the front while the cast members from the first song come out to bow. I screech to a halt when I see not only Lucas come out, but also Anthony, John, and even Jordan. John and Jordan are in full LARPing regalia again. A few people gesture to them in gratitude, and they wave modestly. I have no idea what's going on, but I'm already emotional and seeing so many of my friends unexpectedly up there brings more tears to my eyes. It's not lost on me that Nathan is nowhere to be seen, but I can't dwell on that right now.

I continue clapping and wave to everyone onstage before turning to the group of adults. Mr. Weaver, a white man wearing khakis and a polo shirt, nods seriously to me. He's from the school board. Next to him sits Mrs. Fairfax, a large Black woman with a friendly face who is the Music Boosters president. She's Dawn's mom, and given that Dawn just ran offstage with the other fairy-tale creatures, I'm thinking she'll be the easiest to convince.

I survey them and try to appear my most professional. "Thank you so much for coming today. I'm very sorry I missed the beginning of our meeting time."

Mom steps up next to me. "Hi, I'm Riley's mom. We had a family emergency today, which is why I needed to take her out of school. But I can assure you she's very serious about this spring musical."

"She's not the only one," Mr. Weaver says under his breath.

Miss Sahni stands, her head cocked to the side with a concerned expression. "Yes, I heard all about your father from Hoshiko and the others. I'm so sorry. How is he? We didn't expect to see you today."

"Thank you. He seems to be doing better. In fact, he's the reason I'm here. He insisted I come."

Principle Holloway nods at the stage. "That was quite the performance."

A thrill runs through me, but I force myself to stay calm. "I'm glad you think so. We have so many talented people at the school who are passionate about this. We wanted to show you what we're capable of."

"And that's not *all* you're capable of," Miss Sahni continues, her voice charged with energy. "This group pulled that performance together completely on their own with no budget and only a few weeks to rehearse." She turns to the principal. "Imagine what we can accomplish given some time and resources." She raises her eyebrows and the principal nods gruffly and looks down at the folder in his hand. Those are my folders I put together. I had completely forgotten about them, but after I left school in a rush, Hoshiko must have grabbed my book bag and found them. I'm buying her *so* many chai lattes when this is all over.

"Riley, will you walk us through this?" Miss Sahni asks, holding up a folder.

"Yes, of course." I explain my plans to them, including the different proposed budgets, licensing fees, and cast numbers we would need depending on the musical we choose. Next, I review my thoughts on how we could cut costs compared to the last few musicals and some fundraisers we could think about doing. The group doesn't say anything, but Miss Sahni is smiling brightly as I speak and Mrs. Fairfax is nodding encouragingly.

"This is well conceived," Mr. Weaver says.

"Thank you." Hope fills me to the point I might explode.

"I think we'll need some time to talk, though," Principal Holloway says. His face is a mask. "Why don't you go congratulate your friends on the performance."

I nod, give a quick side hug to Mom, who is now standing by the wall, and head backstage to the wings on shaky feet.

The entire cast is milling around backstage. It's a sea of nervous laughter and wide grins. Paul stands toward the back. He notices me and gives a quick nod before turning away.

I spot Lucas and Hoshiko chatting with John, Jordan, Anthony, and his homecoming date, Kenzie. "You *guys* . . ." My voice is tinged with awe.

Lucas spins and wiggles Hoshiko's arm to get her attention. She turns, squeals, and pulls me into a huge hug. "Riley! Oh my God, I didn't think you'd be here! How is your dad? What happened at the hospital?"

"He's still there, but yeah, it seems like he'll make a full recovery." I shake my head. "The performance was amazing. Hoshiko, your *voice*. And your makeup is perfection." I turn to Lucas. "I didn't know you could do a Scottish accent! And you two skipped LARPing to be here?" I ask, turning to John and Jordan.

"I'm still hoping to get there, but we wanted to see this through first."

"I just—" I break off, getting emotional again. "Thank you all *so* much for being here. It means so much to me."

Hoshiko hugs me again. "There was a moment when we thought about canceling, honestly. It felt like everything was stacked against us with your dad being in the hospital, and no narrator or costumes, but then Nathan suggested—"

"Nathan?" I interrupt. I glance around again to be sure, but he's definitely not here.

She nods. "Nathan convinced us that we could still make it happen. Lucas was pumped to narrate—"

"I never get to use my accents at D&D since I'm always the DM," Lucas adds.

"—and John and Jordan jumped in to help with costumes."

Jordan nods. "John texted me at lunch and I drove over as soon as school finished. We texted some other LARPing friends who had a few things we could borrow and threw together some other pieces."

"If there was more time, we could do a lot more," John adds.

Ah, so that's where the elaborate fairy wings came from. I shake my head in disbelief.

"I don't have any useful skills, but I told Nathan I could help paint sets or something and he said I should stick around too," Anthony explains.

Kenzie loops her arm through his. "Happy to help."

I'm dumbstruck by it all. The boys know next to nothing about musicals or theater, and yet they're here anyway, volunteering like it's no big deal. Hoshiko stepped up, pulling this entire performance together without batting an eye. Really, the whole cast stepped up today. I tell everyone thank you again and walk around to the other cast members, complimenting them and thanking them for being a part of this. Everyone is joyful, in the way they can only be when they've just gotten offstage after nailing a performance, as well as concerned for Dad. They're an amazing group.

At the same time, though, there's a tiny painful hum in the back of my brain, reminding me that the one person I'm most anxious to see isn't here. I check my phone, but there are no missed messages from Nathan. Where is he? Maybe he's covering at the store since both Dad and I are out. The idea lowers my anxiety a bit, but it doesn't stop me from missing him.

I'm about to ask about Nathan when Miss Sahni calls me back out. A few people give me a thumbs-up and I return them. I walk out of the wings, only to realize that Hoshiko and the rest of my friends are trailing behind. I'm not sure if that's appropriate, but I could really use the support, so I don't argue.

The adults blink when we come up in front of them. I guess we are a pretty odd group, given that Hoshiko is currently green and John and Jordan just walked out of the medieval ages.

"Amazing," Miss Sahni whispers, and inspects John's costume.

He steps forward nonchalantly even though his cloak is getting bunched around his legs. "Handmade. We're happy to help with the musical. We don't know much about ball gowns and that sort of stuff, but I'm sure our other friends can help too."

Mrs. Fairfax runs the cloak fabric through her fingers. "The details . . ."

"You haven't seen anything yet," John replies, completely unfazed by their reverence. "Our group is very serious."

"Hi," Anthony says, and he and Kenzie wave to the adults. "We can't sew. And we won't be singing or dancing or acting either, but if you need backstage crew stuff, then we could help with that."

"Yes, we'll need a crew," Miss Sahni replies. "Do you think you could recruit more people?"

He nods. "I can find people."

"And I bet the honor society would help out," Kenzie adds, and smiles at the principal. "We could count it toward our school service."

Did . . . did Miss Sahni just say *we'll*, as in this is something that's actually happening?? My heart rate doubles in speed. Mom does some excited silent clapping behind their heads.

Principal Holloway clears his throat. "All right, we've spoken more about this and—"

The auditorium doors bang open at that moment and my heart jumps into my throat. Nathan strides toward the stage with Lucas's dad and Fred and Arthur, the two retired regulars from the store. I do a double take. I'm thrilled to have Nathan here, but I can't fathom why the others would have come.

Lucas's dad comes up to Mom and shakes her hand. "Boy, Joel gave us a scare. How's he doing? Everything okay?"

"Yes, I think he'll be okay," she replies, startled. "Though he's going to need to make some lifestyle changes."

"Oh, I'm sure he'll love that." He walks over and claps me on the back. "And you're okay?"

I nod, still confused. I give Miss Sahni and Principal Holloway an apologetic look. This is not the professional meeting I'd imagined. It's becoming a circus at this point.

"I'm okay, but, uh, what's going on?" I ask him.

"We're here about the play," Fred explains.

"It's a musical," Nathan replies quietly. I shake my head at him in bewilderment, and he answers with an uncertain smile that makes my heart flip over.

"Nathan came to the store and asked if we'd drive over to show our support for you," Arthur says. He turns to the principal. "I'm happy to build sets or do other work if you need me. My kids went here. I'm always glad to give back."

"My son inherited the Ace Hardware on Fifth from me," Fred adds. "We can donate lumber."

Lucas's dad puts a hand on Nathan's shoulder. "And I can design the program—I'm in graphic design. I'd love to support."

I look at Nathan with huge eyes and his smile grows wider. "I know people," he whispers.

Mom steps next to me. "My design firm can donate paint and materials for the costumes. And I'm sure Riley's father will sponsor as well."

Miss Sahni's eyes widen as she looks around the group and over to her colleagues. "I . . . Well . . . Wow. I'm very impressed. Actually, a little taken aback if I'm being honest."

"This type of community support is exactly what we need," Mrs. Fairfax says.

Mr. Weaver bobs his head. "Absolutely."

"I was very skeptical," Principal Holloway says. "There isn't much money in the budget and I wasn't sure if there'd be the needed interest to make this happen. But I can't argue with the support in this room."

"I couldn't agree more." Mrs. Fairfax beams at me.

The others nod and anticipation makes my hands shake.

"Yeah?" I look around at Hoshiko, then to Lucas and Nathan, and try not to squeal. "So . . . we have your approval? We're going to have a spring musical?"

"Yes!" Miss Sahni says, and claps her hands. "And I'm going to need a lot of help, so I hope you're ready."

"Yes, I'm so ready!"

"Good." Miss Sahni pats my shoulder, and I can feel her pride radiating into me as she says goodbye and walks out with the others.

Mom throws her arms around me after they're gone.

"I'm so proud of you." She looks at my friends, who have circled around me. "I'm going to go back to the hospital and let your father know. I'm assuming you can get a ride back?"

My eyes flick to Nathan for a moment. "I'm sure someone can drive me."

She squeezes me one more time and then ducks out, gesturing for Dad's friends to follow her.

Chapter Twenty-Nine

I laugh giddily, hardly believing it. The rest of the cast—
who were clearly eavesdropping from the wings—come
running out and my world becomes a blur of screaming and
hugging. There's so much to say and so many thank-yous to
give out, but I keep my friends in my peripheral vision. I'm
scared they might sneak out before I can thank them again,
but they stick around until the others have left and we're
alone.

"This couldn't have happened without you all. I can
never thank you enough." I pull Hoshiko into a huge hug.
Then I go around the circle squeezing Lucas, John, Jordan,
Anthony, and Kenzie. Nathan is last and I only hesitate for a
moment before hugging him as well.

Lucas shakes his head. "You already had everything in
place. We just followed through on it. Though I think Nathan
deserves some credit for pushing us to make it happen. We
were too devastated about your dad to think clearly."

"Me too," I say. I love that they all care so much about him. "He's going to be okay, really. He was talking and joking with me and complaining about the hospital food. I wouldn't have left him if I thought he was in any danger."

They nod, looking relieved.

Hesitantly, I turn to Nathan. He's standing slightly away, as if he isn't as much a part of the group as the others. Hoshiko jiggles Lucas's arm. "Um, we should go. We're already late for tap."

"Huh?" he says. She elbows him. "*Oh* right, we should go."

Hoshiko smiles knowingly at me and mimes texting. I nod and they head for the exit.

John shifts and the glass apothecary bottles on his belt clink together. "We should go too. LARPing waits for no man. Glad your dad is going to be okay."

"Yeah, tell him we all say hi," Anthony says.

Everyone waves and backs away, except for Nathan. As soon as we're alone, I can feel the crackle of energy between us. There's so much I need to say to him, but we're still in the auditorium and Miss Sahni and the others could walk back in at any moment.

"I guess you're getting your musical," he says quietly.

"With your help, from what I've heard."

He shrugs off the praise.

"No, really, Nathan, thank you. I never even thought about asking people at the game store if they'd help—that was inspired."

"I had to do something. You put too much into this to let it all go without a fight. Like you said, this is what you love most in the world. I needed to help you get it."

He gives me a small smile and I practically swoon. We ended things so horribly at the dance that I was worried he'd never fully forgive me, despite his earlier text about Dad, but now I can see how wrong I was. I smile back at him, trying to pour every bit of emotion I have into it. We stand for a few moments, grinning and staring at each other like goofballs.

"So, uh . . . ," he says, breaking the moment. "I'm glad to have helped, but I'm getting itchy from being at school too long."

I laugh lightly.

"And we never got to take that drive after the dance. Can I take you back to the hospital . . . the long way?"

My heart swells. "Yes. Please."

We leave the auditorium, our steps slow at first before picking up speed. We're practically running by the time we get outside. I throw myself into the passenger seat of his car and he does the same on his side. We turn to each other.

"Riley—"

"Nathan—"

We both stop and laugh. Omg, this is awkward. I have to get the words out now before they're lodged in my throat forever.

"I'm totally crazy about you," I blurt out, and lean back to gauge his expression. His eyes crinkle at the corners and he doesn't try to stop me, so I push on. "I have been for . . . I don't even know how long. You're going to homecoming with Sophia, and I don't know what that means for us, but I need you to know that I'm out of my mind over you."

The last sentence comes out in a rush and I swallow hard, my nerves about to snap and unravel.

Nathan cocks his head. "You stole my speech. I'm out of my mind over *you*."

His voice is so calm that it takes me a second to comprehend. He shifts closer to me. "I had no idea what was happening at the dance. One moment I was kissing you—*finally*, after wanting to kiss you every day for weeks—and the next moment you were running away and hiding in a bathroom and acting super awkward." He shakes his head. "I thought I must be the worst kisser in the world. Or that you somehow still had a thing for Paul. You can't imagine how sick I felt when you said his name right after kissing me."

I drop my head in my hands. "I'm so sorry. I saw him watching us and I convinced myself that the kiss was fake. That's why I freaked out like that."

"I know that now. Lucas and Hoshiko explained it to me this morning when they found me moping in the hall. But I promise you, he was the last thing on my mind that night. I didn't even know he was watching us until you pointed it out." He puts a finger under my chin and lifts my face. "Nothing I ever did was for his benefit. Well, okay, it was fun making him jealous. But really, he was just an excuse to spend as much time with you as possible."

"And Sophia?"

He slumps back. "She was a mistake. That whole thing was messed up from the beginning. I should never have agreed to go to the dance with her. I left you in the gym Saturday, came back to the car, and called her to break it off."

"But you were so mad at me when you left the dance."

"I was just . . . hurt. And angry at myself for bungling

everything so horribly with you. Either way, I knew I had to end things with Sophia."

"I'm so sorry."

"You were trying to protect yourself. I get it."

I take in his face, and his huge green eyes, and his glasses that have fallen down his nose again. Today has been so full of every possible emotion that I'm barely holding it together. My whole body is shaking and tears are building behind my eyes. Nathan scoots against the driver's side door and tugs me onto his seat with him. I lean my head against his backrest so I can look up at him.

"I love your glasses," I whisper. I gently lift them back up his nose, and he catches my hand in his. He lifts it to his lips and chuckles like I've just told a joke.

"You know, I started hoping Sophia would come to the store every night just so I could do this." He brushes my hair behind my ear. "And this." He presses a kiss to my temple.

I shuffle so I'm even closer to him. It's glorious to be next to him without worrying about faking anything. "Okay, I have to know—how long have you felt like this? How long have we been keeping each other in agony?"

"Since that night you kissed me on the cheek when I was looking for dice," he replies immediately. "You walked away like it was nothing, but if you'd turned around, you would have seen it was like you flipped my whole world upside down." He shakes his head. "I thought maybe I'd get over you once Sophia made it clear she was interested, but that didn't happen. All it did was make me realize how much I wanted to be with you, except I wasn't sure how you felt. You always talked about being such a good actress—which you are—so I figured everything going on between us was just made-up on your end. I was so scared of getting crushed. And . . . well I'm not proud to admit this, but I decided having something fake with you was better than having nothing at all. I would have faked it forever rather than give you up."

"Nathan . . ." I put my hands on either side of his face. "I am so into you. Embarrassingly so. If I could spend every minute of every day just kissing you and talking about Pop-Tarts, it still wouldn't be enough."

He pulls back slightly. "Kissing *and* talking about Pop-Tarts? Is that possibility on the table? Because I'd like to start doing that right now."

I sit up, grinning. "Can I add in musical rehearsals? Because it looks like I'm going to have a lot of those coming up."

"Definitely. What about D&D? Any chance we can add that back into your schedule?"

"Yes," I say, suddenly serious. "I know I said I was quitting, but I don't want to. Even if I don't have time in the evenings to keep working, I'm not giving up the game."

"I'm so glad you came to that conclusion on your own because, if not, I was fully prepared to convince you by any means necessary," he replies with a smirk. "I'm talking pleading, begging, even bribes."

"Bribes, you say? I'm intrigued, but it won't be necessary. We still need to kill that wraith and my show tunes aren't going to sing themselves. Just wait until it hears my rendition of 'Memory.' It'll be absolutely destroyed."

His whole body shakes with laughter. "Wow, I love you."

He says it so abruptly that I wonder if he didn't mean to

blurt that out. But his expression turns nervous and hopeful, and I want to wrap myself around him and never let go. My heart explodes into a haze of glitter and rainbows and show tunes. I kiss him so hard he falls back against the window before pulling me tighter to deepen it.

"I love you a ridiculous amount," I manage to say after a moment.

He breaks into a smile so radiant I'm at risk of being burned by the heat of it. It feels like heaven. He kisses me again. "I'm going to need a way to see you since you won't be at the store every day now. Maybe you'll need an 'assistant to the student director'? I can make coffee runs before my work shifts. And pick you up after. I know all the shortcuts."

I sit back in astonishment. "You'd be willing to stay after school? Because of me?"

"I'm willing to try a lot of new things because of you, Riley."

I breathe in the words. "We're going to have *such* a great time."

Six Months Later

"I can't believe people are going to be stepping on our art," Anthony complains as he stands back to survey his handiwork. "Are you sure you couldn't have the cast walk around the set piece instead?"

I get up from the stage floor, stretching out my legs. "Given that we're painting a set of *stairs,* I think people are going to need to climb them."

He sniffs. "Well, it's a travesty."

I expect Hoshiko to comment since her character will be sweeping up and down these stairs, but she's too busy giggling with Lucas to pay attention to the conversation or the painting. After much debate, we decided on *Legally Blonde* for the musical this year, and Hoshiko is killing it as Elle Woods. We're only a few weeks out from our first show and it's definitely been a chaotic couple of months juggling rehearsals, helping Miss Sahni, plus D&D games and working at the store once a week. But it's also been amazing. I don't want it to end. It's even been okay working with Paul. Not that I have time to think about him when I have many more important people in my life.

"Do you like how it turned out?" Nathan asks me quietly. He comes up behind me and wraps his arms around my waist.

I inspect the stairs. We probably put more work into painting the molding than was strictly necessary since the audience won't be able to see it, but it's not always about that. The more time we put into the set now, the more real the stage will feel for the cast.

Plus, it's fun to spend the afternoon painting with my best friends.

I turn in Nathan's arms so I'm facing him. "It looks gorgeous. Thank you for helping."

"You're welcome." He kisses me lightly on the lips. "I have to admit, the detail work for this was much easier than painting my three-inch-tall models."

"Hey, do you remember back in the fall when you asked me about my favorite color? And we both agreed our favorite was red?"

His eyes narrow just slightly. He's learned to read my expressions and tone much better since September.

"Yeah . . ."

"Well, I wanted to confirm that it's still my favorite." I lift my right hand and brush a smudge of red paint onto his nose. Then I grin beatifically up at him.

"Oh, you do *not* want to start this war." His voice is a growl even as he laughs. He tickles my side, and I shriek and wiggle away.

"Paint fight!" Lucas calls, but Hoshiko puts up her hands.

"No way, *Director.* We're going to get in so much trouble if we get paint on the stage."

"And, as much as I love doing manual labor for free, we need to pack up and get to the store," John adds, and puts the top on the nearest paint can. "You guys aren't ready for what I have planned tonight."

Nathan and I smirk at each other, paint forgotten for a moment. John recently took over from Lucas as DM for our D&D group, and if we thought Lucas was serious, then we had no idea what we were in for with John. Thankfully we switched days so Jordan could join the game too. John's always more chill when he's around.

We clean up the painting supplies and Nathan only gets one smear of paint on my cheek before I'm able to close up the other cans. I can't really complain because right after that he dips me down into a kiss that leaves me breathless and everyone else groaning.

In the parking lot, I pop open the doors of my new-to-me four-door sedan. Nathan climbs in the passenger side as I check my mirrors and adjust my seat even though no one has moved my car since this morning. I feel him watching me and pause to find his lips pressed into a small smile, as if he's trying to keep a neutral expression and failing horribly.

"What?"

"Nothing. You're just cute."

My cheeks heat. I only got my driver's license last month and everything is still new enough that I like to double-check things before I drive.

"No making fun of me!" I warn. "Just be happy you're saving gas today since I'm driving you."

"I'm not teasing you." He puts his hands up in surrender. "It's nice being driven around for once. Gives me more time to mess with the playlist. Although, I *am* still driving us to prom, right?"

I nod.

"Because your dress is so long you can't drive?"

I laugh and mime zipping my lips.

"Because it's so tight you can't move your legs?"

I shove his arm. "Stop snooping around for clues. You'll see my dress when you pick me up Saturday, and you'll have to live in suspense until that moment. I'm getting too much joy from torturing you to tell you a thing."

"And you complain about me!" He sulks and adjusts his glasses. "This is totally unfair. There's no way to keep you in suspense when you already know I'm wearing a tux."

My body warms at the thought of Nathan standing in front of me in a slim-cut black tuxedo. I'm so eager for Saturday I can barely control my breathing. I won't be leaving his arms *all* night.

When we walk into the store, I give Dad a quick peck on the cheek and recap today's rehearsal for him. He grumbles a bit about his dinner—he's made some changes to his eating habits over the last few months, but he still complains daily—before waving us to the back room. After a round of hellos to the regulars, I take my usual seat at the table across from Lucas and Hoshiko.

She gives me a panicky expression and nods at John, who is surveying our D&D group from behind his screen with a very Machiavellian expression on his face.

"Please be the voice of reason with him tonight, Jordan, or he's going to be out of *control*," Hoshiko begs.

"I make no promises," he replies, and winks at John.

"Time to get serious," John intones, his voice low and ominous.

"Oh boy . . . ," Lucas whispers.

Nathan squeezes my hand under the table. "Can you not drive because your dress is so fluffy you won't fit in the driver's seat?" he whispers.

I laugh and slap my hand over my mouth before John sics a dragon on my character. I lean my head on Nathan's shoulder, joy pulsing through me to be so close to him. I can't imagine any place I'd rather be than next to Nathan, teasing him.

"Only time will tell," I whisper back. I glance up and meet his gaze. "But I'll give you one hint. It's red."

Acknowledgments

I am enormously lucky to be able to live out my lifelong dream of writing books and sharing them with readers, and I have many people to thank for helping and supporting me along this ride. I'm so very grateful to editors Wendy Loggia and Hannah Hill for helping this story shine and for laughing in all the right places. Wendy, I'm so happy to have the chance to work with you. Thank you for seeing the potential in this book! I'm also thankful to the entire team at Penguin Random House, including Alison Romig, Casey Moses, Tracy Heydweiller, Kenneth Crossland, Tamar Schwartz, and Sarah Lawrenson. Liz Parkes, thank you for making such an incredible cover and for bringing Riley and Nathan to life inside the game store!

I will never stop being thankful to all the wonderful writers who cheer me on during the highs and commiserate during the lows. Thank you, Diane Mungovan, Becky Gehrisch, Holly Ruppel, Leigh Lewis, and Laurence King, along with my SCBWI friends. Thank you to Keely Parrack for the check-ins, Sabrina Lotfi and Carrie Allen for being awesome beta readers and people, and Kathryn Powers for the MLP gifs and ridiculously long Chinese buffet outings. Debbi Michiko Florence, I'm so glad we met at *Highlights* all those years ago and that we've continued to be such close friends. Thank you for encouraging me to keep working on this book when I felt like giving up.

I needed to research multiple aspects of this book, and luckily many people graciously answered the call. Thank you to my very patient husband for answering *all* the gaming questions. Thanks to employees at my FLGS (friendly local gaming store) for opening your doors and giving me the inside info on running a game store. Rajani LaRocca, thanks for getting on the phone to chat about medicine and for being a cheerleader from the beginning. Thank you as well to Leigh Bauer for answering my theater questions, along with Mary Yaw McMullen and the River View High School theater program for welcoming me back to my alma mater. Who knew when I was a freshman and standing on that stage in a nun costume that I'd someday write a book about it!

As much as I love writing, I need people who will keep my life balanced. Thank you to my parents and mother-in-law for their love and support, and to friends Melissa Beers, Kristy Reel, Courtney McGinty, Rosalee Meyer, Anna Yocom, Kristin Supe, and Beth and David Camillus for always being excited about my writing. No one keeps balance in my life like my son, Liam. I love you, my little gamer.

I'm incredibly grateful to every reader who has picked up one of my books, mentioned it to a friend, reviewed it, or posted a picture of it. Each of you helps this dream of writing continue, and I'd give you all a hug if I could.

The inspiration for this book began in high school when

my best friend and I joined a D&D group, having no knowledge of how to play . . . or that we'd both marry members of that group later in life. I can't imagine what my world would look like had we never met. Thank you Maggie, Emmett, and Mike.